SLOWLY THE POISON

Hugh Frobisher's wealthy family live in South Africa and he, the black sheep, was paid an allowance to go back to England. Now he is killed—apparently by a fall from a horse when drunk, but an autopsy reveals that he was poisoned. Suspicion falls on his beautiful wife Alice, but at the inquest she is cleared by the evidence of Beth Pottergill, her formidable companion-housekeeper. The Frobisher family invite her to South Africa. Beth Pottergill goes too. And there she becomes involved in another murder, and by poison again. So was the verdict at the inquest wrong?

SLOWLY THE POISON

JUNE DRUMMOND

LYTHWAY PRESS
BATH

First published 1975
by
Victor Gollancz Ltd
This Large Print edition published by
Lythway Press Ltd
Bath
by arrangement with Victor Gollancz Ltd
and in the U.S.A. with Walker & Company
1980

ISBN 0 85046 912 0

The quotation opposite is from William
Empson's *Collected Poems*, and is reprinted
by permission of the author and
Chatto & Windus.

British Library Cataloguing in Publication Data

Drummond, June
  Slowly the poison. – Large print ed.
  I. Title
  823'.9'1F   PR9369.3.D7S/

  ISBN 0–85046–912–0

Photoset, printed and bound
in Great Britain by
REDWOOD BURN LIMITED
Trowbridge & Esher

Slowly the poison the whole blood stream fills.
It is not the effort nor the failure tires.
The waste remains, the waste remains and
  kills.

from 'Missing Dates' by W. Empson

PROLOGUE

Hotel Adler,
Zurich,
7th November, 1958

Dear Philip,

If you read this, you will have won your bet and outlived me. It will fall to your lot, poor devil, to administer my estate. I'd like to feel that the task will be an easy one—in the business sense it probably will—but you may have problems with my Frobisher relations.

That would be poor reward for the years of friendship you have given me, so I'm writing to set the record straight.

The doctors I visited in Zurich this week tell me I shan't see in the New Year, which is another way of saying that my wife will survive me. It's on her account that I send you the enclosed documents, relating to what happened in 1911. The start of it you know better than I, but not the latter part.

In November 1911 I set down the story, all the events as I knew them. This was partly an attempt to bring things into order in my own mind, and partly a wish to take out some form of insurance. No man wants to be an accessory to his own murder, and for a while I did run that risk.

1

I believe I took the right course then, though you, as a stickler for the law, can hardly agree with me. A poisoner, you'll say, is the worst sort of animal, and society should be protected against such a one. I believe society was. As for justice and punishment, those abstractions have always been outside my sphere of concern. I've been arrogant enough to think I could look after myself and those I love, and leave retribution to other men. Now of course I learn my error. Time holds a better hand than I.

So Phil, I throw my burden on your shoulders. I've set down the facts. Use them, if you need, to look after my wife. If, on the other hand, you foresee no trouble, then burn the papers, or hide them away in that stuffy vault of yours, to await the Last Trump. When that blows, I hope to see you again, although there would be a better chance of it if you could bring yourself to sin a little.

Thank you for this last office, and for the many good years we shared.

Yours,
Toby

The man reading this letter was deeply disturbed. He fingered the wrappings of the parcel on his desk, folding them back from the faded file within. His large, rather prominent eyes glanced about the room as if in search of

2

reassurance.

The study where he sat was solid and urbane, like him, and like him it gave nothing away. The books on the shelves at his back concerned his profession, the walls were panelled in teak and held no pictures. The furniture was modern and functional. A portable air-conditioner stood in one corner, a high-fidelity set in another. There were none of the trophies, animal or vegetable, that lumber the walls of sub-tropical houses.

Philip Rennie was seventy-two years old and as a successful accountant he was guardian of a great many secrets. He carried them easily enough because beneath a surface affability he was a rather cold and narrow person. He could be kind without committing himself, and could view the death, dissolution and wickedness of the world without being moved.

Yet the letter from Toby Rourke had affected him. He rose and crossed to the window and leaned there, one hand gently massaging his forehead, the other still gripping the letter. He was trying to remember when Toby had last visited Durban. Ten years ago? More?

His mind burrowed back through the years. 1911. Young then, both of them, twenty-five or so, strutting a small town. Harbour undeveloped, mangrove swamps at the Bay's head and round the Island. A shopping and business area no wider than the flat land nearest the sea, and above that, on the slopes of the Berea, the scattered suburbs. Very few roads were surfaced. The red sand wound through natural bush. From this house one looked across seas of green to the Indian Ocean. No more than a couple of hotels on the Front, it was called the Back Beach then. Horse-trams, carriages, pony-carts and some motors. He'd seen his first automobile at his cousin Wyn's wedding. Quaint object it had been, with a fringed canopy, like a girl's parasol.

Damned lucky, thought Rennie. We basked in the after-glow of a great civilisation and we didn't know it was dying. We enjoyed privilege and nobody criticised us for doing so. We were snobbish, sporting-mad; hedonistic and jingo when these were the proper things to be. We were individuals when the wish of the individual carried more weight than the will of the masses.

He had a sudden memory of his father, standing in this room, saying 'we'll go Home next year,' meaning 'we'll visit England.' Oddly enough, that had irked the Frobisher clan. Like the Scots immigrants, and unlike the German, they were good colonists, identifying themselves with Africa and not with Europe. Toby Rourke had said: 'The Frobishers are such egotists they're convinced the centre of the earth is wherever they happen to be. England's the colony, to them. They've sent poor old Hugh to London as a remittance man. They pay him to rot in the white man's grave of Thameside.'

Egotists, yes, and unscrupulous, but attractive.

Rennie's eyes shifted to the flat-top tree that still marked the site of their property, Yellow-wood. Four acres of land, on a gentle slope. The house was neither beautiful nor ugly, a graceful Victorian hotchpotch of verandahs, painted ironwork, a latticed porch, a couple of airy turrets with blue roofs, like fox-glove bells. Geese in the banana-grove, a donkey under the orange-blossom.

Nothing could be more unambiguous, more expressive of middle-class success; yet Rennie's inward eye could seldom see it as he wished, in peaceful sunlight. More often Yellow-wood appeared in black bulk, against a night sky. Light spilled from an upper window where a voice cried out in agony. Down on the front steps, Molly Frobisher stared at him with a face all stark heights and hollows.

'It can't be poison! Phil? It can't be. Such a

terrible thing couldn't happen to us a second time.'

Before he could answer her, Dr Reppley's trap came dashing up the driveway.

★   ★   ★

Philip Rennie heard himself groaning aloud. He straightened up and went back to his desk, sat down and pulled the file towards him. His features resumed their cold composure.

If he read the contents of the folder, and they contained evidence of a crime, his position would be invidious. As a professional man he had certain duties to society. It might be better to hand the thing at once to some disinterested party, someone of standing, of course, who could reach an unbiased decision.

For I, admitted Rennie, am certainly biased. The mere mention of the date 1911 has thrown me into a thoroughly undesirable state of mind. I am an old man. I should avoid stress. I deserve to be left to enjoy an honourable retirement.

Yet even as he thought these things, he was folding Toby's letter and tucking it away in his breast-pocket; reaching for his spectacles; opening the file.

★   ★   ★

The text, in Toby's broad and vigorous hand, offered no introduction, but plunged straight into narrative:

January 21st, 1911. We learned of Hugh's death. Evelyn and I were called about six in the afternoon, by old Mlaas, who was in tears. We'd just come in from the Hockleys' garden party, Eve was still in her finery. We hurried from the cottage to the Big House. Everyone was in the sitting-room; Aunt Delia and Molly on the sofa, Beryl weeping in a wing-chair with Walter patting her shoulder, and Frank and Faith hovering about, trapped by the news and uncertain how to escape.

Aunt Delia beckoned me over. She looked dreadful, like a little white snowman with coaly eyes. She caught at my hand and held on.

'Hugh has been killed, in London. There is to be an inquest.'

Beryl sobbed, and Aunt Delia threw her an impatient glance. 'Why do they require an inquest, Toby?'

I told her that in certain circumstances an inquest had to be held to enquire into the cause of death.

'What circumstances do you mean?'

'If the death was accidental; if they suspect

it was brought about by wilful or negligent conduct by someone or other; or if the cause of death was in dispute.'

'So the circumstances need not be suspicious?'

'No.'

She nodded and thanked me. Evelyn came and stood beside me and began to ask questions. 'What's happened? How did you hear about it? From that woman?'

'From Alice.' Aunt Delia's tone carried a warning. She'll never allow anyone to criticise any member of the family if outsiders are present. 'Alice has been generous, considering that we never made her welcome. She sent me a long telegraph. She is obviously feeling dreadfully alone. I shall write to her at once. Bygones must be bygones. She must come and stay with us.'

'She may not be allowed to,' said Beryl in her chirruping voice. When we stared at her, her soft pink face screwed up. She'd put on a black dress with ruffles, and a string of jet beads that made her look like a baby dressed as a widow. 'I mean, she may be in prison.'

Walter said quite sharply, 'Don't be silly, dear.' Aunt Delia didn't even trouble to speak. She was beginning to master her shock. Her face still had that dead pallor. I couldn't tell if she felt any grief for Hugh. All her

8

energy was bent on protecting the family from further trouble. I'd have liked to read the telegraph from Alice, but I knew it was no go. We'd learn the unpleasant facts in the words of Delia Frobisher, no-one else.

'Hugh,' she said, fixing her eyes on Evelyn, 'was found on the night of January 16th, lying on the Thames tow-path close to a public-house. He had fallen from his horse. He was alive when they found him, but died almost at once. The doctor could not be sure what caused his death, so there is to be a post-mortem, and this inquest.'

Walter said drily, 'It's really nonsense that the doctor couldn't give the cause of death. If Hugh died close to a pub, the chances are he was drunk when he took the toss. And lying in the open, on a winter's night . . . he wouldn't have much chance.'

'Alice gave me no details. She clearly wished to warn us of the . . . the accident . . . before someone else did. She will write as soon as she knows the result of the post-mortem.'

'A letter,' I said, 'will take weeks.'

Evelyn suddenly began to cry, pressing her hands against her face. She dropped down on the floor next to her mother, who put an arm round her.

'Later, we can think of Hugh. At the moment, we must be practical. I know

9

nothing of the law. But it seems to me that Alice faces a very unpleasant situation. Shouldn't we engage someone to attend this enquiry on our behalf?'

I couldn't help admiring the Frobisher nerve. 'We' and 'our' said Delia, brushing aside the fact that they'd kicked old Hugh overseas to go to hell as he pleased, and refused to acknowledge the girl he'd married four years ago.

'Alice may not relish our help,' I said. 'Hasn't she a father living?'

'One can't depend on him, Toby, to consider our interests. I think you and Walter should speak to Seymour Rennie. He'll know what's best.'

Walter nodded. 'I'll call on him tomorrow.'

'Tonight,' said his mother. 'I wish it settled tonight.'

Beryl, who has some lucid intervals, stopped crying and said: 'Why Seymour? Phil Rennie is in London, right this minute. Can't he act for us?'

'Phil's not a lawyer,' said Walter.

'But he must know lots of lawyers.'

Molly spoke for the first time. 'The inquest may already have started.' She was rubbing both hands up and down her arms, and shivering.

'I'll walk down to Mr Rennie's,' Walter

10

said, 'and see what he advises.'

He left soon after. The rest of us stayed. Frank Reppley insisted that Aunt Delia be put to bed, with a sleeping-draught, and Eve and Beryl took her upstairs. I went to the kitchen to talk to the Zulus. They were all very upset, Hugh having been a favourite with them. I tried to explain about the inquest, and old Mlaas said, yes, a good thing, whoever killed the nkosaan must be punished; a statement that did nothing to steady me.

When I got back to the hall I found the Reppleys there, talking to Molly. Although she's such a strapping, healthy girl, she's by far the most vulnerable of the Frobisher clan, and I put my arm round her shoulders.

'Don't worry, old thing. It may not be as bad as it sounds.'

She looked at me in her direct way. 'It's worse, Toby. I had a letter from Hugh, six weeks ago. He wrote such wild things. He said Alice hated him and wanted to be rid of him. I know he was probably tipsy when he wrote that. But what if he's talked that way to strangers?'

'He won't have.'

Frank Reppley blundered in. 'You can't dismiss it, Toby. Something of the sort might be repeated at the inquest. I understand a coroner can allow hearsay evidence.'

'He's not bound to believe it, however. I'd say a British coroner is used to listening to witnesses and can sort out the fact from the fiction.'

Evelyn joined us then and said Aunt Delia was settled for the night. Eve looked very worn. Reppley took her wrist and shook his head at her.

'You must rest, my dear. You're not a hundred per cent yet, you know.'

She pulled her hand away impatiently. 'I'm all right.'

'Better come and see me, all the same. You're still anaemic. We must get you right.'

'Very well.'

On the way back to the cottage I told her Frank was right, she should take better care of herself. She shrugged. 'Oh, illness is so boring.' She walked with a hurrying step, not looking where she was going, and dashing aside the branches that overhung the path so that they whipped back in my face. I knew she was thinking of Hugh. They'd shared a bond. Ganged together against the world.

At home she poured us both a whisky and water. We sat at the dining-room table and drank in silence. After a while she lifted the fringe of her dress that was full of black-jack burrs from the garden, and began to pick them out. 'This post-mortem. Will they be able to bury him after it's done?'

'As soon as the doctor's made his report, and the coroner's given his say-so. There couldn't be a cremation, though.'

'How do you know so much about it, Toby?'

'When I worked on the mines we had to hold an inquest if there was any fatal accident.'

'I heard what Molly said . . . about Alice wanting to be rid of Hugh. I expect she meant a divorce, don't you?'

Eve was staring at me in the intense way she has, as if she could suck the answer out of me. Her eyes were the dark blue of wild irises. I thought how beautiful she was, and how little I understood her, even after two years of marriage. She leaned towards me.

'You don't think he meant murder, do you?'

'Good God, no!' I was afraid she was working herself into another feverish attack. She'd been very depressed since she lost the baby. I said, 'Eve, I'd like you to see another doctor. Someone who isn't a family friend.'

'Oh, Frank's as good as anybody in this dorp.'

'There may be someone in Cape Town, or Europe for that matter. It's no good living under par all the time. I'll take you anywhere, you know that.'

'Don't fuss, Toby. I'm getting well. If we could get into our own house. They promised us the plans last month.'

'Plans always take longer than you think.'

'It's not all that big.'

'Big enough to present problems, darling.'

'You mean money.'

'Among other things.'

'If Walter wasn't so stingy . . . he could lend us anything we wanted.'

'I wouldn't dream of asking him. Besides, it's not necessary.'

'The money belongs to all of us, really. It was rotten of my father to leave it as he did. That's the root of all our troubles. If Hugh had been decently treated, he wouldn't have ruined his life. He wouldn't be dead now.'

The tears began to run down her face. 'It's dreadful. I can't remember him properly. I feel empty inside.'

'Hush, now. You're exhausted. Come to your room and rest.'

She got up slowly. 'What will happen to us?'

'Don't worry. Phil Rennie's utterly dependable. He'll wrap things up right and tight, you'll see. Come along now, come to bed.'

★　　　★　　　★

(They relied on me, thought Rennie, and of course I couldn't let them down. So their disaster became mine. I had no choice in the matter.)

CHAPTER ONE

LONDON

THE MORNING OF January 23rd was cold, but a red-fingered sun fumbled some warmth into the rooftops of Thameside, and drew a flaccid mist across the common-land by the river. The parish had only in the past decade become part of London's sprawl. Its churches, inns and houses still seemed to belong to a rural pattern of life, and it was only on the north-east side that one realised that before long the factories and railyards would gain control.

The two journalists who had come off the early train—'Gaffer' Keech of the *Daily World* and Harry Lodden of the *Southern Review*— ducked through side alleys to Market Square, where the courthouse stood. Keech and Lodden were old friends, accustomed to meeting in and around the courts of London. Both had an astonishing acquaintanceship with people on both sides of the law, policemen, lawyers and pathologists on the one hand, criminals and their cronies on the other. Both were skilled reporters. If expertise had been the criterion, both might have been editors by now, but each had a limiting vice.

Lodden was a lazy man, and Keech drank too much.

Old campaigners, they wasted not a glance on the courthouse, but headed for the top angle of the Square, where the Grey Feather Inn stood. Within minutes they were sitting in the bay window of its dining-room, with veal pies and coffee before them.

'It seems,' said Keech, waving a hand at the surrounding walls, 'that the late-lamented was well known here.'

'Toper, was he?'

'So Sergeant Kerry said, yesterday. "Frequented the public saloons of the Feathers, the Maypole, an' the Bargee down by the river" . . . which is where he turned up his toes.'

'Can't see what we'll get out of today's lark, then. A drunk dead of exposure, nothing in that.'

'Ah, you wait. The widow was a Miss Muirhead. Her dad owns a nice acreage in Dorset and he's a warm man in the City listings. Scandal in the drawing-rooms, my lad. The court will be crowded.'

Lodden made no answer. He had not, like Keech, spent time and brass wheedling the gossip from come-who-might. He turned to watch a hackney cab that was rolling across the cobbles towards the inn. It stopped, a young

17

man alighted, paid off the cabbie, and stood staring about him.

Lodden said, 'He was on the train with us.'

Keech bent to peer through the steamy glass. 'Was he? Never noticed. Looks foreign, don't he? Never got that bronze in England.'

'Frobisher deceased was a South African. This could be his kin, or someone they hired to sweep the dirt under the carpet.'

At that moment the young man lifted his head to gaze directly at the window where they sat. They had time to register clothes of good but conservative cut, a broad high forehead, a sharp chin. Then he hurried forward and ducked through the main doorway. At the same time a number of people trooped into the Square from the western archway, and headed for the red-brick building where the inquest was to be held.

'Queue forming,' said Keech with a chuckle. 'I told you we wouldn't waste our time today.'

*   *   *

The bronzed man edged through the crowd of people in the Inn's hallway, and caught a potboy by the arm.

'Do you know where I may find Mr Wilfred Muirhead?'

The youth shrugged. 'Dunno, guv. Ask Mr Riggs, I would.' He gestured at a thickset man in shirtsleeves who was stationed at the far end of the corridor. The newcomer shouldered towards him.

'Good morning. My name is Philip Rennie. I am a friend of the late Mr Hugh Frobisher. I understand Mr Muirhead is to be found here and I am anxious to speak to him.'

Small blue eyes surveyed him. 'Have you a card, sir?'

Rennie produced a visiting-card, which Riggs studied.

'Lawyer, are you? Retained by Mr Muirhead?'

'No. He has never met me. I'm in London on business, from South Africa. My firm handles the financial affairs of Mr Frobisher's family.'

'I see.' The man handed back the card and indicated a door down a side-passage. 'Mr Muirhead's in there. You could try if he'll see you.'

'Thanks.' Rennie went and knocked on the door-panel. A voice called to him to come in. He did so and found himself confronting two men. The older, a tall rosy-faced man with a shock of greying hair, stood by the open fire. His jacket was thrown back, his heavy fists rested on his hips. Opposite him a slight, dark

19

man in a beautifully tailored suit, paused in the middle of a vehement gesture to stare at Rennie. There was a third person in the room, a young woman seated in an armchair near the window. She leaned a little sideways, her chin propped on her hand. She wore a black silk dress, very plainly cut, and a wide black hat trimmed with tulle cast her face into shadow. She did not move as Rennie entered, or appear even to notice him. The two men watched him enquiringly.

'Mr Muirhead?' said Rennie.

'Yes.' The big man's voice was deep and brusque.

'I am Philip Rennie. I am an accountant attached to the firm of Rennie and Brinkman, of Durban. Hugh Frobisher was a childhood friend of mine. I received a telegraph from his family early this morning, asking me to attend the inquest. I came early, hoping to speak to you.'

Muirhead's chin tilted in a slightly ironic smile. Rennie said, 'I know that things have not been happy between your daughter and Hugh's family. One can't mend that overnight. But I believe we should talk.'

'Well, Mr Rennie, I appreciate your courtesy in coming to see me.' Muirhead held out his hand, which Rennie shook. 'This is Mr Charles Comyns, who represents my daughter's interests. I take it you have engaged someone on the Frobishers' account?'

'No sir. I returned from Scotland late last night, having heard nothing of Hugh's death. The telegraph from home reached me at eight. I had time only to speak to the attorneys who are known to me. If they can arrange for someone to attend, they will. If not, we must rely on British justice.'

'Frank, aren't you?'

'Animosity serves no good purpose.'

'Ay, you're right there,' Muirhead's smile became more friendly. 'Forgive me if I sound rough, Mr Rennie. We've been through the mill since poor Hugh died. I had to carry Alice off to the country because of the crowds round her house, gawking, day and night. Well, we must get over the heavy ground as light as we can, eh? Your name is familiar. Your father, was it, who made the arrangements for the payment of Hugh's allowance?'

'Yes. He carried out the instructions of Bernard Frobisher, Hugh's father.'

'Umph. Did he approve of 'em?'

'That's irrelevant, isn't it.'

'Probably. You say you knew Hugh well, as a child. But as an adult?'

'I knew him well enough, and recently enough, to guess that he was drunk when he

21

died.'

'He'd been drinking. You'll hear it all at the inquest. D'you mean to speak of his character in court, Mr Rennie?'

'Only if I have to. Please understand, I was fond of him. We lived more or less next door to each other in a small town. I know things about him . . .'

'Yes?'

'That explain his shortcomings. He didn't get on with his father. They quarrelled viciously. You know the terms of his father's will?'

'In outline, not detail.'

'Bernard Lawson Frobisher left a secure income to his widow. The bulk of his estate, however, went to his older son Walter. His daughters, Evelyn and Molly, received token amounts. Hugh got nothing.'

Muirhead scowled. 'Unwise, and mean-spirited. I've always disliked the idea that a dead man should bully the living. Of course, there may have been provocation.'

Rennie ignored that tangent. 'Walter Frobisher has tried to set things straight. When Bernhard died two years ago, he not only continued Hugh's allowance, which he had no need to do, but doubled it.'

Muirhead grunted. 'So Hugh got a monthly hand-out from his big brother, which he regularly spent in two weeks. He was a man, to be blunt with you, with a load of charm and no sense at all.'

'I accept he must have been difficult to live with. Self-indulgent and at times dishonest. I repeat, he was, in some sense, a cripple.'

Comyns, who had been listening in silence, now intervened. 'May I ask, Mr Rennie, whether you have spoken of all this to anyone else? The police, for instance, or the coroner's officer?'

'No. There's been no time.'

'Ah.' Comyns seemed pleased with the answer. Rennie saw a certain satisfaction in his smile.

'I think, Mr Comyns, you could satisfy me on one or two points.'

'Perhaps.' Cautiously.

'I'd like to know why there has to be an inquest at all? Did the doctor refuse to sign the death certificate? Is it merely because the death was termed accidental? Who asked for a post-mortem?'

'I did.' The voice came from the woman by the window. She was sitting bolt upright, staring at Rennie with lifted chin. Rennie, who had forgotten her presence, was startled into confusion.

'I asked for the post-mortem,' she repeated. 'I'm Alice Frobisher.'

23

Rennie, thinking of some of the things he'd just said, bowed clumsily.

'It's all right,' she said, as if she read his mind. 'Nothing you said about Hugh was untrue . . . or new to me.'

Her mouth was curved in something not quite a smile . . . self-mockery, perhaps. Her figure was slight, but upright. Her pose was neither contrived nor bold, but it held the eye. All three men in the room seemed to have come to attention when she spoke. Rennie judged her age to be twenty-three or -four. Her face was oval, the skin drawn smoothly over a delicate jaw and prominent cheek-bones. The eyes, very large and brilliant, were grey-brown, and had a magnetic effect. They gazed up at him from the shadows of a wintry day, the shadows, it might be, of recent suffering. He found that without conscious thought, he had crossed the room and was standing close to her chair. She put out her hand, on which a ring sparkled.

'Hugh often spoke of you. He liked to talk about home. You played polo with him, didn't you? And rugby?'

'Yes, we were friends until he came to England.'

She nodded. She appeared to be quite composed. Yet she must know what an ordeal she faced? Was she very brave, or merely very stupid?

Again she seemed to read his thoughts. 'Mr Comyns has warned me there'll be a lot of questions about my life with Hugh. I've accepted that.' She leaned forward a little. 'I'm glad you're here in Hugh's interest. Perhaps someone can do something for him, now he's dead. No-one could help him while he was alive. There was something in him I couldn't reach. A sort of monster, that fed all the time on misery. The liquor he drank was quite secondary. It's a pity the doctors don't know more about misery. If they could cure that . . .'

She seemed almost to have forgotten Rennie, to be about to drop back into her reverie; but Comyns made an impatient sound, and she recalled herself. Straightening in her chair, she said, 'I asked for the post-mortem, Mr Rennie, because the people here in Thameside were saying that I poisoned Hugh.'

*   *   *

'Bit of a come-down, eh?' said Keech.

Until recently, Thameside inquests had been held in the disused billiard room of Rothsey House. Its Regency panelling and its three tall windows looking across grass to the

25

river had lent some grace to the coroner's courts. The new building in the Square, with its raw red brickwork and yellow varnished doors, had no grace to lend. As the two journalists tramped along the main corridor, they caught the stench of formaldehyde from the neighbouring post-mortem room. The court itself was cold and stuffy, still empty of the public. Opposite the main doors was the coroner's bench, raised on a dais. On the left was the jury-box, on the right the witness-stand, and below the bench were tables and chairs for counsel, solicitors, or such expert witnesses as might be called to attend.

The Press seats were next to the jury's. Keech and Lodden took their places. Almost at once a side door opened and four men came through, approaching the legal table. Two were evidently clerks, but Lodden's eye was not on them.

'Is Charlie Comyns for the lady?'

'Seems so.'

Lodden hissed through his teeth. 'Then you're right, laddie, they're expecting trouble.' As Keech made no answer, he added, 'Charlie'll cost 'em.'

'Her father has the dibs.'

At this point, Comyns caught Lodden's eye and gave him a brief nod, then turned to speak to his companion. It was the young man they'd

26

seen alighting from the hansom cab. Keech got up and strolled down to the well of the court.

'Morning, Mr Comyns.'

'Good morning to you, Mr Keech.'

The journalist looked enquiringly at the young man, but the advocate did not introduce him. Keech let it pass. He'd get the name when he needed it. He drew the lawyer a little to one side.

'You're in the widow's behalf, are you?'

'Yes.'

'Big crowd out there.' Keech glanced up at the windows high in the south wall. 'Courtyard's packed. There's been talk.' As Comyns began to frown, Keech's eye became more benign.

'People don't like the Crowners' Courts, y'know. Think they're too piddlin' to deal with big cases. And give rise to talk into the bargain.'

'I'm not sure,' said Comyns, at his silkiest, 'what is meant by "big cases"?'

'Oh, one that could become a cause célèbre, I suppose.'

'You let your professional hopes outrun the facts, Mr Keech. As to the idea that a coroner's court is too . . . ah . . . parochial . . . I would suggest that's precisely their advantage. They save a great many people a

27

great deal of time and money, and they bring the law down to local level. Furthermore, they are, in my view, very ably administered. A coroner like Mr Kerr-Jenkins, for instance, is one of the most knowledgeable men in the field of medical jurisprudence.'

'Oh, I know,' Keech grinned. 'Lookin' for a story, y'see, is my job. Think this one will run more than a day?'

'I wouldn't think so. One never knows, though.'

Lawyer and journalist parted affably, having given and received useful information. Keech had warned that there was a large public excitement over the inquest, and that the rumour went that it might lead to action in a higher court. Comyns had reminded him that Kerr-Jenkins was in charge, and would probably wrap up a straightforward matter like this by evening.

Philip Rennie, standing close by, heard the exchange. He was beginning to see in Comyns a man of large ambitions, who made a point of playing along with the Press. He would have been happier in the hands of someone less aggressive than Comyns, less well-known, less likely to suggest by his very presence that there was scandal brewing.

He moved to the front row of public benches. As he did so, the journalist overtook him and extended a hand.

'My name's Keech. "Gaffer" Keech, *Daily World*.'

'Philip Rennie.'

'Friend of the deceased?'

'Yes.' Rennie's face was closing against the expected questions, but Keech merely nodded. 'If you want advice about anything, ask Sergeant Kerry. He's the Coroner's Police Officer.'

'Where do I find him?'

For answer, Keech gestured towards the side door, which had just opened to admit a uniformed policeman, followed by a tall man with a ruddy complexion and a slight, dark young woman. At the rear came a second woman dressed in a black woollen gown and an old-fashioned bonnet.

'That's Kerry,' said Keech, 'with Alice Frobisher and her father.'

'And the other woman?'

'Mrs Beth Pottergill, Mrs F's housekeeper.'

Outside in the Square a clock began to strike the hour. Keech nodded affably and moved away. Comyns approached the group at the side entrance, and herded them towards the front row of seats. Sergeant Kerry walked to the rear of the court and gave three warning knocks on the big double doors there. A minute or two later he swung them open to

29

admit a stream of people. Heavily muffled, pale or ruddy from their wait in the cold, they crowded to fill the benches. A number of them, Rennie saw, were well-dressed. One woman wore a full-length sable cloak.

When there was no more space, two policemen checked the flow of humanity and closed the doors. One of the last to gain admittance was a short, purplish, bearded man of about fifty, who sat down at the back of the court. Through the closing doors, Rennie glimpsed a solid pack of men, women and even children. The murmur of their voices dwindled and died. The lock was turned.

Within the court, Sergeant Kerry called for silence. He moved to the clerks' table and began checking names on a list, glancing about the court to make sure certain people were present. Once he said irritably:

'Where's Mr and Mrs Sopwith? I don't see 'em.'

One of the clerks shrugged. 'They were in the courtyard earlier on. I saw 'em.'

Kerry beckoned to a constable. 'Go and find the Sopwiths, Pierce, will you? Natterin' somewhere, most like, and we've only five minutes to go.'

The couple named arrived with seconds to spare, and went to sit in the space reserved for witnesses. Rennie studied them closely.

The man was thickset, with a face that seemed to be composed entirely of circles: round pale cheeks like sallow cheeses, round snub nose, round almost colourless eyes. His reddish-gold hair was parted in the middle and heavily sleeked down with pomade. He was dressed in a tight tweed suit, a brown wool waistcoat and a shirt with very high, starched collar-points. A brown Derby hat was tucked under his left arm. He did not glance about, but moved to his place with deliberate decorum, put his hat under his chair, spread his knees and bent his head as if he had entered church.

His wife seemed less conscious of the solemnity of the occasion. She wore purple: a long woollen skirt with a full-sleeved jacket moulded tightly across a great swell of bosom; and over that a short black velvet cloak. A bunch of artificial violets was pinned to her black toque. Rennie, sitting close to her, saw that she was handsome, despite a too-heavy jowl. Her skin was white, with large pores, like the pith of an orange. The hair looping from under her hat was glossy brown and still rich, although she must be past the fifty mark. As she turned to search the benches behind her, he saw a curling red mouth that made constant, involuntary movements, and black eyes that missed nothing. There was a pale

31

mole on her left cheek. She had large, white, strong hands. She would, Rennie imagined, be a good manager at the bar, she'd rally the drinker with saucy stories, humour him as long as he stayed within bounds, and lay him flat with a sweep of that fleshy palm if he exceeded them.

It was ten-fifteen. The air in the room was already tinged with the smell of bodies in damp clothes.

Sergeant Kerry rapped for attention. The side door opened, the crowd rose to its feet. There entered a very tall, very thin man with close-cropped, tightly-curling, iron-grey hair, and rimless glasses that glinted so brightly one could not discern the eyes behind them.

The figure made for the Coroner's chair. A voice, very deep and beautiful, said, 'Be seated, please.' A bony finger signalled to Sergeant Kerry.

The court of Mr Bevil Kerr-Jenkins, Coroner for the Borough of Thameside in the County of London, was in session.

★   ★   ★

'You good men of this county of London summoned to appear here this day to inquire for our Sovereign Lord the King, when, how, and by what means Hugh Malory Frobisher came to his death, answer as you shall be called, every man at the first call, upon the pain and peril that shall fall thereon.'

While the Officer of the Court rolled out this command, the Coroner drew a sheet of paper towards him, wrote a heading across it with practised speed, set down his pen and gazed at the occupants of the public benches.

Bevil Kerr-Jenkins was one of the best-known of London's coroners, and one of the first to hold the dual qualifications of lawyer and doctor of medicine. He had a deceptively mild manner, this erudite, silvery man, but those who took his benevolence for weakness, generally lived to regret the error.

'Alfred Kirk...' As the Officer named the first juryman, a man rose in response and muttered, 'Aye, here sir.' He was a butcher from the next parish, a big-nosed, nervous person with watery eyes. Several other names were called and answered. Rennie viewed the owners with some dismay. Most of them seemed confused and overawed. It struck him that this was a frightening way to hand out justice, this random choice of men with nothing in common save a geographic closeness to the place of death.

Kerr-Jenkins administered the oath to the jurors, each in turn. 'I swear by Almighty God that I will diligently inquire and a true

33

presentment make of all such matters and things as are here given me in charge on behalf of our Sovereign Lord the King, touching the death of Hugh Malory Frobisher, now lying dead . . .'

(Rennie had a sudden picture of Hugh as he had seen him last, standing on the deck of a liner leaving Durban, waving as the streamers stretched and broke.)

'. . . and will, without fear or favour, affection, or illwill, a true verdict give according to the evidence, and to the best of my skill and knowledge.'

(But Hugh had always demanded favours. He'd been a perennial special pleader. 'No hard feelings, Phil, old boy. Life's too short . . .')

'. . . duly sworn,' said the Coroner. He removed his pince-nez and gazed at the jurymen. His eyes were opaque and yellow-brown, like butter-drops.

'We are here,' he said, 'to assist at an enquiry, not a trial. I want you to remember that it is not the objective of this court to arraign any person, to judge any person. You have sworn that you will allow malice no place here. What we desire today is accurate information given on oath before God and man. Receiving this, our task is to enquire when, how and by what means the

34

unfortunate man, Hugh Malory Frobisher, came to his death. Before the inquiry begins, you will accompany me to view the body. In some cases it is not deemed necessary that the jury carry out this duty, unless a majority of its members wish to do so; but in the present circumstances I do insist upon your sharing with me this melancholy task. We will go at once, if you please.'

He rose. The jurors followed suit, shuffling from their benches, stumbling down the wooden steps, trooping through the door. They were away some ten minutes, and in their absence the coldness of the courtroom seemed to intensify, as if the collective mind of the watchers dwelled on the icy place where Hugh rested, with its white enamel, its silence, its smell of disinfectant. On Rennie's right, Wilfred Muirhead stretched out a hand to his daughter. She ignored it, sitting bolt upright, staring straight ahead.

Does she appreciate her danger, wondered Rennie? According to Comyns, the Coroner could have ordered a post-mortem to be done without holding an inquest. He could have ordered Hugh buried, without further question. He could, had he wished, have told the world he believed the death to be due to natural causes. But the inquiry had been called, the question posed, the suspicion

35

aroused in thousands of minds. By evening, the Press would be pumping out reports.

Returning footsteps echoed in the corridor. The jurors filed back into their places. A sigh went round the courtroom. There was a shifting of bodies, a leaning forward, as if some libation had been poured to the gods, and the gates of the arena opened.

★　　★　　★

The first witness to be called was Herbert Sopwith, owner of the Bargee Public House, on River Road. It was there that the dead man had spent the last evening of his life. The Coroner's patient questioning drew from Sopwith answers at first hesitant, then expansive.

'Mr Frobisher came into the public bar about a quarter of ten o'clock ... it was bitter cold out, starting to snow ... he came up to the bar where I was serving and asked for a double brandy to keep out the chills ... sat and drank it very quick ... he was cheerful and excited ... he talked about money...'

Bit by bit there emerged the picture of the winter's dark on the river bank, the tap-room noisy with Friday-night drinkers, the smell of beer and sweat. Mrs Sopwith and two bar-maids toiled to keep the orders filled. The house was in a working area, used by riverside folk who drank as hard and as often as they could manage; very different from the Grey Feather in Market Square. Yet it was at the Bargee that Hugh Frobisher, gentleman, had spent most of his leisure time.

'A regular patron?' suggested the Coroner.

'Oh yes, sir. All the four years he lived hereabouts, he'd come in two-three times a week, or more. He counted me and the wife as friends, said as much, many's the time.'

'You say that on the night of January 16th he was "excited". Could you expand on that statement?'

Sopwith's pale eyes blinked as if he had not understood. 'Well ... he was like that, sometimes.'

'Like what, Mr Sopwith?'

'I dunno, sometimes he'd get a bit up in the air. You know, talk racy, and tell jokes, or laugh rather loud.'

'Was he sober when he came into your saloon?'

'I don't like to say, exactly.'

'But you are an experienced judge of such matters, are you not?'

'Oh yes, your honour. You could say it's my job. But if you're asking me, was Mr Frobisher noisy because he was drunk, then I'd say, "It's hard to tell." He wasn't slurring

37

his words, nor staggering. Just strung up. Excited.'

'Had you seen him drunk before?'

'Yes, but not often. Mr Frobisher carried his liquor well, very well.'

'He was accustomed to drink brandy?'

'Yes.'

'What was his usual consumption?'

'If he was in the bar for the whole evening, then he'd take four or five.'

'Double brandies, or singles?'

'Double.'

'A hard drinker, would you say?'

'Yes.'

'And on that night of the 16th, how much did he drink?'

'He was only in the bar about half an hour.'

'In that time, what did he drink?'

'He took two doubles. Brandies.'

'What effect did they have on him?'

'They seemed to calm him down.'

'He was no longer excited?'

'That's right. He calmed down and talked more sensible. He spoke of buying a motor-carriage. Told me he was going to sell his horses and buy one of these new De Sotos instead.'

'Did he name the horses he intended to sell?'

'There was one horse he named. Asked was

I interested. He wanted fifty pound for it and I said it was a bit above my touch but I'd pass the word around.'

'Which horse did he name, Mr Sopwith?'

'Azrael.'

'Was this Azrael one of Mr Frobisher's carriage horses?'

'No, no, sir, a hack. One that Mrs Frobisher used to ride.'

'Did you discuss that point with Mr Frobisher?'

'What d'you mean?'

'The fact that Mrs Frobisher used to ride Azrael?'

'Not overly much. I think I said, would she ... Mrs Frobisher ... mind, and he replied "Pride goes before a fall, Herbert".'

A rustle went round the courtroom. Sopwith looked uneasy. The Coroner's face remained bland.

'Later, you say, Mr Frobisher became quiet?'

'Yes, very quiet.'

'Did this quietness seem to you to be normal?'

'No. I thought the poor gentleman was feeling ill, your honour. Sat with his head hung down, and then he laid forward on his arms. I asked if he was all right and he mumbled that he was. He was shivering. I thought it might be one of his attacks coming on.'

'What sort of attack do you mean?'

'Well, he'd had the malaria in Africa. He was a man you could never describe as in the pink. Pale, always, and he sweated a lot. I'd seen him go down with the fever before, and I thought it was the same that night. It was only later I knew different.'

'One last point. Mr Frobisher's mood, by your account, changed very quickly . . . from excited and elated, to quiet and lethargic. Was this the usual pattern with him?'

'He was moody at times. Depressed.'

'To what extent?'

'He'd be very depressed.' Sopwith was suddenly galvanised to rage. 'But don't let anyone tell you he did himself in. I've never heard him talk of suicide, never once. Anyone who says so is telling lies. He was far from the thought of death, your honour. That last night, he was making plans. He was talking of tomorrow!'

The Coroner sat a moment, staring thoughtfully at Sopwith. Then, at a movement at Counsel's table, he glanced down. 'You wish to question this witness, Mr Comyns?'

'Later, please, your honour.'

Again the silvery regard was bent on

40

Sopwith.

'At what time, Mr Sopwith, did Mr Frobisher leave your premises?'

'About ten twenty-five, sir. It was near to closing time. He finished his drink and went out.'

'Did he bid you goodnight?'

'No.'

'Did you actually see him quit the building?'

'No. It was a busy night, a Friday, and there was a crowd pushing for the last round.'

'Did you feel Mr Frobisher was in a suitable state to ride home?'

Sopwith shot the Coroner a sharp look. 'He was all right, or so I thought. He was a good horseman. His horse knew its way home. White Lodge, where he lived, was no more'n a quarter of a mile from the Bargee.'

'At what time did you close the premises?'

'Eleven o'clock I finished locking up. Closing time was ten thirty, and nobody hung about talking. It was snowing and the wind was bitter. The yard was clear by a quarter to eleven.'

'What happened after you locked up?'

'We retired to bed. Me and the missus and the two girls that sleep in, we were all abed by quarter past eleven. I'd no sooner climbed into bed that I heard Mr Frobisher's horse coming

41

back.'

'Will you tell the court about that?'

'I heard the sound of hoofs. Turning into the yard, that's cobbled, y'see. I sat up in bed and listened, and heard the animal stamping about, so I took my watch from the pocket on the bed-head, and took a look, and it was twenty-five minutes to twelve.'

'What did you do then?'

'I pulled on some clothes and went down to the back door that leads to the yard. I saw it was Mr Frobisher's horse, a big bay called Chesham with a white blaze. I brought him into the stable, and looked him over. He wasn't hurt, though shivering and blowing hard. Sam Fisher, that's my cellarman, has the room over the stables, he also came down to the yard. I told him to dress quick, and we'd go along the tow-path, which we did. We headed for White Lodge, which was the way the horse's tracks led us. About three hundred yards along, we found Mr Frobisher.'

'What time did you reach him?'

'About ten minutes to twelve.'

'Can you describe the circumstances?'

'He was face down, your honour, half in a drift of snow. His head was turned to the side and his knees drawn up, like he'd tried to crawl and then slid down sideways.'

'Did you touch him?'

'Yes. I turned him more on his side, to see if I could feel his heart. There was a faint beat still. I took off my topcoat and put it over him, and I sent Sam to fetch Dr Bell, who lives on the far side of the Common. But before the doctor came, Mr Frobisher died. It was only a few minutes after we reached him. He was breathing so faintly, and then it got louder, as if he was choking, and then there was nothing. I mean, I couldn't feel anything in his chest or wrist, and he'd no breath coming. I tried what I could to revive him. It was no good. So then I left him as he was.'

'Did you form any opinion about how he came to be lying on the tow-path?'

'There wasn't much to show what happened, because it had been snowing. I couldn't see any tracks but Sam's and mine and Chesham's leading to the place, and then the drag mark to where Mr Frobisher was lying. Chesham's marks went from the tow-path up onto the Common, the snow was quite thick up there. I think he must have bolted after Mr Frobisher came off, and galloped about on the open ground, before he turned back for the Bargee.'

'Would he not have made for his own stable at White Lodge?'

'He'd have had to jump over Mr Frobisher's body, sir. There's a steepish bank beyond

43

where that was lying, and the animal was maybe scared. A horse hasn't got much brain, especially when he's frightened.'

'How long was it before Dr Bell arrived? Judged from the time you found Mr Frobisher?'

'About a quarter of an hour. Not more. He told us Mr Frobisher was dead, and said we, that's Sam and me, should fetch the handcart from the Bargee. We did that, and we put Mr Frobisher on it, to take him back to White Lodge. The doctor went ahead of us to warn Mrs Frobisher.'

'You took the body back to the Lodge, before informing the police there had been an accident?'

'Well, sir, it just looked like he'd taken a toss, there was nothing suspicious. We carried him home, and Mrs Frobisher told us to put him in the ground-floor bedroom. Which we did.'

'Did you remain at White Lodge after that?'

'No. Sam and me came away.' Sopwith shot a sidelong glance at Alice Frobisher, sitting quietly in the front row of benches, her eyes fixed on space.

'She never spoke to us,' he burst out. 'Never spoke a word nor shed a tear. Her husband stone dead and she never . . .'

'Order!' The Coroner's hand rose sharply,

and Sopwith checked in mid-sentence.

'That is all, thank you, Mr Sopwith. I have, as you will have noticed, taken down in writing the facts and circumstances which you have related to us this morning. I shall ask you to sign a formal deposition, and I shall also sign it myself. You understand?'

'Perfectly, your honour.'

Kerr-Jenkins turned to the lawyers' table. 'Mr Comyns?'

Charles Comyns rose and prepared to question the publican.

* * *

'Mr Sopwith, you have told the court that the dead man, Hugh Frobisher, offered to sell you a horse named Azrael, for fifty pounds.'

'That's right.'

'Was Azrael the property of Mr Frobisher? Think carefully, please, before you answer.'

'It was . . .' Sopwith's eyes screwed up, as if he recognised a lurking danger. 'So far as I knew, it belonged to him, yes.'

'Had you ever seen Mr Frobisher ride Azrael?'

'Well . . .'

'Had you?'

'No.'

'And Mrs Frobisher?'

'Yes, she rode him.'

'When you were offered the horse, did you think fifty pounds was a fair price?'

Again a hesitation. 'Well . . .'

'You seem unsure. Would it surprise you to know that the original purchase price of Azrael, as a yearling, was six hundred guineas?'

'I knew he was a good horse.'

'Yet you refused to buy him for fifty pounds?'

Silence.

'Will you tell us why you refused such an opportunity, Mr Sopwith?'

'I told you, I couldn't afford it. Anyway, I didn't take Hugh serious.'

'Were you perhaps aware that Azrael was not the property of Mr Frobisher?'

Sopwith started to answer, changed his mind, and shrugged.

'Were you aware of that?' repeated Comyns.

'They were man and wife, weren't they? I was bound to think that when they wed, the horse was his by rights, same as all her property? He spoke as if it was his.'

'Was Hugh Frobisher in the habit of describing his wife's material assets as "his by rights"?'

'He spoke of his house, and so forth, the

way any man would.'

'So it will no doubt come as a surprise to you when I tell you that Mr Frobisher owned neither White Lodge nor Azrael, but that in terms of her marriage settlement, those assets, together with all her silverware, furniture, and jewellery belonged to Mrs Frobisher exclusively, and could not be sold without her consent?'

'That does surprise me, yes.'

'You say Mr Frobisher offered to sell you Azrael. He made the offer in your public bar-room, in the presence of several other people, naming fifty pounds as the price. Did you ask him whether Mrs Frobisher was in favour of the sale?'

'I thought they must have agreed upon it.'

'Having rejected the price of fifty pounds, did you suggest a lower figure?'

'I said ... I think I said something about forty.'

'Did Mr Frobisher respond?'

'He said he couldn't take less than fifty, he needed fifty at once.'

'Did he say why he needed money so urgently that he was prepared to sell a thoroughbred horse for that figure?'

'No, he didn't. Anyway, it was none of my business.'

'Of course not.' Comyns' sleek head dipped

47

for a moment, then lifted. 'Mr Sopwith, you were talking across the width of the bar counter for some twenty minutes to Mr Frobisher. You have said he looked ill. You noticed his changes of mood. Did you study his face closely?'

'His face? No, not really. I was busy, coming and going. We chatted 'tween-times. I thought his eyes had a feverish look.'

'Bright, would you say?'

'Glittering, yes.'

'What colour were they?'

'Eh?'

'What was the colour of Mr Frobisher's eyes?'

'Very dark brown. And when he'd been drinking heavy, they'd be bloodshot.'

'Were they bloodshot on the night of January 16th?'

'Not particularly, not so I noticed.' The publican made an impatient gesture. 'I wasn't likely to gaze into any man's eyes, with the saloon packed out on a Friday night!'

'Quite so. Later that night, when you and Mr Fisher found the unfortunate man on the tow-path, you knelt down beside him, did you? Yes. And his face was turned sideways? Yes, I see. You shifted him onto his side. Did you lift his eyelids to see if he was still conscious?'

48

'Yes, I did.'

'You studied his eyes then?'

'Yes, but not for long. The poor lad was dying . . .'

'Did you notice the pupils of his eyes?'

'Well . . . yes. I saw the black part was very big. The black part in the middle.'

'The iris of the eye was distended?'

'Yes. It gave me a start, see, like he was alive, but I knew he didn't see me. He was a goner. It was only a matter of minutes with him.' Herbert Sopwith shuddered suddenly. 'You don't know what it was like, out there. I was alone with him once Sam had gone for the Doc.'

'One last question. The way Mr Frobisher was lying when you found him, half in and half out of the snowdrift . . . was his nose or his mouth in the snow?'

'No. He would have been able to breathe all right. There was snow under him, but it wasn't deep under his face, and the fold of his coat had kept him out of it. I thought myself he might be choking, but that wasn't so. I made sure.'

'Thank you, that's very clear.'

Comyns indicated that he had no further questions, and Sopwith returned to his seat. Rennie saw that his high collar points were soaked with sweat.

*   *   *

The next witness was the cellarman at the Bargee; Sam Fisher, large, fair-skinned and fair-minded, answering the questions in a West Country burr. He had little to add to Sopwith's evidence.

He had seen Hugh Frobisher leave the public-house just before closing-time. Frobisher had staggered as he crossed the stable-yard where Chesham was tethered. Sam, thinking he looked 'very under the weather', spoke to him but received no answer. Instead, Frobisher had turned aside and vomited into the gutter. This Sam took to be because of the alcohol he had consumed. He helped Frobisher up into the saddle, where he sat 'limp-loike, but arl right'. Chesham started forward at a steady walk, and turned out onto the tow-path. He'd carried his master home before now, and Sam let the pair go without much misgiving. 'Oi washed down the cobbles, where Mr Frobisher was took bad, with a bucket or two o' water. Then up I went to my larnin'.' Sam, it seemed, was teaching himself to read, going to night school, and he'd been busy with his homework. He had worked until, like Sopwith, he had heard Chesham return to the

50

stable-yard.

His evidence corroborated Sopwith's except on one point. When Comyns asked him how Alice Frobisher had received the news of her husband's death, Sam's expression softened. 'Poor maidie,' he said, 'it were a terrible blow. She were struck to stone, yeu could see. Sim'ly struck to stone.'

*   *   *

Dr Bell and Mr Kerr-Jenkins were old acquaintances, having dealt together on a number of cases in Thameside. The doctor was in appearance the direct antithesis of the Coroner, being short, pudgy, and given to snappish gestures. But the two men understood that to reach the truth, one must study not only the facts but the eccentricities of men and women.

Once sworn in, Bell identified himself to the court and agreed that he was a general practitioner working a large practice in the borough. His home and consulting rooms were a quarter-mile from the Bargee, on the north side of the Common. He was therefore the doctor nearest to the scene of the accident on January 16th. He had visited Mrs Alice Frobisher professionally three or four times in the past four years, but had never attended Mr

Frobisher. The latter, being a medical student, got medical attention at St Joseph's.

On the fatal night, continued Dr Bell, he had been roused from his bed 'just on midnight', by Sam Fisher, who told him that Mr Frobisher had been found 'hurt bad' on the tow-path. He dressed hastily, took his bag and a paraffin lamp and went with Fisher to a point a little west of the Bargee where the injured man lay. He found Mr Sopwith waiting there. As he came up, Mr Sopwith said, 'I think he's gone, Doctor.' He had made a cursory examination of Mr Frobisher by the light of the lamp.

'What did this first examination reveal, Dr Bell?'

'Hugh Frobisher was dead, your honour. I tried to revive him, without success. He had evidently fallen heavily from his horse. There was a contusion on the right side of his head, though not a large one. There were no bones broken that I could find. As Mr Sopwith has said, there were obvious signs that Mr Frobisher had moved after he struck the ground, dragging himself a yard or two. He had also vomited a very small amount of material, but because of the muddy and sodden condition of the ground, it was not possible to recover this for examination. His clothes were sodden, probably because he had lain in the snow for an hour and a half, but one must also consider that he may have been sweating profusely, earlier in the evening. Death was very recent, the covered parts of the body being still quite warm. The face was darkly flushed, and the pupils of the eyes much dilated.'

'This enlargement of the pupils . . . what significance did you attach to it?' asked the Coroner.

'It suggested to me that the deceased might have died from asphyxia . . . suffocation. This could have come about by blockage of the breathing passages. I looked for such a cause, but could not find any sign that Mr Frobisher had inhaled any vomited material. He could possibly have suffocated in the snow-drift. The snow was thin under his head, but it might have been deeper when he fell. I questioned Mr Sopwith and Mr Fisher and learned from them that the dead man had consumed a considerable amount of liquor at the Bargee during the evening, and that he had been sick in the inn-yard. I decided that I must make a closer examination of the body in a proper light. I therefore requested Mr Sopwith and Mr Fisher to convey it to White Lodge. I went ahead to warn Mrs Frobisher that her husband was dead.'

'Will you describe what happened at White

Lodge?'

'When I reached the house it was in darkness except for one upper room. I knocked loudly and Mrs Pottergill, the housekeeper, came downstairs to admit me.'

'She had been awake, then?'

'Oh yes, sir, she was fully clothed. I started to tell her why I had come, and while we were still speaking Mrs Frobisher came to the head of the stairs in her night attire and asked what was the matter. She hurried down to the hallway and I told her the sad news. She collapsed into a chair that stands close by the door. I thought she might faint, her pulse was very irregular. I asked Mrs Pottergill to bring a glass of brandy or wine for her mistress, and was told there was none in the house. When I expressed surprise, Mrs Pottergill said. 'It was by Mrs Frobisher's orders. We tried to keep it from him.' I then sent Mrs Pottergill to make strong sweet tea. While it was being prepared, Mrs Frobisher recovered sufficiently from her shock to talk. I told her some of the circumstances of how her husband had been found, and that Herbert Sopwith would be coming with the body at any minute. When I told her that she became very angry, and demanded to know how Sopwith dared approach the house when he was the cause of all that had happened. I asked what she meant

54

by that, and she said, 'If Hugh had been sober, he would never have taken such a toss.'

'I explained to her that it was, in my view, more likely that her husband had been taken ill, and had fallen from his horse because of that, than that he had been fatally injured by the fall itself. She replied, 'If drinking is an illness, then indeed Hugh was ill.' I said I must make a more complete examination before passing an opinion on the cause of the accident.'

'How did Mrs Frobisher receive that?'

'She made no comment. She was still very distressed, very shaken, and unable, I think, to absorb what was being said to her. The two men arrived with Mr Frobisher's body. I asked them to place it in a bedroom on the ground floor of the house. They did so, and left. Mrs Frobisher then became very distraught. I left her in the care of Mrs Pottergill. I removed the outer clothing from the body and made a more careful examination than I had been able to do on the river-bank.'

'Did this further examination settle any questions in your mind, Dr Bell?'

The little doctor glanced across the courtroom to where Alice Frobisher sat, and hesitated, as if choosing his words with extra care.

'I spoke to the widow again. I told her I

could not reduce the cause of death to a single factor. I said it was probable that several factors had combined to kill him ... his fall from the horse, exposure to the cold, a constitution weakened by malarial fever. I knew something of his history, though not recent history. I asked her whether she could tell me anything that might be a further guide to me.'

Again a pause. The Coroner nodded encouragingly. 'She told me,' continued Dr Bell, 'that her husband had become addicted to alcohol. As I questioned her, she described to me the classical symptoms ... the fact that her husband had lapses of memory when he was unable to recall events in which he had taken part ... his hiding liquor about the house ... his drinking alone ... his secretive and sly ways of obtaining liquor after it was barred from the house. She told me that her husband had failed his university examinations, and of late had not troubled to attend lectures. About two months before Christmas he gave up all pretence of studying, and stayed at home.'

'What was her attitude, in telling you this.'

'She showed, I think, an unusual degree of tolerance and understanding. She repeated that she felt her husband was ill. She saw his drinking as a symptom of something deep-seated, a chemical defect over which he had no control. Right at the end of our conversation, she mentioned that for the past three months he had appeared to be mentally unbalanced. He would swing from depression to a state of almost hysterical elation. He suffered from childish tantrums, and from physical ailments which she described as "stomach troubles", periods of retching and diarrhoea. I explained that these were very likely the result of his excessive drinking. I told her I would return the following morning to talk with her. We discussed whom she would inform of the death . . . her own father, and her husband's family in Africa. I told her to leave other arrangements, with the undertakers and so on, to me. There seemed to be no friend . . . in London, that is . . . to whom she could turn. I asked if she required a sleeping draught, but she refused. She said Mrs Pottergill would look after her. She showed great courage, I thought, and great self-discipline.'

'Did you return next day?'

'I did, sir. In unpleasant circumstances. Soon after breakfast, as I was about to set out on my early round, Mrs Dora Sopwith of the Bargee came to my house and demanded to see me. She was insistent. I admitted her, and she made a certain statement about Mrs Frobisher. It was scurrilous. I warned her that

57

if she spoke so she would soon find herself in deep waters, legally. I sent her packing. But later, as I made my rounds, several people questioned me on Mr Frobisher's death and one or two repeated Mrs Sopwith's charge.'

'Which was?'

'That Mrs Frobisher "knew more about it than she'd tell".'

'How did you respond to these remarks?'

'I told them,' said the doctor, with an angry glance round and a jerk of the jaw, 'that Hugh Frobisher might be alive today if he'd taken less alcohol and they'd do well to learn the lesson of that.'

'And what was your next step?'

'I called at White Lodge and reported the remarks to Mrs Frobisher. She is, to my mind, a woman who prefers to face facts. I told her I had no intention of heeding such scandalmongers, and that I had decided the terms in which I would define the cause of her husband's death.'

'Do you mean, the terms in which you would sign a death certificate?'

'Yes. I intended to give as cause a chronic addiction to alcohol, with contributory factors of malarial fever, a heavy fall and exposure to the cold—more than enough to account for death.'

'Yet you did not in fact sign such a

certificate?'

'No. Because Mrs Frobisher herself said a rather astonishing thing. She told me she was not satisfied to leave it at that. She said, "Dr Bell, I want a post-mortem to be conducted on my husband".'

A buzzing swelled in the courtroom. Like many others, Rennie turned to look at the widow. What sort of woman could ask that her husband's body be dissected? One so cold that she did not care? Or so self-disciplined, to use the doctor's words, that she did not allow herself to flinch from the idea of that final indignity?

Her profile was calm. She was watching the Coroner. Rennie saw a faint colour rise in her cheeks. So she was aware of the public gaze, although she did not deign to recognise it. He thought her too proud for her own good. A clever woman would show distress. It would be more seemly.

Mr Kerr-Jenkins finished writing a note and looked at Dr Bell. 'Mrs Frobisher asked you to arrange for a post-mortem, and you agreed?'

'Yes, your honour.'

'Umh. Mr Comyns, would you like to question the doctor.'

'No thank you, your honour.'

'Then Dr Bell, you may stand down, but I

ask you to remain in court, since it may be desirable to recall you later.'

Dr Bell, with one final glance at Alice Frobisher, did as he was bid.

*　　*　　*

'Amen,' said the man in the witness-box, and pushed aside the Bible with an almost peremptory speed. Mr Laurence MacQuern, decided Rennie, did not look like a pathologist. His long red cheeks, his carefully sleeked sandy hair, his large red hands would have fitted a ploughman at a fair, and he repeated the oath in an almost comical North Country accent. Yet he gave his evidence with a confidence, both in his facts and his ability to convey them, that was clearly won of experience. MacQuern, it seemed, belonged to the new group of medico-scientists that was lifting pathology from the despised levels of the past, and making it a vital part of criminal jurisprudence.

Above all, he was likeable. He was at pains to see that his answers were clear to the laymen in the court. When he referred the Coroner to his written report, already in the court's possession, he did so with diffidence. The Coroner afforded him the closest attention.

MacQuern began by giving an account of

the clothes worn by Hugh Frobisher on the night of his death. He went from there to his examination of the body itself, its exterior condition, the opening of the thorax, head and abdomen, the meticulous study of interior organs. It was a gruesome enough category, yet MacQuern's matter-of-fact voice somehow avoided the sensationalism that had crept in with Herbert Sopwith and Dr Bell. His detachment was the detachment of death itself, and Rennie saw the widow's face lift with an odd expression of gratitude.

'There was a slight contusion on the right frontal area of the skull . . . high up here, on the crown.' MacQuern traced the position on his own head. 'It was made before death. It was in accordance with the bruise you might expect to find if a man fell from his horse, but did not pitch straight onto his head. There was a much more extensive bruising of the right shoulder, upper arm, and side,' . . . again, a hand demonstrated the area . . . 'and it's my belief deceased fell shoulder first, striking his head on the ground in a secondary manner. He may well have rolled from the saddle quite slowly. He was a big man, a hundred and seventy pound in weight, and he'd fall heavily, d'you see? There was no fracture of the skull, nor of any other bone of the face or hands. He fell limp, and there were no lacerations of the skin, no gravel-rash. I don't consider there was any dragging of the body by the horse. That would have showed on the clothing Mr Frobisher wore, or on his skin. I'd say the horse was not travelling at speed, but ambling along quite quietly, or even standing still. The injuries sustained in the fall were not serious, not serious at all.'

'Not such as would cause death, you mean?'

'Not in the general rule, your honour. But one must consider the effect of shock, and exposure, as Dr Bell pointed out quite rightly.'

'Dr Bell and Mr Sopwith have suggested that Mr Frobisher crawled a yard or two. Would that fit the facts known to you?'

'Aye, it would. He fell, but was able to crawl a couple of yards. He then collapsed into the half-crouched position in which he was found; passing within a few minutes into unconsciousness, and then into death.'

'Was he unconscious when he fell from the horse?'

'I can't tell you that, sir, but in my view he was close to it, for reasons which I'll explain later.'

'I see. Pray continue.'

'I examined the organs of the body for signs of injury or disease. There was fatty degeneration of the liver, and signs of cardiac and renal involvement such as one may find in subjects who have been addicted to alcohol, although the presence of these symptoms does not necessarily mean there was such addiction. There were also signs of granulomata in the brain, which can occur after malignant tertian malaria. Mr Frobisher's own doctor will no doubt be able to assert the frequency and seriousness of his past malarial attacks.'

'Do you think deceased was undergoing such an attack at the time of his death?'

'There was nothing to support that theory. I would just say this. My examination was of a body that had been damaged by previous illness, the body of a malaria subject who may well have been a heavy drinker, and who had sustained at least minor injuries and shock in falling from his horse.'

'Now, this is very important, Mr MacQuern. Does this total of contributory factors amount, in your opinion, to the cause of Mr Frobisher's death?'

MacQuern paused, and the silence in the courtroom seemed to be something he held in his hand. At length he shook his head.

'No. Although it could have been sufficient cause, I did not feel satisfied. In my examination of the chest cavity and certain of the major blood-vessels, I found evidence of asphyxia.' He glanced at the jury, and then began to go into some detail about the symptoms of death by suffocation. One of the jurymen suddenly leaned his head on his arms. A policeman passed him a glass of water. MacQuern waited until he had drunk it and then continued. 'The dilation of the eye and redness of face noticed by Dr Bell and Mr Sopwith, and confirmed by me; the evidence of asphyxia I found at post-mortem; these signs were not supported by evidence of how the deceased could have suffocated. He did not lie face down in the snow, he did not damage his facial bone structure, nor fracture the carotid bone, nor choke on his own vomit, nor bleed into his lungs. I wanted to know how he came to suffocate. I accordingly sent certain organs to Mr Theodore Fox, for chemical analysis. The results of his series of tests are in my report, which you have there, your honour.'

'I will be glad if you will repeat them for the benefit of the court, Mr MacQuern.'

'Yes. Well. The analysis showed that Hugh Frobisher had in the last hours of his life consumed a lethal dose of the drug morphine.'

All round Rennie, noise exploded, noise and movement as people stood, or craned, or burst into conversation. For a moment the crowded benches surged like a stormy sea. In this commotion, Rennie was aware of three points of stillness; the Coroner, who gazed serenely at Alice Frobisher; Alice, eyes closed, face chalky, about to slide sideways against her father's shoulder; and Beth Pottergill, staring up at MacQuern with an expression of furious dislike.

*   *   *

Order was restored. Alice Frobisher had not, in fact, fainted. Mr MacQuern was speaking again in his deep voice.

'The analysis showed a definite reaction for morphine in most organs. I have noted the distribution, sir. The amounts present indicate that Mr Frobisher absorbed a large dose of morphine, nearly one and a quarter grains, some three hours before death.'

'Can you be more precise about the time?'

'I can say he swallowed the morphine not earlier than 7 p.m. on the 16th January, and not later than a quarter past nine. The most likely time is close to nine o'clock.'

'What effects would have been visible to an observer?'

'Such a dose would affect the parasympathetic system of the taker to a considerable degree.' MacQuern cleared his throat, turning to the jury. 'That means, the

65

taker would display signs, pin-point pupils, a slow pulse, sweating and a mood at first excited and later depressed. There might be vomiting. There would eventually be a depressive effect on the breathing functions, perhaps strong enough to endanger life. In other words, such a large dose of morphine, combined with several brandies, and exposure to shock and cold, could be enough to result in the failure of the respiratory system. This would mean, simply, that the victim would suffocate. This in turn would cause the dilation or widening of the pupils of the eyes, the redness of the face, noticed by Mr Sopwith and Dr Bell. It is my opinion, your honour, that Mr Frobisher died of suffocation brought about by an overdose of morphine. The alcohol and the accidental fall and exposure to cold were contributory factors.'

Charles Comyns questioned MacQuern. He wanted details about the size of the dose of morphine and its probable effect within the first half hour, the first hour, three hours. Would the amount found in Mr Frobisher's body inevitably prove fatal?

MacQuern explained that as morphine was habit-forming, a tolerance to it might result, so that large amounts might be taken without fatal effect. Mr Frobisher had ingested more than double the usual dose recommended for medical purposes, which was a third to a half a grain.

Comyns pounced. 'Ingested, Mr MacQuern? Will you tell the court, did you form any opinion as to how the morphine entered Mr Frobisher's body, was the ingestion oral, or by injection?'

'I could find no trace anywhere of injection.'

'No mark on the skin?'

'Nothing to indicate injection at all.'

'You have described how there was a trace of morphine in many organs of the body. Does the drug remain in the system for long periods?'

'Morphine is absorbed rapidly,' said the pathologist, 'through the intestinal mucosa, the average dose being destroyed or excreted in about three to five hours. The presence of oxydimorphine in Mr Frobisher's body showed that breaking down of the morphine had taken place.'

'Did you form any opinion, upon post-mortem findings, about the ingestion of morphine? Was it a single occurrence in your view?'

MacQuern leaned his elbows on the bar of the witness-box, as if warming to his subject. 'Morphine does not continually build up in the system, sir, like some drugs. It is eliminated, as I have said, in a matter of hours. You want to know if the drug had been taken by the dead man on more than one occasion. Well now. There was no sign of the skin-punctures you often find in an addict, but of course one can take morphine orally, in tablet or crystal form. It looks like Epsom Salts, y'know, and it tastes bitter, but you can swallow it in coffee, for example. At post-mortem, I found certain conditions that do occur when morphine has been taken repeatedly. Trophic disturbances of the skin, loss of hair, brittleness of the nails. Again, I do not say that these are infallible proof of morphine addiction, but they are consistent with that state. One can't rule it out. I've been sitting in this court today, listening to the descriptions of mood change and personality change, suffered by Mr Frobisher. They tally with the changes brought about by morphine addiction.'

'Is it fair to say that one should consider the possibility that Mr Frobisher was in the habit of taking drugs?'

'It is fair to say so. I could go further. What I found at post-mortem is consistent with what I would expect to find in a man who had begun to take morphine, but had not been addicted for more than a few months.'

Comyns, apparently satisfied, sat down.

Rennie found that his hands were shaking. He would have given anything to sneak out of the court and light a cigar. He looked at the jury. In the wintry light, darkening as the morning wore on, their faces looked drawn and bloodless.

Well, he thought, we're all in the same boat, and the rapids straight ahead.

Accident, suicide, murder? One of those, one knew that now.

The two journalists were scribbling away. How fast did the news appear? Tonight, probably, tomorrow certainly. And in Africa? Very soon. Headlines. Morphine. God, when was the old man on the Bench going to get on with things?

The Coroner finished writing, conferred briefly with Mr MacQuern, signed something. Raised his head.

'Call Sergeant Grimbold, please.'

The Sergeant took the stand and gabbled the oath, explained that he was the officer in charge of the sub-station of Police situated in Thameside half a mile from the Bargee, and stated that he had lived in this Division for the past twenty-two years. He then went on to relate, as if it were the most ordinary of events, how on the morning of January 17th Mrs Dora Sopwith of the Bargee had come to the said Police sub-station, asked to speak to him, and

69

made a certain allegation; to wit that Mr Hugh Malory Frobisher had not died of natural causes but had suffered death by poisoning.

'What,' asked the Coroner, 'were Mrs Sopwith's words?'

The Sergeant produced notes. 'She said, your honour, "Hugh Frobisher was a man in his prime, he was not ready for death, it was brought to him before his time. His wife did it, she did for him. She wanted him dead. I heard her say so".'

'Silence,' said the Coroner, as once more the court buzzed like wild bees.

'Did you ask Mrs Sopwith to amplify those remarks?'

'I did, sir. She told me that on Friday, January 16th, she and her husband Herbert Sopwith did call upon the 'ouse of Mr and Mrs Hugh Frobisher at approximately five-thirty in the afternoon. Mrs Frobisher was not at 'ome, as she was out 'orse-ridin'. Mr and Mrs Sopwith were entertained for an hour by Mr Frobisher. Mrs Frobisher then returned. She appeared to be angry at findin' guests present. There was an argument, in the course o' which Mrs Frobisher struck her husband in the face with 'er ridin'-crop. She also said, "If you touch Azrael or anythin' else of mine, I will kill you".'

'That was the substance of Mrs Sopwith's

70

report to you.'

'Yes, your honour.'

'How did you respond to it, Sergeant?'

'Well, sir.' The Sergeant swung a cold eye towards the publican and his wife. 'I warned Dora Sopwith that it don't do to go about making accusations without she could produce proof there was truth in 'em. I warned 'er she could fall foul of the law that way.'

'Did she accept your warning?'

'No sir, she did not. By next day, it was coming to me from all over the manor, Dora Sopwith says Hugh Frobisher was poisoned. I ignored it. But then Mr MacQuern's report came through to us. In view of the contents thereof, I thought it my duty to report to you, sir, about Mrs Sopwith's allegation on the morning of January 17th. Which accordingly I did.'

The Coroner gave the Sergeant an almost affectionate nod. 'Thank you. And now, I think we will hear what Mrs Sopwith herself has to tell us.'

*　　　*　　　*

Dora Sopwith took the stand. A bold woman, moving lightly despite her size, gathering up her sober purple skirts with fingers thick and pale as lily roots.

Her voice as she took the oath was muted, but with an earthy timbre. She was, she told the Coroner, a woman of Thameside, born there and married there. She gave the courtroom a queenly nod, as if the people there were her subjects; and maybe they were, brooded Rennie. How many of the jury were known to her?

She had a certain blowsy frankness that might have appealed to Hugh. She spoke of him in affectionate terms. He had been a reckless man, but lovable. A gentleman, lonely, unhappy and hungry for companionship.

'We knew, Sopwith and me, that Hugh shouldn't 'ave come to us so often as he did. He should have been with his wife, going to the theatre and the like. He was a man needed company all the time and Mrs Frobisher never held parties. Perhaps that was to keep him at his studies, I don't know, but it was never going to work with a man like Hugh, your honour. He was never a student. He wanted flesh and blood about him, not books, and that's why he came to the Bargee. It wasn't just for the drink.'

Mr Kerr-Jenkins asked for her account of the last evening of the dead man's life.

'How did you come to visit Mr Frobisher's

home?' he asked. 'Was it by invitation?'

'We had a standing invitation, your honour, from Hugh. Herbert and I would go to White Lodge every so often. The pub don't leave us much time for visitin', but sometimes of a quiet afternoon we'd leave Sam or my son in charge and go off. Hugh was always glad of a chat, particularly since his health made him leave off studying for a doctor.'

'When was that?'

'Before Christmas, about three months ago, as I recall. He'd been workin' hard, but then the fever came back, and he lost so much time with his books he said it was no use finishin' the year. He was upset about it, very nervous. Mrs Frobisher was out a great deal, being as it seemed a very busy woman, and when he was lonely, he'd ask us over to the Lodge.'

'How often did you call there during the past three months?'

'Oh . . . I reckon . . . four or five times.'

'Always in Mrs Frobisher's absence?'

'That's right, sir.' Mrs Sopwith shrugged delicately. 'The truth is, Herbert and I couldn't feel easy with her. We knew Hugh before he was married, you see, he had one of our rooms at the Bargee for a while. But when a man takes a wife things change. We were the ones found White Lodge for them, but once they'd moved in, well, it was a case of who's gentry and who's not, and who may sit down to dinner and who may not. I don't hold it against Mrs Frobisher. She was brought up so, and people don't change easy, to my way of thinking. But she and us didn't get on, that's the truth of it.'

'You called at the Lodge on 16th January, then. What time?'

'Ha' past five.'

'Who admitted you?'

'Beth Pottergill.'

'Did you enquire for Mrs Frobisher?'

'Yes. But Hugh said she'd gone out, ridden to Kew to attend one of her meetings.'

'What sort of meeting?'

'One about Votes for Women, your honour.'

Someone at the back of the court sniggered. Mr Kerr-Jenkins peered over his pince-nez and the sniggers stopped.

'Mrs Sopwith, did you, while you were with Mr Frobisher, take any sort of refreshment . . . food or drink?'

'Well, sir, we took a little brandy.'

'Provided by your host?'

'No. No, we took a bottle with us. It was by way of a Christmas gift to Hugh, you see. He'd been away over Christmas, staying with his wife's father in Wiltshire or Dorset or somewhere, so we couldn't give him the

74

brandy before.'

'Dr Bell has said that later that same night, when he asked for a little brandy to give to Mrs Frobisher, he was told by Mrs Pottergill that liquor was not permitted in the house. Did you know of that rule?'

'Hugh never spoke of it, sir.'

'Did you know that Mr Frobisher was in the habit of consuming a good deal more alcohol than was good for him?'

Mrs Sopwith drew a careful breath; but she faced the Coroner squarely. 'Mr Frobisher was a heavy drinker, your honour, too heavy. I know that. But I also know that if a gentleman is that way inclined, he'll get the drink. You can't treat a man like a child. Better to have a bottle on the table in plain sight, I say, than hidden somewhere, or taken in the street, secret-like.'

'Had you discussed that view with Mrs Frobisher, at any time?'

'No. As I've said, we didn't meet. She didn't come to the Bargee, and I didn't take tea at White Lodge.'

'Let us retrace our steps a little. You have said that Mrs Beth Pottergill admitted you to the house. Did she do so readily?'

'Well...' The heavy shoulders rose... 'No. She tried to pretend Mr Frobisher wasn't home.'

'Did she say so?'

'Yes. She said he was out, and started to close the door on us, but I saw Hugh's hat and coat in the hallway, and gave a call, and he heard. He came out from the drawing-room and made us welcome.'

'What happened then?'

'We went into the drawing-room and sat there, talking.'

'You opened the bottle of brandy you brought?'

'Hugh did. We each drank a glass to welcome in the New Year.'

'Did you empty the bottle?'

'We certainly did not, your honour. I don't take spirits as a rule, and nor does Herbert. We had a small glass apiece. Hugh had more.'

'How much more?'

'Two or three drinks. I didn't count.'

'Tots, or double tots?'

'Double tots, I think.'

'Did Mr Frobisher show any signs of intoxication?'

'No. He was depressed. Shaky. He wasn't feeling well.'

'How long did you remain at White Lodge?'

'About an hour. Until Mrs Frobisher came home.'

'Describe what occurred then, please.'

Mrs Sopwith folded her hands in front of

her waist. She seemed to be marshalling her thoughts. 'It would be . . . a little before a quarter to seven . . . we heard someone walking up the back path. That's on the garden side, where the stables are. The drawing-room where we sat runs right through the house, you see, from front to back, with the river in front and the Common at the back. I could see it was Mrs Frobisher coming home. I stood up and told Hugh we'd not stay, but he told me to sit down again, and before I could make shift, the door from the hall opened, and in she came. She was brushing water from her shoulders, for it was raining. She looked up and saw me, and said "good evening". She went over to Hugh and gave him a kiss. Then she saw the brandy bottle on the table with our three glasses.

'She just stood there for a minute. Her face was kind of stiff. Then she put out her hand and grabbed up the bottle. Hugh said something like "You leave that alone," and caught hold of the back of her skirt. She lifted the bottle away from him and looked at Herbert and me. "Mr and Mrs Sopwith," she says, "I do apologise for not asking you to stay for dinner, but I have no cook at the moment. Her son is ill and she has gone to look after him." It was plain she was asking us to leave, and I stood up right away and said we must be off. But Hugh shouted to us to sit down.'

Mrs Sopwith spread her arms in a gesture of simple bewilderment. 'It was hard, your honour. We'd done the wrong thing, bringing the brandy, I know, but the more I said we must go, the more Hugh shouted to us to stay. He stood up and got in front of the door and yelled that he wasn't having his friends insulted. Then Mrs Frobisher said she didn't intend any insult, and we'd be welcome to stay, but she was dirty from her ride and must go upstairs and wash. She started towards the door, where Hugh was still standing. He didn't move. He was shaking like a leaf. I said, "Careful, Hughie boy, you'll make yourself ill." And he said, "If I'm ill, it's the fault of this..." He used bad language, sir, which I won't repeat. "She'll be the death of me," he said.

'Then Mrs Frobisher stepped away from him and held up the bottle. "This is what's killing you, Hugh," she said, "and you know it." And she went over to the window on the river side, and put up the sash, and poured the rest of the brandy out into the garden. At that Hugh seemed to go kind of crazy, for he fairly jumped past me and grabbed hold of his wife and started to shake her and shout like a madman. He had her by the throat. She still had her riding-whip in one hand, and she

78

lifted it and hit him in the face. He let her go, then, but he still kept shouting. Herbert tried to quiet him, and he kept shouting, "I'll take what I like in my own house, I'm master in my house as you'll learn." He kept pointing at his wife. "You'll not go gallivantin' after Women's Rights and the rest, but stay home where it's your place to stay. I'm going to sell that horse of yours tomorrow," he said, "that'll keep you at home, by God, unless you mean to walk all the way to Kew.""

Mrs Sopwith drew breath. She took a lace handkerchief from the sleeve of her dress and dabbed her forehead with it. Her black eyes shot a look at Alice Frobisher, who was watching her intently. For a moment the gaze of the two women held. Then Mrs Sopwith turned back to the Coroner.

He spoke mildly. 'Did Mrs Frobisher respond to this . . . ah . . . warning?'

'She did. She said, "Hugh, if you try to sell Azrael, or anything that's mine, I'll kill you." Then she just walked out of the room, and up the stairs.'

'Did Mr Frobisher answer her?'

'No. He said no more. He flopped down in his chair and put his head down in his hands. Herbert and I left as quick as we could. Y'see, we never guessed Hugh was in any danger, we never thought she meant it . . . but next day . . .'

'Wait a moment, Mrs Sopwith.' The Coroner wagged a thin hand. 'Are we to understand that when Mrs Frobisher said, "If you try to sell Azrael or anything that's mine I'll kill you," neither you nor your husband took her seriously?'

'Well . . . you don't, do you?'

'What did you take her to mean?'

'I thought she was just angry. As you might say, speaking without thinking.'

'Did you take her words literally?'

'How do you mean?'

'Did you believe her to be threatening her husband with violence?'

'Not then, I didn't.'

'Let us be quite clear about this. Were the words spoken in such a way that you felt you must take action to protect Mr Frobisher? Did you, for instance, warn the police?'

'No, of course not. I mean, I thought she said it as anyone might. You know, "I'll kill you". You can't blame me for not . . .'

'Nobody blames you, Mrs Sopwith. As you have pointed out, people use the words "I'll kill you" without meaning them. And you took Mrs Frobisher's words in that sense?'

'Yes sir. But the same night Hugh came to the Bargee and said to Herbert he was going to sell the horse and, as Herbert says, it was a firm offer, not just talk. A lot of people heard it. And by next morning, Hugh was dead of poison. Well, when I realised that, I thought different about what I'd heard and seen at White Lodge. I went to Sergeant Grimbold and told him the whole. I felt awful about it, but what else could I do? Hugh was my friend. Nobody else was going to see him right. I did my duty.'

'Mrs Sopwith, you have just said, "By next morning, Hugh was dead of poison." At the time you spoke to Sergeant Grimbold there was nothing to indicate the presence of poison. Why then did you suggest it?'

For the first time, Mrs Sopwith looked wary. 'It's true, no-one had spoken the word. But I'd eyes in my head, hadn't I? I'd seen Hugh go thinner and thinner, all those months. The attacks he had, vomiting and purging, those weren't normal. He was a sick man, anyone could see it. He was being poisoned.'

'You mention attacks of vomiting and purging. How long had you been aware of these attacks?'

'Well, Hugh had the gastric trouble for some time.'

'How long? Think carefully.'

'I suppose ... about a year. Since last Christmas but one.'

'To what did you attribute them a year ago?'

'Well ... how can I tell ... I'm not a doctor, your honour.'

'Did you at any time during the past twelvemonth notice a change in the drinking habits of Mr Frobisher?'

'He was drinking more.'

'Did you ever refuse to serve him at the Bargee?'

'A few times, when I thought he'd had enough.'

'As his friend did you reason with him or try to make him give up alcohol?'

Mrs Sopwith's lip jutted. 'It's no good reasoning with a man that wants to drink.'

'Did you ever think that the alcohol he consumed might be the cause of his attacks?'

'I'm in the trade. I know what hard liquor can do to a man. I've known a deal of heavy drinkers, I've seen men die of it, but Hugh wasn't so far gone. When he died so sudden, I had to speak up.'

'Very well. You spoke to the Sergeant; and to anyone else?'

'Perhaps I did.'

'Did you suggest to anyone other than Sergeant Grimbold that Mr Frobisher died of poisoning?'

'I may have done.'

'To how many people did you so speak?'

Suddenly Mrs Sopwith's temper flared. 'To quite a few. I spoke my mind, I'm not ashamed of it, I wanted to see justice done!'

The Coroner did not question her further, but left it to Charles Comyns to check certain points. Mrs Sopwith was a good witness in that she did not contradict herself. Rennie, hearing her, felt sure that her description of the scene at White Lodge was substantially accurate. But there was a slyness about her. She was too clever, she was twisting something. Surely the jury would sense that? Surely they would see that those attacks of Hugh's were due to alcohol and no other poison? Yet would they? Since the Crippen case, every gastric symptom was the subject for doubt, every sudden death a matter for gossip.

Leaning forward in his seat Rennie watched Mrs Sopwith step down from the stand. A small smile touched her lips. She was pleased with herself. Why? Why did she want to fix such a terrible crime on Alice Frobisher? What malice possessed her?

Rennie felt the beginnings of panic. He swung round to look at the Coroner and encountered the direct gaze of that enigmatic eye. The Coroner seemed to be looking right through him, and for a moment Rennie felt that he, too, was being weighed in the balance.

83

Then Mr Kerr-Jenkins took from his vest-pocket a large silver watch, tapped it and laid it on the table before him. 'There is, I think, time to hear one more witness before we adjourn for luncheon. Mrs Beth Pottergill, please come forward.'

*   *   *

Mrs Beth Pottergill, housekeeper to Alice Frobisher, was one of the plainest women Rennie had ever seen. She was a mulatto, her skin sallow, her jaw long and thrusting, her nostrils wide and flaring. Her black hair was drawn back tightly under a black straw bonnet of antiquated style. One of her front teeth was chipped. But Rennie saw that she had fine eyes, deep-set, grey, observant; and that her hands moved with delicate grace. When she spoke her voice had a burr, not of the tropics, but of the English south-west. She stood in a posture erect yet relaxed, her hands resting lightly on the bar of the witness-box. Looking at her, Rennie decided that what she said would be believed.

She described herself as a widow, twenty-eight years old, and added that she had been in the employ of Mr and Mrs Frobisher since they married four years ago.

The Coroner asked her whether she had

84

been at White Lodge throughout the afternoon and evening of January 16th.

'Yes, your honour.'

'You admitted Mr and Mrs Sopwith to the house at about five-thirty?'

'Yes. And I'd like to say, sir, that I never told them Mr Hugh was out. I said he was not at home to them.'

'Why did you say that?'

'He was resting. He'd been poorly all day, and after tea he fell asleep in his chair. I didn't want him disturbed. And I saw Mr Sopwith had a bottle under his coat. I knew they meant to give liquor to Mr Hugh, and that was not what Mrs Frobisher wished. I thought to send them about their business, but Mrs Sopwith called out quite loud, and Mr Hugh heard, and I had to let them by.'

'Having done so, what did you do?'

'I went back to the kitchen to prepare the vegetables. Cook was away, and I told Mrs Frobisher I'd see to the dinner.'

'Your mistress was out riding?'

'She'd ridden over to Kew for the Women's Franchise Meeting.'

'Did Mrs Frobisher tell her husband where she was going?'

'I don't think so, sir. Mr Frobisher was against votes for women.'

'Quite right,' called a voice from the back of

the court, and the Coroner rapped sharply.

'Silence. This is not a mart for the exchange of unsolicited political views. If there is further interruption, I shall have the offenders removed from this place.' He turned back to the woman in the witness-box.

'At what time did Mrs Frobisher return from her outing?'

'Just on a quarter to seven. She came in through the back door and went straight to the drawing-room.'

'Mrs Sopwith has told us that an altercation followed between Mr and Mrs Frobisher. Do you agree?'

'I was in the kitchen, your honour, but I heard voices shouting, angry-like. I don't know what words passed. Later I heard the mistress go upstairs and, a minute or two after, she rang for hot water and I took it up to her bedroom. As I climbed the stairs, Mr and Mrs Sopwith left the house by the front door.'

'How was Mrs Frobisher when you took up the hot water?'

'She was crying.' Beth Pottergill turned to look at Alice Frobisher. It was a look of intense pity, of love and steadfastness, and it made the woman's plain features almost radiant. Turning back to the Coroner she said, 'It was the first time I ever saw her cry. She was bitter upset because those people brought drink into the house and tempted Mr Hugh. They were always helping him to stumble. I told her not to worry about their sort, but she caught a hold of my hand and said, "How can I ignore them, Beth, when they're killing Hugh before my eyes? How can I be calm under that?" I told her she must, for her husband's sake. I said she must talk to Dr Bell about him. He couldn't go on as he was, or there'd be nothing left of him, or the marriage.'

'Did Mrs Frobisher agree to your suggestion?'

'Aye. She said she'd speak to the doctor the very next morning. She said, "I've tried to deal with it by myself, and I've failed. I've let Hugh down. If I can't help him, perhaps someone else can." She talked that way, oh, for quite a long time. She needed to quieten down. After a while she washed and changed into fresh clothes, and brushed her hair, and we went downstairs. She peeped into the drawing-room and saw that Mr Frobisher was reading his evening newspaper. She didn't go into the room. We went out to the kitchen and got on with preparing the dinner.'

'You prepared it together?'

'Yes, that's right. Mrs Frobisher wanted to tell me about the meeting at Kew.'

'She'd interested you in women's rights, eh?'

Calm grey eyes surveyed him. 'No, your honour, I interested her. She joined our Group for Reform six months back.'

'I see. Now tell me, did Mr Frobisher leave the house at any time during the evening?'

'No.'

'Are you sure?'

'Sure as I can be, sir. I kept looking to see if he wanted anything, as he'd been poorly. He slept a lot, that day, in his chair. At about eight o'clock, when the dinner was ready and I went to call him, I had to waken him. I had to shake him by the shoulder.'

'What food did you serve at dinner?'

'There was a nice chicken casserole with vegetables, and a roly-poly pudding with syrup, because it was such a cold night.'

'Was any drink served with the meal?'

'Just fresh lemon cordial from the jug. Mr and Mrs Frobisher both drank a little of that.'

'Did they both taste everything on the table?'

'Yes. Mrs Frobisher ate a little of everything, as usual. Mr Frobisher seemed out of sorts. He never spoke a word, except to complain. He took a few mouthfuls from his plate, and then pushed it aside and told me it wasn't fit to eat; but that was not true sir, for I had some of everything afterwards in the kitchen, and it was good wholesome food that would have done him good had he taken it.'

'You say your master was out of sorts. Do you mean ill?'

'Peevish, your honour, and only half-awake from his sleep. His hands were shaky, too.'

'What happened after the meal ended?'

'Mrs Frobisher asked me to build up the fire in the drawing-room, and she sat in there with her needlework. Mr Frobisher went up to his bedroom.'

'What time was that?'

'About a quarter to nine. He left the dining-room, and at the door he stopped and said, "Beth, bring me a large pot of coffee, upstairs." I made the coffee and took it through to Mrs Frobisher on the tray. She didn't want any herself. I asked should I take the tray up to Mr Hugh, but she said no, she'd do it.'

'And did she take the coffee to him?'

'Not exactly, your honour.'

'Explain, please.'

'She took the tray from me and carried it half-way up the stairs. I was watching from the hall. Before she reached the top Mr Hugh came and stood on the upper landing and called out, "Leave it on the table," meaning the table on the half-landing, at the turn of the stairway. Mrs Frobisher said something like, "Please, Hugh," and he shouted again, "I tell you, leave it there." So she set down the tray on the table and came down the stairs and went into the drawing-room and shut the door. And when the door was shut, then Mr Hugh came down and collected the tray and took it up to the top floor.'

'You watched him do this?'

'Yes, for it was in my mind to speak to him and tell him what hurt he gave his wife, but I saw it wasn't my place and I went back to the kitchen.'

'Was there sugar and cream as well as the coffee-pot and cups on the tray?'

'Cream. No sugar. We none of us took sugar.'

'Later, we are told, Mr Frobisher left White Lodge. Did you notice what time that was?'

'Yes. He went out at half-past nine, through the back door and down to the stables. Mrs Frobisher came out to my sitting-room at the back of the house and told me not to put the chains up on the door, as she didn't intend to wait up for her husband. She went up to her room. I went to Mr Frobisher's room which was next to hers, and collected the coffee-tray. The coffee was almost finished, but there was enough left in the pot to make half a cup. I added cream from the tray, and drank what was left, using the cup I'd set for Mrs Frobisher.'

The Coroner's chin dropped. He gazed steadily at Beth Pottergill and she met his gaze. 'After I'd drunk the coffee,' she said deliberately, 'I washed the cup, the cream jug and the coffee-pot, and polished them and put them away.'

'Mrs Frobisher never drank any of the coffee?'

'No sir. Just Mr Frobisher and myself.'

'When you collected the tray from his room was there any sediment or residue in the cup he had used?'

'Nothing I could notice.'

'Mrs Pottergill,' the Coroner leaned forward to emphasise his words, 'you have stated that you and Mrs Frobisher shared all the food eaten by Mr Frobisher?'

'That's right. There was nothing he took that one or the other of us didn't eat.'

'Or drink?'

'The lemon cordial was drunk by the Master and Mistress. The coffee by the Master and me.'

'Did you, on that night or any other occasion, see any unusual substance in White Lodge, any new medicine, for instance, or any packet you did not recognise?'

'No. It wasn't a house for medicines. I mean there were Gregory powders, and Sedlitz powders, and some embrocation for a sore back . . . and a small bottle of quinine tablets Mr Frobisher took for the malaria, and a bottle of *sal volatile*. Those were all in the closet in Mr Frobisher's dressing-room. I tidied it out only the week before he died. There was nothing new. Mrs Frobisher didn't like medicines.'

'Were there any crystals or salts? Epsom Salts, for instance?'

'None. Mr Frobisher said once that Epsom Salts was fit only for savages, not civilised beings.' Mrs Pottergill raised her shoulders in a faint shrug. 'I understand what you need to know, sir, you need to know if I ever saw any of that morphine at White Lodge. Well, I never did see any. If that's what he took, then I don't know where he got it.'

'It is indeed important for this court to know, if possible, the source of the morphine, and how it came to White Lodge. It is not a commodity one can buy over the counter in a pharmacy, and any man who possessed such a drug would treat it with caution, and keep it in a safe place.'

Mrs Pottergill appeared to think this over. At last she shook her head. 'I never knew him to have such a thing but, as you say, sir, a man with a wicked drug like that would treat it carefully, he'd maybe hide it, or carry it with him? I never looked after Mr Frobisher's

92

clothes. He looked after himself, and sent his things to the laundry or the valet-service for cleaning.'

'After Mr Frobisher's death, was any search made for the drug at White Lodge?'

'Yes. The morning after he died, I mean on January 17th, Dr Bell came and spoke to the Mistress. The three of us went round the house together. We found nothing.'

'Thank you. Now, Mrs Pottergill. Had you formed any opinion about Mr Frobisher's health during the past few months.'

'Hindsight is easy, isn't it, your honour? Now, I can see he might have been taking more than liquor. Then, I didn't see it. A person doesn't think of poison nor of drugging. Not in their own home. A person doesn't think of anything so terrible.'

'I'm sure that is often so, Mrs Pottergill. What happened at White Lodge after Mr Frobisher left the house at nine-thirty?'

'Mrs Frobisher went to bed, sir. I looked in on her about ten-thirty and she was asleep.'

'You did not yourself retire?'

'No. I had mending to do, and I read some tracts too. Then I reckon I fell asleep in my chair, for I was awakened by a great hammering on the front door. I thought it was Mr Frobisher lost his key, and went to let him in. But it was Dr Bell. I opened the door to him. He told me he must speak to my Mistress, for Mr Frobisher was dead. And then Mrs Frobisher came downstairs herself.'

The rest of Mrs Pottergill's testimony confirmed what Dr Bell had said. But as she was about to stand down, she turned back and addressed the Coroner.

'Can I say something of my own wish, your honour?'

'If it concerns this inquiry, Mrs Pottergill.'

'It's just that I want to say, I lived at White Lodge with Mr and Mrs Frobisher for four years. You get to know people in that time. She never said or did anything to harm him. She was as loyal and loving a wife as you'll find this side of heaven, and his best friend. She stood by him, always.'

Beth Pottergill went quickly back to her place in the well of the court, looking neither to right nor left of her. Charles Comyns, apparently well satisfied with the impression she had made on the jury, did not seek to question her.

★　　　★　　　★

The court adjourned for luncheon.

Rennie, easing stiff limbs, found himself hustled from the courthouse by a crowd bent on reaching the Grey Feather.

Outside the sun smouldered behind clouds.

94

Morphine, thought Rennie, as he crossed the courtyard. A grain and a quarter of it would taste strongly enough to alert any man, even in black coffee. Hugh must have swallowed it knowingly.

Suicide?

Sopwith said not.

An accidental overdose?

A lethal dose swallowed in the belief that it was not morphine, but something innocuous?

The women knew the truth. Alice Frobisher and Beth Pottergill. Beth was an extraordinary woman. Obviously devoted, yet independent. Convincing, very . . .

He entered the Inn, one of a crowd, yet isolated by his own conjecturing.

★ ★ ★

Not everyone went to the Public House to eat. Of the people in the court, many refused lunch, preferring to remain outside the courtroom so that they could regain their seats there.

The jury, shut away from their fellow men, were served sandwiches and hot drinks in the jury-room. They talked of the morning's revelations.

The Coroner did not leave the courtroom. He remained at his table, apparently im-

95

pervious to cold and hunger, taking only a cup of beef tea. He studied his notes, one slender hand supporting his forehead, the other holding a gold pen. From time to time he added or deleted a word. After some fifteen minutes, he laid the pen aside, leaned back in his chair and closed his eyes. He was not asleep. The policeman on duty at the door could see that his lips were moving gently, as if he murmured to himself.

*   *   *

'Ah, she did it all right.'

Rennie, temporarily blocked in his progress across the tap-room, turned his head to observe the speaker. This was a skinny man in a long black overcoat, the collar trimmed with greasy serge. A black bowler hat was tilted to reveal a narrow brow, and thick glasses grossly magnified a pair of greedy eyes. A hungry carp, thought Rennie, that will eat any unwholesome thing.

'You can't say that,' a second voice reproved, 'can't say that until it's at an end, Josh.'

'Put it in the coffee,' said Josh, undeterred.

'Mrs Pottergill drank some, didn't she? Didn't 'arm 'er.'

'She took only a half-cup, that's why. Mind,

96

not that I blame the widow. Provocation. She was provoked. There was the 'orse, and more, I can tell you. There was a brooch of 'ers, brought it in to me, did Mr Frobisher, oh, a matter o' three months ago, and "What'll you give for that?" 'e says. I give 'im twenty pund. Next day but one, in comes Mrs Frobisher. Redeems the brooch for cash on the nail. Nothin' said, but by the way she looked, I could tell 'e'd popped it without 'er say-so. Proper wild, she was. Well, if that was 'is line, you can see it'd provoke a woman. Eh?'

'Not to murder. Not to poison.'

'You can't tell.'

'No more can you, Josh Riley. You didn't oughter say what you can't rightly know.'

Josh buried his nose in a pint-pot and his spectacles glinted above it. 'Poison,' he said, with relish, as he lifted his head, 'is the weapon of a fiend. What sort 'o woman 'ud use it? Imagine waitin', after you'd give it, watchin' to see it take effeck. Cruel, that is. And careful what's more. A poisoner is a careful one. Thinks about it careful, and measures the time an' the dose with a steady 'and and 'eart. And then watches the victim careful, to make sure 'e's good an' done for. I thought about it, sittin' there in the court. An' I thought, if I was up there, on the Crowner's bench, there's three things I'd want to know.

97

'First, I'd ask myself, 'oo's interested, 'oo's concerned, 'oo's to be the lucky one once the dear departed is safe in the coffin? For there's some'll kill for a sixpenny-piece, or because of a few 'arsh words spoken in anger.

'Second, I'd ask, 'oo ad the chance to do the deed? 'At's a question for yer. Opportunity.

'And last, I'd look at the way people be'aved arter the crime was done, yuss, and some while arter, too. Because people will give 'emselves away. By their fruits ye shall know them, as the Good Book says. Mrs F. 'ad the interest to kill. She 'ad the opportunity to kill. But there's the last question, 'ow did she carry on arter 'e was dead? There's the answer we don't 'ave.'

'Yes, we do. Went to bed and to sleep, as Mrs Pottergill told us. A loyal wife, Beth said, and I'll take 'er word when I wouldn't take others.' The second man wagged a finger. 'An' I'll say more. Beth doesn't tell lies, but 'Erbert Sopwith does, and so does that wife of 'is, as well you know. They'd 'ave the skin off of their old Gran for a 'earthrug.'

The crowd in the taproom shifted, and Rennie was able to reach a table, where he sat sipping his whisky and thinking over what he'd heard. Josh was the local pawnbroker, evidently, and could vouch for at least one attempt by Hugh to sell his wife's possessions.

Comyns should be warned about that.

Rennie became aware of someone at his side. It was Keech, who had spoken to him that morning in court.

'Mind if I join you?' The journalist swung his chair round and squeezed into it. 'Well,' he said, 'finding it interesting?'

Rennie, feeling the tug of anger, said nothing. Keech grinned. 'Oh well, it's distressing for anyone who's close to the dead person.'

Rennie shifted to face the other man. 'May I ask you a question?'

'By all means, old man.'

'You know the courts well? From your work?'

'Palm of my hand.'

'How about Mr Kerr-Jenkins?'

'Ah. Him.' Keech swilled beer dregs round his tankard, and drank. 'Sharpest old bugger on the Crowner's bench, anywhere in the four proud realms.'

'Indeed?'

'Indeed. This affair now. Today. You're probably wondering if he expects a verdict of murder. Wondering what's in his mind. So are we all. I'm here because my editor was tipped off this could be more than your common-or-garden case. Then, the Coroner summoned a jury. That's significant. He could have

99

dispensed with it, if he'd thought the death was due to natural causes. As to whether he smells murder . . .'

Keech beckoned to a potboy, and was at once provided with a fresh tankard. He paid, and looked back at Rennie. 'If you want my real opinion of the Crowner, he scares me out of my wits.'

'Why?' Rennie could see that Keech was not entirely joking.

'Because he's a man who backs his own judgement to the limit.'

'But surely, most people . . .'

'Oh no, dear boy.' Keech cocked a bloodshot eye. 'Most of us leave room for human error, for reasonable doubt. Enough change in the pocket to cover the last bus home. Not Kerr-Jenkins. He's one hundred per cent sure, once he's made up his mind, that he's right. Now, nobody's that good. Nobody's God. One day, he'll make a mistake, and he'll push it through to the mouth of Hell and beyond. So you see, Mr Kerr-Jenkins is like the performer on the high wire. We're all watching to see when he falls, and who he takes with him when he does.' Keech paused. 'It could be Alice Frobisher. You know her well?'

'I never saw her until today.'

'Then let me speak freely. There are stong

100

rumours going about that she poisoned her husband. My paper heard of it before the results of the post-mortem were known, so the talk must have been pretty virulent. There was no mention of other men, but plenty about quarrels between the lady and her husband. He chose his friends badly, as you've seen. That's a rough crowd at the Bargee. The police have been interested, so I'm told, about some of the patrons; but ask for details, and they tell you "nothing known".

'Thameside is hostile to Alice Frobisher. As to the Coroner, with him it's one of two things. Either he isn't sure how Hugh Frobisher died, and means to find out; or he is sure, and intends to nail the guilty party. Either way, by tonight I'll have a good story. And for Alice, fair Alice, that old man on the Bench will be saviour or executioner. God save us all from justice, is what I say.'

'But the Coroner said himself at the outset, we were not conducting a trial.'

Keech laughed loudly. 'We're always conducting a trial old man, every day of our bleeding lives. Say what you like, Mrs Frobisher is being judged, both in this court and outside of it. Did you see those society women sitting there in their silks and furs? That's the jury, dear boy, the jury of her

101

peers. I'm telling you, public opinion is likely to condemn her.'

'Why?'

'Any number of reasons. She took agin' the Sopwiths, and showed it. She's gentry. She wouldn't let Thameside rob her. She supports votes for women. She owns her property instead of handing it over to her husband, which of course is unnatural vice.'

'If she'd let Hugh have it, he'd have gone through it all, I know.'

'You going to say so?'

Meeting the sharp eye, Rennie hesitated, then decided that Keech had earned the confidence. 'Yes. If I'm asked. I told Mr Comyns I'd give evidence if it was needed.'

'Umh. Character stuff? Scion of a respected family, I take it?'

'The Frobishers are respected.'

'And toffee-nosed?'

'Why do you say that?'

'Made Hugh the black sheep, didn't they?'

'I suppose so.'

'Would he be likely, in your opinion, to take to drugs?'

'Are you interviewing me for publication?'

'Not if you say not. But I'll tell you, old man, I'm interested in this case. It's on two levels, you know. There's the surface level, what we're hearing about Hugh Frobisher,

102

the inquest; and there's a deeper level, something we've not been told yet, and that's where the real story may be.'

'What do you think will happen? I mean . . .?'

'At the moment my bet would be on a verdict of murder.'

'But Mrs Frobisher had no opportunity . . .'

'On her side, aren't you? Well, she's a spellbinder, give you that. But either she or Beth Pottergill could have tipped morphine into that coffee-pot, don't you see?'

'Beth Pottergill drank some of the coffee. So it wasn't . . .'

'She says she drank it.'

'You mean she was lying?'

'Someone in that court was lying. Felt it in my bones. What would you say was the relationship between those two women?'

'Relationship? I thought Mrs Pottergill showed loyalty. Devotion.'

'Devotion as what? Servant? Friend? Something more?'

'I certainly did not feel that there was anything unnatural. Nothing to suggest perversion.'

'Except a dead husband on a river-bank.'

'Oh come.' Rennie's annoyance was rising. 'You're building up a sensational story and

103

blackguarding two women without the slightest evidence to support you. I don't believe there is anything . . .'

'You don't want to believe it.' Keech suddenly chuckled. 'I said, you're on her side. She's like that. Makes you for or against her. Well, if it's any comfort, I'm for. My report of the case up to the luncheon break will tend to favour the good-looking widow. But you watch Mr Kerr-Jenkins, sitting up there like the Archangel Gabriel.

'And one thing more. I've said society judges, and it loves to kill, too. It hounds down, and tears apart. I know what I'm talking about. I'm paid huntsman in the biggest blood sport of them all. That's why I drink too much. I've been in at too many kills.'

He rose to his feet and began to shoulder his way towards the bar. Rennie took the opportunity to escape. He went out of the Inn and stood in the Square, breathing in the cold and heavy air. After a while he made his way back to the court-house. Two men he had noticed that morning were standing on the steps, in close conversation. One was the Coroner's Officer, Kerry. The other, a rock-like person, had arrived late and sat at the back of the courtroom.

They glanced up at Rennie's approach, and

moved away out of earshot. It crossed his mind that the big man could be a plain-clothes policeman. Scotland Yard might well be waiting for the outcome of this inquest.

★   ★   ★

'Ten days before he died,' said Mr Wilfred Muirhead, 'I told Hugh he must mend his ways.'

The court had resumed promptly at two o'clock. Where MacQuern had spoken with the authority of his knowledge, Muirhead spoke with the confidence of his caste. To the voice and bearing of a country gentleman, he added a conversance with business circles. He was the first lay witness who did not seem to be in any way in awe of the Coroner.

'Mend his ways . . .?' prompted Kerr-Jenkins, and Wilfred nodded.

'Hugh was killing himself. His behaviour was affecting my daughter's happiness. I always feared that might happen. They met four years ago. It was a rapid courtship. I tried to dissuade Alice from the engagement, but she was very much in love with Hugh and believed his faults arose from loneliness, and would dissipate on marriage.'

'What faults?'

'He drank too heavily. Although he was

clever, very good company, and a fine sportsman, he was erratic. I was fond of him, but thought him a bad risk.'

'Did you forbid the marriage.'

'Lord, no.' Muirhead glanced at his daughter, whose lips curved in a faint smile. 'Alice is independent. She was almost of age when they met, and I've never thought it either the duty or the right of a father to impose his will on a grown woman. I took steps to ensure financial and material security for her. I talked to Hugh about his plans for the future. He was already enrolled as a medical student at St Joseph's College of Medicine. He received an allowance from his family. It was not big enough to support two people in comfort. My lawyers and those of Hugh's father drew up a marriage settlement, fixing a certain income upon Alice, and giving her ownership of a house, which I bought for her. Also of the equipment of the house, her horses and jewels. Hugh, on his side, was to receive from me the sum of five thousand pounds invested in sound stock when he qualified as a doctor.'

'That was a generous settlement on your part.'

'No sir. I am comfortably established and have one child only. I could afford the money. In a sense, I was seeking my own peace of mind by bestowing it as I did. I think now I was wrong.'

'In what way?'

'I made Hugh dependent upon Alice for house, food and transport. He resented this. Instead of giving him freedom to study, as I had hoped, I made him bitter towards me and even towards Alice herself. He talked about finding employment, but that came to nothing. He studied, but without dedication. He failed examinations, missed lectures. Perhaps I should have given him nothing at all. Perhaps I should have allowed him free access to whatever Alice owned. I don't know. Certainly my arrangements made neither Hugh nor Alice happy.'

'What was Mr Frobisher's state of health during the time you knew him?'

'He was never a fit man. His drinking weakened his constitution, and he deteriorated very sharply this past year. My daughter brought him to spend Christmas with me on my farm in Dorset. Twice during that time he suffered rather frightening lapses of memory, and often he was half-drunk. I persuaded him to see my doctor, who warned him he was on the way to killing himself. I spoke to him and begged him to take a cure. There is a doctor in Zurich who specialises in such cases. I told him I was prepared to make a fresh settlement in the monetary sense, and he smiled at me and said, "Don't do it, Father. I shall spend it all on brandy, and die the quicker." He could be very honest when he was sober. I pitied him deeply.'

'It has been suggested here today,' said the Coroner, 'that in the last three or four months of his life, he showed signs of emotional disturbance, a change in character. Is that your view?'

'Yes. He became very much more moody. Lethargic at times, then up in the air. Almost hysterically excited. He began to ... to sell my daughter's possessions, or pawn them. Brooches, small articles from the house, harness from the stables. She would let them go, as a rule, to avoid scandal. But once, he pawned a brooch that had belonged to my wife. On another occasion, he sold a carpet I had given to Alice. It was imported from China, and quite valuable. Hugh sold it to Mr and Mrs Herbert Sopwith, of the Bargee.' Muirhead's eyes shifted to the couple seated behind his daughter. 'They gave Hugh five pounds for the carpet. When I learned of this, I went to see them, explained the actual and sentimental values of the rug, and redeemed it.'

'For what sum?'

'For one hundred and thirty-five pounds.'

'Have you a record of this transaction, Mr Muirhead?'

'I have. When I went to redeem the rug, I argued with Mr Sopwith about the legality of the original sale. He showed me a receipt for five pounds, signed by Hugh, which he claimed "made all right". I pointed out that the rug was not Hugh's to sell, and that I could if I wished take legal action to recover it for my daughter. Mr Sopwith replied that his wife would "cut up rough" if she lost the rug, but suggested that one hundred and thirty-five pounds would reconcile her to her loss. I did not wish to bring a case which would expose Hugh's weakness to public view. I paid the price named. At the same time, I warned Mr and Mrs Sopwith that if I heard of any further attempts to "buy" Alice's possessions without her permission, I would have the law on them. I left them in no doubt what those possessions were. I told them, for instance, that Azrael belonged to Alice, and not to Hugh.'

Rennie felt a surge of triumph mingled with apprehension. Muirhead's words showed that the Sopwiths had been both grasping, and untruthful in their testimony at this inquest. But they also showed that Hugh had for some time been cheating his wife of her property. That could be a powerful source of hatred, and therefore a motive for murder.

'One last question,' said Kerr-Jenkins. 'Did you at any time try to consult Mr Frobisher's medical advisers?'

'Yes.' Muirhead lifted his head and spoke with great emphasis. 'Perhaps it was unethical, but I believed Hugh was heading for an early grave. In September of last year, without informing Hugh, I went to St Joseph's College and spoke to Professor Sidney Wendell, head of the Department of Medicine. I told him of Hugh's drinking and asked him to help if he could. He promised to do so. But a month later Hugh was sent down from the Medical School.'

'He was sent down? He did not suspend his studies of his own accord?'

'No, although he told us so at the time. It was only after his death that I learned the truth.'

'On what grounds was he sent down?'

'I will explain.' Muirhead paused to collect his thoughts. 'When my daughter told me, two days after Hugh's death, that there were rumours she had poisoned him, I went to Professor Wendell for a second time. I questioned him closely. I learned that in October last year there was a party held at the College, a party which was attended by students only, and which became very rowdy. College authorities were forced to intervene to

110

end the disturbance. Several of the students present were found to be suffering from the effects of morphine and were sent down for the remainder of term. Hugh was one of them.'

'What was the date of this "party"?'

'October the 19th.'

'And you learned the details, the facts, only on January 18th of this year?'

'Yes.'

'How did you respond to this information?'

'I told Professor Wendell the circumstances of Hugh's death. I told him there was to be an inquest. I told him that Dr Bell, my daughter's doctor, already suspected that Hugh might have taken something that hastened his death. I told him of the rumours going about Thameside. I asked him, in view of all these circumstances, to speak to Dr Bell and to the police in the light of his knowledge of Hugh's previous use of morphine. He agreed to do so.'

'You acted very properly, Mr Muirhead, and very promptly. What you did must have been painful for you, but I'm happy to say that, as a result of your advice, Professor Wendell did consult both Dr Bell and the police authorities, and is present in court today.' The Coroner's smile was benign. 'Mr Comyns? Have you any questions you wish to put?'

'No, your honour.'

'Then Mr Muirhead may stand down, and I will ask Professor Wendell to come forward and take the oath.'

There advanced from the back of the court the short and purplish man Rennie had noticed earlier. He wore a frock coat and striped trousers, an old-fashioned spade-shaped beard. His eyes were small and of a very bright blue. He had the look of being pompous and quick-tempered, and that he was also wary emerged from the fact that he had already submitted written testimony to the Coroner, who duly read this aloud.

There had been, averred the Professor, no reason prior to the incident of October 19th last year, to discipline Mr Frobisher. He was a third-year student, older than most. He 'lived out', and his drinking habits had not impinged upon his studies 'to any marked degree', although recently his health appeared to have declined. On October 19th, however, the party had been held in the rooms of a senior student. Some of those present had behaved disgracefully, broken furniture and tossed the College porter into the ornamental fountain in the courtyard. As a result of this behaviour, four students had been sent down, Hugh Frobisher among them.

When he had read the statement, the Coroner laid the sheet of paper aside, and sat for a moment in silence, considering Professor Wendell with an expression of detached interest.

'Professor,' he said at last, 'did you and the other members of the disciplinary committee attempt to discover the cause of this riotous behaviour?'

'We enquired. We enquired, naturally.' The little man was blustering, and Rennie suddenly had a picture of St Joseph's as a college of small account.

'What was the outcome of those enquiries?'

'In what sense . . .?'

'What did you learn from Mr Frobisher to explain his conduct?'

There was a long silence. Then, unwillingly, the Professor said, 'He told us he had acted that way because he had taken morphine.'

At this point Rennie saw Alice Frobisher, who had sat so still up till now, swing round in her seat to stare at the witness on the stand. The Professor glanced at her almost nervously, then back to the Coroner, who posed another question.

'At the disciplinary Committee, held on . . . let me see . . . October 20th, Mr Frobisher admitted to taking morphine. He named the

113

drug to you, did he?'

'Yes. He told us he'd taken half a grain of morphine in a glass of brandy and water. When he was asked why, he said he wanted to test the effects on himself, in the spirit of scientific experiment.'

'Did he say how he had come to possess the drug?'

'He said he had been given morphine crystals by a friend. He refused to divulge who this person was. He said he had shared the supply with others at the party, and they had consumed all he had.'

'You believed his statement?'

'At the time, yes, I did. So did the other members of the committee. Students are at an age when experiment is natural. It is the purpose of a university or college training to encourage the spirit of adventure, of innovation. Of course, I warned Mr Frobisher of the extreme folly of such an experiment.'

'Did he observe that warning?'

'I am unable to say. He went down the same day, and I did not see him again.'

'Did the College authorities try to determine the source of supply of the morphine?'

'Yes. Without success. The other students confirmed it was supplied by Frobisher. Where he got it, nobody knows. It certainly

114

did not come from St Joseph's Hospital stocks.'

'Did you report the matter to the Police?'

Before Wendell could answer, Alice Frobisher was on her feet.

'This is infamous. I was not told. I was not warned. How dared this man keep such a thing from me...?' Tears were pouring down her face, she could hardly speak. The Coroner held up a gentle hand.

'Please, Mrs Frobisher, sit down. I appreciate your shock. But I must ask you not to interrupt.'

Abruptly, Alice sat down, turned towards her father and bent her head. He put his arm round her shoulders. The Coroner addressed Professor Wendell.

'Did you report the matter of the morphine to the Police?'

'Not then. The whole matter was thrashed out. We ... the disciplinary committee ... felt that the affair was not malicious. It seemed to be a single incident, which was not repeated. To inform the Police would have brought scandal to the College, and possible disgrace to some young men at the outset of their promising careers.'

'Professor, you know that morphine is an addictive drug, do you not?'

'Naturally, sir. I am a doctor.'

'So am I, and for that reason I ask you this. Did it never occur to you that Hugh Frobisher, and the other students, having once tried the drug, might acquire a taste for it, and become addicted?'

'I didn't think of it that way.'

'Did you think of it at all, Professor?'

The Professor's face was flaming. He burst out, 'I had the reputation of the College to consider.'

'I see. You were in court this morning, and heard Mr MacQuern's evidence. You heard him suggest that Mr Frobisher might have been taking morphine for some months, in other words, he might have begun taking it before the party on October 19th. As a doctor, you are familiar with the signs of morphine addiction. Did you notice any such signs in Mr Frobisher, before he was sent down?'

'No.'

'Can such addiction pass unnoticed by people close to the victim?'

Wendell shrugged. 'Unnoticed is a relative word. We notice what we wish to notice, we notice what we expect to see. It's not uncommon for the family and friends of a drug-addict to persuade themselves for a surprising length of time that nothing is amiss. And in the case of Mr Frobisher, his habit of drinking too much might have masked the

116

signs of morphinism.'

'But you have said you were not aware of his drinking.'

'Not quite that, sir. I said it did not noticeably affect his studies, until recently. He missed some lectures . . .'

'Other witnesses have said he was seriously ill as a result of what he took. Do you refute that?'

'I can't keep track of every student in my faculty.'

'After you received a visit from Mr Wilfred Muirhead, on January 18th, you went to the Police, I understand.'

'Yes. I visited the Station nearest to St Joseph's. They put me onto Inspector Malcolm Rowan, of the Thameside Division. I went to see him next day, January 19th. I told him about the October party, and the morphine.'

'That was just three calendar months after the incident at the College?'

'Yes.'

'Thank you, Professor Wendell.'

Rennie, watching the doctor stumble down from the stand, felt almost sorry for him.

The next witness to testify was Inspector Rowan, the rock-like being Rennie had seen talking to Sergeant Kerry outside the court-house.

*   *   *

Seen close to, the Inspector was formidable. His broad pale face shone as if polished. He had large white teeth in a wide, thick, down-turned mouth. His hair was receding from his forehead. His suit was tight across the bunched muscles of shoulder and thigh. Everything about him, his hardness, his air of massive patience, made him seem more like marble than flesh. Only his eyes were alert and quiet, like a weasel watching from a hedge.

'Inspector Rowan, you are in charge of the Thameside Division of the Police Force?'

'Yes, your honour.'

'The report of Sergeant Grimbold of Thameside West Station regarding a statement made to him on January 17th by Mrs Dora Sopwith, was referred to you?'

'Yes.'

'That same day,' the Coroner glanced at a paper before him, 'you informed my office that there might be a need to call an inquest upon the body of Mr Frobisher. You reported to me that you had seen Dr Bell, who advised that a post-mortem should be requested. You said further that the widow of the dead man, Mrs Alice Frobisher, had asked for a post-mortem. You mentioned that Mrs Sopwith had suggested, to Sergeant Grimbold and to others, that Mr Frobisher had "died before his time". Have I those facts correct?'

'Quite correct, sir.'

'Did you yourself interview Mr and Mrs Sopwith?'

'Yes. I called at the Bargee at three-thirty p.m. on January 17th, and spoke to them. Sergeant Grimbold accompanied me. I cautioned Mr and Mrs Sopwith not to discuss the circumstances of Mr Frobisher's death with anyone, but to leave matters in our hands.'

'Did you interview Mrs Alice Frobisher?'

'Yes. I went with the Sergeant to White Lodge, and saw her there.'

'Can you give an account of your actions at White Lodge?'

'Having offered my condolences to Mrs Frobisher,' the bright eyes flashed towards Alice, 'I informed her of Dr Bell's visit to me. She said she knew of it and had invited it. She knew of the accusations made by Mr and Mrs Sopwith, and said she wanted the matter cleared up.'

'Did you ask whether, to her knowledge, her husband had taken any poisonous substance?'

'Yes. She told me that she and Mrs

Pottergill had shared everything that was eaten or drunk by her husband the night he died. Except for one thing, that is.'

'Yes?'

'Neither of them shared the bottle of brandy that was brought to the house by Mr and Mrs Sopwith that evening.'

'Did you enquire about the bottle?'

'I did, sir. Mrs Frobisher told me that when she came home about six-thirty that Friday evening and entered the drawing-room, the bottle was standing on the table near her husband's chair. About two-thirds of the contents had been drunk. She poured what was left in the bottle out of the drawing-room window. She left the empty bottle on the table.'

'Did you ask for it to be handed to you?'

'Yes, but it was no longer at White Lodge.'

'Did you learn what had become of it?'

'No sir. It seems that Mrs Pottergill took a basket of empties round to the local shop about ten o'clock on the morning of the 17th, but there was no brandy bottle among them. Liquor was not kept in the house, so any such stuck out like a sore thumb. Mrs Pottergill never saw the bottle anywhere at White Lodge after that evening.'

'Did you search the premises?'

'Sergeant Grimbold and I made a thorough

search of the house, the stables and the grounds.'

'Thorough, Inspector, is a big word.'

'Well, as thorough as can be expected in two hours.'

'Could the bottle have been hidden? Buried, for instance?'

'To my mind that wouldn't be necessary your honour. The river runs right past the house. Anyone wanting to get rid of a bottle had only to pitch it in. If the cork was driven home, it could be floating in the Channel by now.'

'What was Mrs Frobisher's attitude to your search?'

'She was co-operative. She conducted us round the house herself, and showed us where things were kept.'

'Did you, while you were searching, look for anything else beside the bottle?'

'We looked for poisonous substances.'

'Did you find any?'

'Every house has poison in it. There was weedkiller in the potting-shed, rat-poison in the cellar and lofts, and some medicine for conditioning the horses in the stables. That contained antimony, according to the label. I examined all the containers of these noxious substances. None of 'em had been opened for some time. The lids were rusted in.' The

Inspector flexed his shoulders. 'And we didn't find any morphine, your honour, not anywhere at White Lodge.'

'Were you looking for morphine at that stage? Surely you had not yet received the post-mortem results?'

Slate-grey eyes surveyed the Coroner. 'I looked for poisonous substances, sir, such as are known to me. I found no morphine, crystals or pills.' Again, Rennie was aware of some undercurrent in the court, some secret that rolled almost to the surface, like the body of a drowned man, and then sank out of reach.

'Did you,' said the Coroner, 'question Mr and Mrs Sopwith about the brandy bottle?'

'Yes, at seven thirty-five on January 17th I again, in the company of Sergeant Grimbold, called at the Bargee. I asked Mr and Mrs Sopwith about the bottle. They stated they had left it on the table in the drawing-room at White Lodge.'

'Have you since been able to determine who moved it from there?'

'No, your honour.'

'Did you search the premises of the Bargee?'

'For one brandy bottle in a public house, that would have been a needle in a haystack.'

'Mmh. I see. Then, Inspector Rowan, according to your statement, you received a

122

visit on January 19th, from Professor Wendell?'

'Yes. He called to see me and told me the circumstances relating to October 19th last, when Mr Frobisher consumed morphine.'

'What was your response to this information?'

'I expressed my concern that the matter had not been reported to me at once. There has been a great deal of illegal traffic in drugs along the Thames over the past three years and, as I told the Professor, it doesn't help the Police to apprehend the criminals when the public fails to report cases like that. I told him too, that if we'd known about the morphine being available to Mr Frobisher, we might have caught him at it and he might be alive today.'

'Did you question the other students concerned?'

'Yes. They all tell the same story. Mr Frobisher gave them the morphine to try "just for a lark".'

'Have you come across that sort of "lark" before?'

'Well, sir, it's an old trick of the man who's caught in the drug habit, to try to involve others. Drugs are expensive, and sooner or later an addict runs short of the cash he needs to buy supplies. Then the pusher ... the seller ... may use him to find new clients. A party where drugs are handed round is one way of doing that.'

'How was the morphine presented on October 19th?'

'In the form of crystals, which was mixed with the drinks. None of the students ook much, I gather. But Mr Frobisher urged them to try it, and gave the impression he could get plentiful supplies.'

'Have you made enquiries about the morphine that was taken by Mr Frobisher on the last night of his death?'

'I have, your honour.'

'Have you traced the source?'

'No, but it's early yet. Enquiries of this nature take time. We have not found any evidence of any morphine sold legally to any member of the Frobisher household, nor of any missing from St Joseph's College.'

'In other words, you don't know where he got it?'

'That's about the size of it, sir. We'll keep looking.' Inspector Rowan's mouth bunched in a humourless smile. 'In my view, Mr Frobisher will be found to have bought his supply illegally. Morphine is being sold every day along this reach of the Thames. London's a big port, the drugs come in and are dispersed by water as well as overland.'

'Is this crude opium, or refined?'

'Both. The refined opium . . . morphine in the crystalline form . . . fetches a better price. But the degree of refinement can vary. Illicit drugs are often impure, and that means uncertain strength. A man can take several doses of a weaker type, building up the amount he takes as his addiction grows. Then, one day, he gets a package that's a lot stronger. He takes his customary amount, and it kills him.'

*　　*　　*

At the request of Mr Comyns, the Coroner recalled to the stand the two medical witnesses. Dr Bell came up first.

'Doctor,' said Comyns, 'when you went to White Lodge on the night of January 16th, to warn Mrs Frobisher that her husband was dead, you spoke at some length both to her and to Mrs Pottergill?'

'Yes.'

'Did either of these two women show any sign of suffering from the effects of morphine?'

Dr Bell shook his head. 'No sir.'

'Yet they had shared all that was eaten or drunk by Hugh Frobisher that night?'

'Apparently, yes.'

'That being so, is it reasonable to suppose that Mr Frobisher consumed the fatal dose in some medium that was not shared by his wife or his housekeeper?'

'That is reasonable, I think.'

'Thank you, Dr Bell, that is all.'

MacQuern stepped up to take his place.

'Mr MacQuern, you have told us that morphine is bitter to taste. Could it have been taken in brandy without Mr Frobisher's noticing the flavour?'

'I would say not.'

'If Mr Frobisher took morphine between six-thirty and seven p.m. on that night, and took it in brandy, what would be its effect?'

'The brandy would increase the speed of absorption into the system, and intensify its effects. Mr Frobisher would in my view have collapsed earlier than he did.'

'You have also said that taken in coffee, the bitterness of the morphine would be less noticeable?'

'Yes, that is so.'

'You have heard that Mrs Pottergill drank what remained of the coffee. Would she have noticed the taste, had it contained morphine?'

'I think she would, certainly. In my view, the morphine could not have been added to the coffee in the pot without being detected by Mrs Pottergill. That does not mean, of course,

126

that Mr Frobisher did not take it in coffee. He might have placed it in his own cup.'

'You have told us that he took one and a quarter grains, a large dose. Would he do so deliberately?'

'I think deliberately is the wrong word.'

'Will you explain that?'

'We're talking about a man already suffering from alcoholic poisoning, to the degree where he has memory lapses, fits of extreme depression, emotional crises. A man in that condition might misjudge the quantity he had taken; or he might simply forget that he had taken an amount, and repeat the dose. It is conjecture, though.'

★   ★   ★

In the courtyard, the clock struck four and the sky took on a bruised and sullen hue. In the court-house, the Coroner was pulling together the threads of evidence for the guidance of the jury. His voice, silvery and deft, spun fact across fact, stretching a shining web . . . for whom? Rennie looked at Alice Frobisher, her profile touched now with shadows as someone turned on the courtroom lights.

'. . . the exact circumstances of death on the river-bank are conjecture . . . but we can accept that death occurred very close to midnight on January 16th ... you have the testimony of Herbert Sopwith, of Sam Fisher, of Mr MacQuern, and of Dr Bell about that ... you have been given expert opinion that the primary cause of death was an amount of morphine, something close to one and a quarter grains, and that this, acting in conjunction with the deceased's poor state of health, his over-indulgence in liquor, his fall from his horse and exposure to the bitter cold of a winter's night ... caused him to die of suffocation. Mr MacQuern has given it as his view that the morphine was probably taken by Mr Frobisher some three and a quarter hours before death, that is at about a quarter to nine on the night of January 16th.

'You have been told what the dead man ate and drank in the course of that evening. At six-thirty, he shared the greater part of a bottle of brandy with Mr and Mrs Sopwith ... his dinner included chicken in casserole, vegetables, a steamed pudding and a glass of fresh lemon cordial, all of which was shared by his wife, and the housekeeper Mrs Pottergill. After dinner, at a quarter to nine, Mr Frobisher withdrew to his own room, allowing no-one to follow him. We have the picture of his telling Mrs Frobisher to leave the coffee-tray halfway up the stairs, and when she had done so, of his collecting it and taking it up with him.

'His actions in the next fifty minutes are, as Mr MacQuern has said, a matter for conjecture. But we can take it that some time between going upstairs, and leaving the house at nine-thirty, he consumed nearly a whole pot of coffee.

'Mr MacQuern's considered opinion is that between the lower and upper limits of seven-thirty and nine-thirty, Mr Frobisher also ingested the morphine. He has told us that the likelihood is that it was taken close to nine o'clock. You have heard that the drug is bitter to taste, and while it would be easily noticeable in most foodstuffs, it could be masked, though not concealed, by the flavour of strong coffee.

'You may decide that the likelihood is that Mr Frobisher took the morphine in his after-dinner coffee. You will notice that having swallowed this bitter-tasting drug, he did not make a complaint to anyone, nor try to rid his stomach of the poison, but went off to a public house and there behaved in a perfectly ordinary way, drinking several tots of brandy, and talking about the sale of a horse to Mr Sopwith.

'You have been told by people who knew him well that Mr Frobisher was not a man likely to contemplate suicide, but that he was also a man who had recently suffered fits of

129

depression and unnatural excitement ... that his family and friends knew him to be a hard drinker ... that he was at times shaky, and that he suffered from lapses of memory. You have also heard that the post-mortem revealed signs which could support the theory that deceased had been taking morphine for some time, although not for a very lengthy period ... say for months rather than years.

'Inspector Rowan has told you that it is not yet known to the Police how Mr Frobisher obtained the morphine he distributed at the St Joseph's party, on October 19th last; nor have we any evidence on who supplied him with the morphine that caused his death. But you may consider the likelihood is he obtained supplies by illicit means, and that he had been doing so at least as long ago as last October.

'The total picture, you may feel, is that in Mr Frobisher we see the unhappy picture of a man addicted to alcohol and to drugs, which twin poisons caused the deterioration in his health and his personality described to us by many people today.

'There is remaining, the vital question of precisely how the morphine taken on January 16th, was administered to Mr Frobisher. Did he himself measure one or more doses into his coffee, or was it given him by a hand other than his own? If the latter case is in your opinion true, then you may bring in a verdict that Hugh Frobisher came by his death by murder or by manslaughter. I must warn you that if you bring in such a verdict, it must be a verdict built upon solid grounds. You must set forth in your verdict the person, if any, whom you find to have been guilty of the offence; and if the name of such person is unknown to you, then that person may be referred to as "a person unknown".

'In the event that you do not find that the deceased met his death by murder or manslaughter, then you should say so. You should make it clear in what manner you think he died, whether he did deliberately take his own life, or whether he died by misadventure, that is by taking through accident, ignorance or carelessness, or any other ill-chance, a dose which proved fatal to him.'

Mr Kerr-Jenkins paused a moment, gently patting into position the pile of notes in front of him.

'I must remind you again that you must base your verdict on the facts placed before you, the concrete evidence you have heard in this court. Supposition and rumour should not influence you, nor are you required to make moral judgement of the lives, the social behaviour, the attitudes of those concerned in this very tragic occurrence. You are here, as I told you at the beginning of the day, to decide how, when, and by what means Hugh Malory Frobisher came to his death.'

* * *

When the jury withdrew and the Coroner retired to his own office, Rennie and the rest of the observers remained in the courtroom. He did not speak to anyone. He could not bring himself to follow Alice Frobisher, her father and her lawyer, when they walked out into the corridor.

He sat on, elbows along the rail before him, head bent. He thought of Hugh. A hundred images came to him of a young man, cantering his horse across a sun-baked polo-field, lying on his back to watch an eagle rise, laughing, arguing, alive.

The clatter of the jury's return startled him. He looked up. The benches were packed. The Coroner mounted his stand. In the journalists' row, Keech leaned forward and caught Rennie's eye, with a faintly quizzical smile.

'Gentlemen of the jury, what is your verdict?'

The foreman rose from his seat.

'We find that deceased. Hugh Malory Frobisher, of White Lodge, Thameside, did by misadventure on January 16th of this year,

132

swallow a fatal dose of morphine. We further find that no person or persons other than Mr Frobisher himself was concerned in the administration of this poison.'

*   *   *

Outside in the corridor groups of people lingered in avid discussion. Rennie, thrusting between them, felt his arm grasped, and found Charles Comyns beside him.

'Mr Rennie, Mr Muirhead and his daughter would like to offer you some refreshment before you go back to London. They're in the private sitting-room.'

Rennie hesitated. The hearing had depressed and upset him more than he would have believed possible. The verdict of accidental death was a relief, but it could not place on record the suffering and mis-management that had led Hugh to a sordid end on the tow-path. An inquest, it seemed, cleared the living of blame by shifting it onto the dead. Rennie felt a fierce resentment against all the protagonists of the day's events. He wanted to be rid of the lot of them.

However, it would be grossly discourteous to leave without saying goodbye, so he went with Comyns across the Market Square, and slipped through a back door of the Grey

Feather, and made his second entry of the private parlour there.

This time, he found father and daughter sitting over a tea-table. The old man looked weary, but Alice Frobisher turned to Rennie with a brilliant smile.

'I'm so glad Mr Comyns found you. I wanted to thank you. I didn't do so properly this morning.' The hand she extended to him was warm, he could feel the vitality in it, and her face was flushed. 'Since Hugh's death, I've been living in a nightmare. Every day there was some fresh horror. Questions, police, humiliation. People threw stones at my windows. I knew the Sopwiths were out to prove I killed Hugh. They're evil people. I knew we had to beat them, to show them up, and we did, didn't we?'

Her manner was excited. There was an almost animal triumph in her voice that both fascinated and repelled Rennie. So much for the cool detachment she had shown in the court. She was a good actress, it seemed.

Muirhead interrupted these thoughts. 'Mr Rennie, Alice and I are staying in London tonight, at Brown's Hotel. We'll be honoured if you will dine with us.'

'That's kind of you, sir, but I must write letters tonight.'

'Ah yes, of course. You'll want to set things

134

out for Hugh's family. We'll be taking the train down to Appley early tomorrow. The funeral will take place there. Will you be able to come down?'

'I'm afraid it's impossible. I am due in Paris tomorrow afternoon, an arrangement I can't alter. I shall be away for a fortnight.'

Muirhead bowed politely. 'Then it remains only to thank you for your support today, and to say that if ever you are in Dorset, we hope you will come and visit us. This is our address.'

'Thank you,' said Rennie, taking the card. He then took his leave. Comyns followed him out into the corridor, which was now deserted.

'Will you be acting for the Frobisher estate, in the financial sense? May I communicate with you, if there is any need?'

Rennie nodded. 'Certainly.' They exchanged cards. As they did so, Comyns remarked, 'White Lodge will be sold. Mrs Frobisher doesn't wish to remain there. Can't say I blame her. There'll be gossip for some time, yet. It's best she should make a fresh start.'

They parted, and Rennie headed for the courtyard with some haste. But he was not yet free. As he stepped out into the Square, he encountered 'Gaffer' Keech. The journalist was talking to Inspector Rowan. Both men

135

turned and Keech called out,

'Hullo there, Mr Rennie. Going for the train?'

'Not immediately. I have something to do first.'

'I'll walk a way with you. Coming, Inspector?'

The three men crossed the cobbles, went through the archway and started down the narrow main street of what had once been Thameside village. Keech said, 'Well, what did you think of the day's work?'

'I thought the jury reached a true verdict.'

'Yes. At least the gal's cleaned of some of the mud. A little always sticks. She leaving the district?'

'I understand so.'

'Good thing. She's been lucky.'

'Lucky?'

'What would have happened if Beth Pottergill hadn't finished off that pot of coffee?' Before Rennie could answer, Keech swung round to the Inspector.

'What do you think. Was it a fair verdict?'

The cold grey eyes lifted. 'Yes.'

'You don't believe she killed her husband?'

'There was no case against her, was there? The Sopwiths witnessed a domestic quarrel. And they're a couple of liars, who fight worse than that in their own home.' The big man gave his bunched and mirthless smile. 'It wasn't facts that convinced the jury, though.'

'What then?'

'I'd say it was the moment that Professor Wendell admitted he never told her her husband was on morphine.'

'Yes, it's possible. She cried. The crowd liked that. A show of womanly feeling.'

The Inspector shrugged. 'It's my opinion those were tears of pure rage. Furious, she was, with the old fool, and I can't say I blame her. If she'd known in time, she'd have acted. She's a very forcible young lady, is that one. Ah well, now she's in the clear, and I think rightly so. Yes, the jury reached the only verdict possible on the facts . . . reached it for the wrong reasons of course . . . that's often the way.'

They had come to the station turn-off. Keech said his goodbyes, and hurried off. Rennie remained facing the policeman.

'Inspector Rowan, there was a lot left unsaid at that inquest.'

'Always is, sir.'

'I believe the Sopwiths supplied Hugh with morphine.'

'What makes you say that?'

'No reason you could use in court. But . . . they're guilty people. One feels it. Liars, as you said. I think they were trying to shift attention from themselves, by accusing Alice Frobisher. The things Hugh sold to the Sopwiths, and other people . . . he could have been trading them for drugs, couldn't he?'

The Inspector was still watching him carefully. Rennie demanded, 'Why don't you search the Bargee?'

'We wouldn't find anything there. Not now.'

'I suppose not.'

'Don't worry sir, we know our job. We can deal with the Sopwiths when the time comes. There's questions still to be asked about all this, and people to be kept in mind.'

'Of course.' Rennie was now impatient to be alone. 'Can you tell me how to get down to the tow-path? I would like to walk along it. To tell Hugh's family . . .'

Rowan gave him instructions. Rennie followed them, walking through narrow lanes until he came to the glint of River.

The Thames at this point was not majestic, but a broad and fairly populous highway. A string of barges went down-stream as he watched, their lights throwing blood-red reflections.

He turned westward along the path, passed yards stacked with timber, a tannery, a clump of cottages. He came at length to the Bargee. It was already doing a brisk trade. No doubt half

Thameside would be in tonight, to talk about the inquest. Already, the ballad of Hugh Frobisher was taking shape, on the pen-tip of Keech and Lodden, on the tongues of men and women. One couldn't stop it.

He walked on. The buildings gave way to open Common, and here the tow-path was wider, and edged by ragged bushes. Rennie could not know at which point along it Hugh had died, but he felt obscurely that it would comfort his people at home to know that someone had visited the place.

He reached the end of the open ground, and saw ahead of him a large house fronting directly on the River. The name 'White Lodge' was chiselled on stone gateposts. Beyond the garden wall rose bow windows, a grey slate roof. Not a mansion, but a graceful, well-found building.

Rennie stared at it, trying to imagine Hugh living here. He could not conjure up that ghost. Instead, he received an impression of someone quite different; of Alice Frobisher, clever, vibrant, determined. This was her house. Her presence dominated it still. Her face shone in Rennie's mind, eliminating all else.

Angrily, he turned away.

Damn the woman.

He would send a telegraph to Delia

139

Frobisher first thing in the morning, telling her of the verdict of the inquest, and then his responsibility would be over. That would be that.

* * *

Rennie soon found he could not escape so easily. The day after the inquest he sent his telegraph, bought the morning papers and clipped out every reference made to the hearing, and included these in a long letter to Hugh's mother.

That afternoon he left for Paris, and in hard work tried to drown the memory of what had happened. It proved impossible. As he had feared, the public appetite had been whetted. When he returned to London he found that one rather scruffy journal was running an article on drug-running. Another, more respectable, was publishing letters that criticised the whole institution of Coroners' Courts, saying they often amounted to trials. And in polite drawing-rooms, the guilt or innocence of Mrs Frobisher and Beth Pottergill was still eagerly discussed. In fact, one unpleasant quatrain was often heard:

For wives who rue the wedded lot
The remedy lies handy;

For morphine in the coffee-pot
Kills quicker far than brandy.

Some six weeks after the inquest, Rennie's
hand was forced. He returned to his rented
rooms to find two letters awaiting him.

The first was from Walter Frobisher, and
its message was brief. The family was grateful
for Phil's presence at the inquest, and his kind
letter to the family afterwards. His mother had
been greatly comforted by it. But her mind
was not at rest. She felt extremely unhappy
about the position of Hugh's widow, and had
written to her, inviting her to come out on a
visit to Durban. What did Phil think of the
plan? Was Alice likely to accept? And what
sort of woman was she, what must they
expect? Walter would be glad of such
guidance as Phil could give him.

The second letter bore a Dorsetshire
postmark, and was from Alice. She wrote:

*I have had a letter from my mother-in-law,
Mrs Delia Frobisher. I would very much like to
have your advice before I answer it. She wants
me, you see, to go out to South Africa, to stay with
her for some time. 'To make amends for the past',
she says. I must say, I'm very torn. My life here is
so empty now. I'm in limbo. So one half of me
longs to travel, to meet Hugh's people. The other
half feels I'd be mad to do so. You are the only*

person I know who can help me to decide. You know the Frobishers. What sort of folk are they? Do they really want me? What should I do?

I know I should come to London and see you, but I have been so unhappy there, and I dread the crowds. My father suggests that if it is not too much to ask, you might come down to Appley for a short spell . . . or a long one if you have time . . . we would so welcome you, and I would be so eternally grateful to you. Of course, if you can't leave London, then I'll come up to Town to see you. But the weather is lovely now, and you might enjoy being in the country for a day or two? If you can come, I will meet you at Wimborne station whenever you wish.

Will you let me know what you would prefer? Father sends his salutations to you.

Rennie spent that evening striding the streets, trying to sort out his emotions. His instinct was to dash off an answer to both letters, saying that he could not undertake to settle problems that existed within the Frobisher family. It was not fair to expect him to do so.

Yet faces rose before him. Walter, earnestly trying to do what was right and kind. Alice, a woman who had suffered a great deal and was asking for help.

That night he wrote to Walter, saying he would be going to spend a few days at Appley

142

and would write again when he had had a chance to talk about the visit with Alice and her father.

On Friday, he took a train for Wimborne in Dorset.

*　　　*　　　*

That journey through the Dorset farmlands, riding in an ancient pony-cart with a woman recently suspected of murder, was a turning-point in Phil Rennie's life. He had spent the past weeks in the smoke and sprawl of cities, and had not realised how much he longed for clear skies and clean earth. Now he was looking at some of the most beautiful country in the world. There unfolded to left and right prospects of hills that lifted round green shoulders to the sun, of streams that ran over beds white as bone. Much of their route lay along the banks of one such rivulet, and it seemed to Rennie that the valley before him was a cornucopia, so richly did it spill forth orchards and pastures and prosperous homesteads. Above him were broad uplands where he could see sheep grazing against a frosty skyline.

'Magnificent,' he said, gazing up at this horizon.

Alice smiled. 'Appley is round the corner,

in the Inch valley, but we often ride on these hills. Do you like riding?'

'Very much.'

'Good. We can find you mounts very easily. Riding is one way of shaking off the chains, don't you think?'

'I wouldn't have thought you carried any.'

'Every woman does.'

'And having shaken them off, what would you choose to do?'

She gave him a quizzical look. 'Explore the Amazon.'

'Good God.'

'I could have said, "enter politics" or "attend university" the choice doesn't matter. I want the freedom to make it.' She laughed suddenly. 'Once, just after I left school, I asked Father to let me go to Vienna to study medicine. He was very surprised and asked me why I wanted to. I said, "If I was a boy, would you ask me why? I just want to." Anyway, it came to nothing, because I married Hugh instead. You know, one reason I fell in love with Hugh was because he was like me. Discontented. He wanted something different, without being sure what.'

The road they travelled now curved towards the broader valley of the Inch. Fingers of sun leaned from a cloud to pluck at the ploughland, and this burst of light seemed to lift a sullenness from Rennie's mind. He said abruptly, 'Hugh did know what he wanted. He wanted to be a musician.'

She stared at him wide-eyed. 'He never spoke of it to me.'

'It was long ago.'

'Tell me about it.' She was as eager as a child asking for a story. 'You were friends, weren't you? Tell me?'

*   *   *

'We lived,' said Rennie, 'about a quarter of a mile apart. We went to the same prep school, and the same boarding-school in the country. Our families were close. Still are. Hugh and I paired off, both being the youngest of large families. He was much more brilliant than any other boy I knew. He had the sort of brain that is quick at mathematics, and music, neither of which were much valued in my little world. Luckily he was also a good athlete. He made the first rugby and cricket teams, and was a splendid horseman. But he didn't take sports very seriously.

'When he was six, he could play the piano and violin better than average, and kept badgering his parents for more lessons. His father thought this effeminate. They never got on, they used to go out of their way to irritate

145

each other, and as the years went on they frankly hated each other. Bernard Frobisher was an ambitious man, and a cruel one in some ways.

'He took the line that there was no chance of Hugh's becoming a first-rate musician. "You'll end up scraping a fiddle in a second-rate band. You've a small talent, you're no prodigy. You'd best go to university and qualify for some real profession." Hugh was dreadfully frustrated. He felt that if he were allowed to go to Europe and study with teachers there, he could make a career of music.

'Bernard wouldn't give him that chance. He was quite happy to stake Hugh to a future he didn't want, but not to one he did want. He said, "If you're so keen to go to Europe, go. Work your passage over, as I did at your age. Show us what you're made of." The point is, he knew what Hugh was made of, and it wasn't anything like tough enough to leave home at seventeen and fend for himself. Eventually Hugh went to university in Cape Town, to study commerce, of all daft things. From that time on he never tried an inch. He never opened a book. He started drinking and ran up debts.

'Bernard stood bail for him for two years, and then refused to hand over any more. Hugh simply left university and stayed at home. Bernard was too concerned about scandal to throw him out on the street. Hugh loafed round the house, sponged on his mother, his sisters and his friends. Women always liked him and took his part. Men too, for that matter.

'He took pleasure in annoying Bernard. Turned up at home with unsuitable girls. Made a nuisance of himself at the Club and other places. Bernard still refused to consider a musical training. By this time of course the battle-lines were drawn. I really believe Bernard's rage against Hugh was turning his mind. The whole family was being made to suffer. Finally someone . . . I don't know who . . . persuaded Bernard to make a settlement. Hugh was to come to England, and attend St Joseph's. As long as he did so he would receive an allowance that would keep him in comfort. Once he qualified, he was free to do what he liked, of course.'

'Why medicine?' said Alice.

'Hugh chose it. He said it was the longest and most expensive training he could think of, and he was going to get as much as he could out of his father.

'So, he left for England. At first he wrote to me quite often. He seemed to be enjoying himself. He found friends, Hugh always found friends. He even passed his first-and second-year examinations. He went to concerts and enjoyed the music in London. Then one day he wrote to say he'd met you. After that, I didn't hear much.'

'Tell me, how did the family react, when they heard about us?'

'None too well. Bernard ranted and raved. Said Hugh had no prospects, no income, how dared he become engaged? Who did he think was going to support him? Said you must be an adventuress, and after the Frobisher money. He said he was going to go to London and knock some sense into Hugh.'

Rennie paused, staring at the road ahead, and then turned to the girl beside him. 'Did you meet him? Bernard, I mean?'

'Yes. In London. It was a disastrous encounter. Father wanted to go with me, but luckily I refused. Otherwise there'd have been bloodshed. Mr Frobisher was incredibly rude, mad, as you say. I think he'd hoped I'd turn out to be some barmaid that he could buy off. When he realised I wasn't, he insulted Hugh so grossly that I couldn't stand for it. I simply told him I wasn't going to change my mind, that I was going to marry Hugh, and that if he cut off Hugh's allowance, I had money enough to support us both until he qualified.

'After I left, Hugh and his father had a
148

blistering row. I went home and told my father what was happening, and he went to London to see Mr Frobisher. I don't know what passed between them, Father can be pretty terrifying when he wants to. Finally, the two of them sat down with their lawyers and worked out a financial settlement.

'When it was done, Father said to me, "Bernard Frobisher isn't right in the head. Money is an obsession with him. Don't ever deal directly with him, work only through your lawyers. In fact, steer clear of the whole litter of Frobishers if you can. You don't need them".'

Alice smiled somewhat ruefully. 'In fact, I never had the chance to snub them. They snubbed me first. They sent us wedding-gifts, and wrote one formal letter apiece, but once we were married, silence. Hugh was very hurt about not hearing from his mother and sisters. He thought they were fond enough to stand by him.'

'Bernard probably spun them a tale. You mustn't think of them as demons of selfishness. They all depended upon him to some extent.'

Alice did not reply to that. Instead she said, 'Tell me about them.'

'Well. They're a clannish lot. No feeling for matters of culture, or intellect, but fond of

149

good living. Extravagant. They support charities, but they don't really care much for anyone outside their close circle. Millie is the exception, she works with the poor.'

'You mean handing out soup and worn-out clothes?'

'No. She really works.'

'They sound horrid.'

'No. They aren't. They have . . .' Rennie tried to define their quality of attraction, and failed. 'They're like Hugh. You may have disapproved of him, but you loved him.'

She nodded slowly. Then she said, 'Thank you for telling me what you have. I think, you know, his father gave Hugh a contempt for money. It was a symbol that represented his father, and so he treated the symbol with contempt. Of course, once he started to drink, then it became important.' She shook her head. 'I couldn't get through to him. You know, he was like a deaf and dumb man. I felt so helpless. It was all such a terrible waste.'

Her face twisted into the ugly grimace of someone trying not to cry. She gave the reins she held a sharp flick, so that the cob broke into a trot. 'I'm still in a very silly state.'

'Please,' he said. He could hardly bear to watch the trembling of her hands, but he sensed that she didn't want sympathy. After a while she said in a normal voice, 'I'm so grateful to you, Philip, for coming down here.'

They topped a small hillock and ahead the road dropped to the valley bottom where the village of Appley lay, tucked between two spurs of land like a bone between the paws of a mastiff. Alice pointed to the flat fields on the far side of the river, and to a group of trees set in their midst.

'That's my home.'

They passed from rosy shreds of light into blue shadow; crossed a stone bridge, wound up a long drive between massive lime and chestnut trees, and reached the house.

⋆   ⋆   ⋆

The guest room allotted to him was large, with a northern prospect across open fields. Curtains of thick embossed velvet the colour of wheat straw clothed the three tall windows. A log fire crackled in the grate. The smaller room next door had been converted into a bath-room, with an electric geyser. Philip wondered how it was powered. Possibly by the huge old water-wheel that he had seen on the far side of the house as he arrived?

Wrendale, he decided, must have started life as a farm-house and been altered into something grander as the family fortunes

151

improved. It had a well-proportioned façade of stone, and there were graceful fanlights over the front and inner doors. On his way upstairs he had seen none of the abominable pictures so common in English country houses, no animal heads, no weapons from the battle-fields of Empire. It struck him rather as the home of a man who was up-to-the-moment, well-informed and comfort-loving. The novels on his bedstand were new, but had been read. Over the bed hung a pastel sketch of the Loire valley, rather pleasing. The man servant who carried up his bag had offered to unpack for him.

'No shortage of money,' thought Rennie. 'Keech was right there, at least.'

Against his will, his thoughts kept returning to the inquest. As he bathed and dressed for dinner, faces and phrases crowded in on him. It was a trick of imagination played on him all too often, but never had any person proved so intrusive as this Alice Frobisher.

Did she always have that effect on people? She seemed to work no conscious wiles, yet she appeared to have this powerful force in her, that made one remember . . . there was no peace near her . . . she was a witch . . .

He caught sight of himself in the looking-glass, a longish, narrow, smooth face that showed its no-nonsense Scots-English ancestry. The eyes had the stare of a scared rabbit. It was ridiculous, bloody ridiculous. He must get a grip on his nerves.

At seven o'clock he went downstairs to meet his host. Wilfred Muirhead was in the drawing-room on the ground floor. Chairs had been drawn up to the hearth, and the flames twinkled on decanters and glasses on a pewter tray. Muirhead came forward to welcome Philip, and thanked him for making the long journey in winter.

The two men chatted amicably for some time. They spoke of politics, of France, of Appley, of everything but the reason for this visit. Presently Alice joined them and they moved into the dining-room. She was not wearing mourning, but a dress of dark amber velvet, trimmed with écru lace. Her hair, he saw, was not worn in the current high pompadour style, but cut short and allowed to curl naturally about her face and neck. The simplicity of her dress and hairstyle gave her an appearance that was neither modern nor old-fashioned, but singular, as a fine Chinese vase is singular. As she took her place at one end of the dinner-table, the light from the central cluster of lights touched her pale skin with points of colour, like the lustre on a pearl.

She kept the conversation to trivial matters. Yet Hugh was in all their minds. They were like fakirs, walking on knives. At any moment, their self-hypnotism might break down, and truth cut to the bone.

Muirhead seemed to be aware of his guest's unease. At half-past ten, when Alice excused herself and went to bed, he said abruptly:

'This visit to Africa; is it feasible for Alice to go?'

Philip took his time answering. 'It's a genuine invitation on Delia Frobisher's part. I'm sure she's anxious to meet Alice, and to make amends to her. Whether it will come off, I'm not so sure. I had a letter from her older son, Walter, asking that very question, will it work? I think a great deal will depend on Alice herself.'

'She's very keen to go. But isn't it very risky? To be frank with you, she's in an awfully distressed state, though she hides it well. The way Hugh died and that damned inquest have left a mark. She doesn't feel safe. The findings of a jury can't wipe out the knowledge that people have made an accusation. Strange, isn't it, that if a jury finds a man guilty, then everyone accepts the verdict, but if it finds him innocent, then doubt always lingers. Alice has been sleeping very badly. Nightmares, and so forth. She's a bundle of nerves. If she was put under strain, I don't know what might happen.

'But that's not all.' Muirhead straightened up in his chair and gazed intently at Rennie. 'The people around here . . . her friends . . . not all of them have stood by her. Some of them avoid us. Doubt remains, y'see. You yourself, after we left the court, you wanted to be rid of us. Oh I don't blame you. Friend of Hugh's, naturally you felt that way. But our friends and neighbours shouldn't disclaim us so easily, d'you think?'

'Perhaps,' said Rennie uncomfortably, 'they feel you need privacy for a while.' He encountered Muirhead's sardonic smile.

'No, not they. That jury brought in a verdict of accidental death, but some of our friends judge Alice of causing her husband's death, not because she might have put morphine in his cup, but because she neglected her wifely duties. To them, any man whose wife believes in female franchise is bound to take to drink.'

He paused, sank back in his chair once more and said, 'One of our closest friends married off his daughter last week, and Alice was not invited to the wedding. Mere cowardice on their part, but hurtful. It will blow over in time, but meanwhile Alice has to bear it. I'd like her to get away for a spell. See what I mean? I'm between Scylla and Charybdis, eh?'

Philip said slowly, 'It's difficult to answer since I don't know your daughter very well. But I'd say she's going to have a bad few months, wherever she is. Some of the problems might be avoided if she was in a town where nobody knew her. As to the Frobishers, all I can tell you is that I like them. Mrs Frobisher is a generous woman, and she really loved Hugh, and only lost touch with him to spare her other children. Walter is a solid citizen, and his wife, though a rather bird-brained creature, will certainly see that Alice meets pleasant people. Evelyn, the younger of the two daughters, is married to a chap called Toby Rourke, and they live in the Cottage in the Yellow-wood grounds, so they'd be close at hand. And Molly, the older sister, has the kindest of hearts.'

'You think they'll accept Alice without reserve?'

'They've invited her, so they must want her.'

'Perfectly true.' Muirhead got to his feet. 'And it's unfair of me to expect you to say more, at this juncture. I'm glad you're here. You know you're welcome to stay for whatever time you can spare us, the longer the better.'

'It can't be for more than three or four days, sir. I've several things to settle before I leave for home.'

'When do you sail?'

'On February 20th. I'm taking the steamer *Falstaff*. She's small, but new, and I must say I'm looking forward to the voyage.'

'That's West Coast, is it?'

'Yes, calling at Madeira, St Helena and the Cape ports.'

They walked to the door. 'I have an early start tomorrow,' said Muirhead. 'Business in Inkpen. Alice rides at ten. Would you like to go with her?'

'I'd love to.'

'Good, then Lomas will saddle a gee for you. Brought your togs?'

'Yes.'

They climbed the stairs. As they started round the gallery leading to the bedrooms, Rennie's eye was caught by a flicker of movement along a lighted passage on his right. A figure stood there, arms arrested in the act of drawing a curtain. A face turned towards him, a dark-skinned, lantern-jawed face with luminous eyes.

'Goodnight, Beth,' Muirhead called, and added, as they passed out of earshot, 'Marvellous woman, that. Devoted to Alice. Never thought she'd stay, after what happened, but she insisted. Makes herself useful here in a hundred different ways.'

157

Before he climbed into bed, Rennie opened one of the windows. The night was still, frosty, and he could hear clearly the turn of the water-wheel at the far end of the house.

It was a peaceful sound, a peaceful countryside, a warm and restful house. Yet Rennie, perhaps because of the strange surroundings, found it difficult to fall asleep.

★　　　★　　　★

Next morning, Rennie breakfasted alone, Alice having gone early to the village on some errand.

At ten, he was in the stableyard, where two horses were being saddled; a big bay for Rennie, and an exceptionally fine chestnut for Alice. If this was the Azrael that Hugh had tried to sell for £50, then it was hardly surprising that his wife had been furious.

A minute or two later, hearing a step behind him, he turned to see Alice approaching. Her appearance gave him something of a shock.

She was wearing what he at first took to be some sort of fancy dress; baggy pantaloons of fine brown wool tucked into short red boots, a white shirt, and a long narrow suede coat that fitted closely to the waist and then flared out. The hem and cuffs of this coat were beautifully embroidered in red, brown and amber. On her head was a knitted cap, from which her hair flowed free to her shoulders. She called 'good morning' as she came up, and her face broke into a smile at his expression.

'Do my trousers bother you?'

'I think they look very dashing. What is it, some sort of national dress?'

'It's a hotchpotch. I like to ride astride. I have a proper habit for polite company, but the trews are what I really prefer. My father bought them in the Argentine two years ago. The boots are Russian, the jacket came from Persia. The cap was knitted by Mrs Rees, in the village. It's all warm and comfortable.'

'And becoming,' said Rennie, finding he meant it.

A groom brought the horses up to them. Azrael was decked out, caparisoned almost, in saddle and bridle trimmed with Mexican silver. He danced and sidled as if aware of this splendour.

Alice and Rennie mounted and set off down the drive, then took a lane that circled the village and cut diagonally towards the steep hill they had passed the day before. The route gave them several chances to canter. Rennie's bay was feeling his oats, but well-mannered.

As they climbed the slope the air grew more stark, and so quiet that one could hear the soft flutter of the wind in the grass tussocks. At last they reached the top, a wide crest that stretched unbroken for miles. Alice pointed to a distant speck of white. 'That's the survey beacon. We can gallop as far as there, but watch out for potholes.'

Away she went at once, urging Azrael on. Rennie let the bay have his head, and the two horses surged across the uneven turf, through sheets of standing water, past outcrops of rock. Alice was a superlative horsewoman but, to Rennie's cautious mind, a horribly reckless one. By the time they drew rein he was soaked in sweat.

She grinned at him. 'All right?'

'Fine, thanks.'

They had ridden straight into the wind, and her cheeks were scarlet, her eyes sparkling. It was the first time he had thought her beautiful. She pulled off her cap and let her hair blow about her face.

'In summer,' she said, lifting an arm, 'you can see the sea from here, but today it's too hazy.'

'My ship will leave from Southampton.'

'The *Falstaff*. Father told me.'

'Perhaps you'll be coming with me.' He was so startled by his own words that his mouth fell open. What in God's name had made him say such a thing?

She tilted her head. 'Perhaps I will. Time

will tell.'

She started along the track that would lead them down the south-western side of the hill. Rennie followed, furious with himself. The last thing he wanted was to travel to Africa with this turbulent woman. He hurried so that his horse drew level with hers.

'Alice. I must be frank with you. Life's no different in Africa, you know. You'll find them busy building a world very like the one here. Same churches, same offices, same institutions and amusements. Same prejudices against women's suffrage.'

'You don't think I should go?'

'I'm not saying that. I'm just warning you . . .'

'Beth doesn't want me to choose Africa.'

'Choose?'

'She's keen on my going to the West Indies. She says no good will come of meeting Hugh's family. She's very superstitious in some ways.'

'But should you be influenced by Mrs Pottergill?'

'Why not?' Alice seemed surprised. 'Beth is far more than a servant to me, you know. She's a companion.'

'Of course. I expressed myself badly. I meant, should you be influenced by anyone, at this stage? Shouldn't you do precisely what you feel you want to do?'

'The trouble is that I don't know what I want.'

'Then wait until you do know.'

They spoke little on the way home, each being occupied with private thoughts.

*　　*　　*

That afternoon Philip spent in the library of Wrendale. The supply of books was not great, but it included a good selection of reference works. He chose a folder of old maps of Wessex, and a modern atlas, and a history, and sat comparing the three. He had, on previous visits to England, found Dorset one of the most fascinating of all its counties. It seemed to him that here the distant past had not been obliterated by the more recent. Rather, past and present co-existed. The ruined abbeys still spoke of the Saxon kings, the novels of Hardy described a people not much changed. There was something reticent and mysterious under the surface warmth of Dorset, something ancient and intractable.

At four, Alice came in and found him absorbed in his reading. Seeing the maps, she asked whether he would like to see some of the country round about.

'I have to drive down to Poole some time this week, by car. If you'd enjoy the run we could go tomorrow.'

'That's very kind of you.'

'You don't feel nervous of a woman at the wheel?'

'Terrified. But I'll brace myself.'

She laughed, and went and found the road map, spreading it on the sofa and pointing out the roads they might take. Her hands were small and deft. She was wearing some sort of afternoon gown of dark silk that fitted smoothly over her breasts, and her hair when she bent her head had a delicate scent, like a lemon tree in the sun.

★   ★   ★

They set off soon after breakfast next day.

The car was a Rolls Silver Ghost, the sun shone and Rennie was thankful to find that Alice drove a good deal more cautiously than she rode. She was obviously enjoying herself, and chattered away as they followed the route south. The ploughed fields gave way to downlands, and just before noon they stopped at an inn outside Swanage, to have lunch. It was warm enough to sit outside, sip their wine and eat thick wedges of leek-and-potatoe pie. Alice plied Philip with questions about the Frobishers. She wanted everything he could tell her, anecdotes of their childhood, details

163

of their marriages, their work, their interests.

He described their house, Yellow-wood, how the timber had been brought to Natal from the Tsitsikama forests by Bernard's father, who made his money as a transport rider in the early gold-rush days.

'So they're what you might call comfortably off?'

Something in her tone made Rennie glance up sharply. Alice met his eyes, smiling a little.

'Before you snub me, Phil, let me point out that they did allow me to support Hugh for four years. They made Hugh live on my charity as well as theirs.'

'I think Walter acted generously.'

She shrugged. 'I got the impression Walter thought so too.'

'No, Alice, you're wrong. Walter may sound stuffy, but he'll do anything for his friends.'

'I'm sorry. I know I sound hateful. I'm still so full of rage and bitterness. I know I must stop feeling that way, but I can't. If I had a child . . . we wanted children, but we never had any. Now there's nothing left but total failure, total loss.' She began to gather up scarf and purse. 'We'd better get on. I've some legal papers to sign in Poole. Then if you like, we'll drive along the coast. We can look at Portland Isle. I walked over it, once, and a man showed me the hole where St Paul's came from.'

★　　★　　★

It proved to be a day of small events that were to shape Rennie's life. Her own words, that everything added up to a final destiny, were true, for him, not of the years but of one Saturday.

While Alice visited her lawyers, Philip wandered about the town, gazing at shop windows, walking down to the front to stare towards the Isle of Wight. From that shore, his own forebears had set sail for Africa. How deeply symbolic the sea was, to all who were unhappy or beleaguered. One crossed the sea, and left the past behind.

Alice needed that release.

He realised that he was already too involved with her problems to drop them. He even saw the wry humour of it, that the impeccable Mr Rennie should be losing his head about a woman so unsuitable.

He made his way slowly back to the centre of town. It was lunch hour, and the streets were packed. He came upon a small square where a building had been demolished, and here found a crowd gathering. At the back of the cleared space was a ramshackle pile of timber and metal, and on this makeshift

165

platform stood a man. He was addressing the watchers in the high, resonant voice of the professional speaker, a voice that for all its roughness of accent, yet treated words as living things. The gift, thought Rennie, of poets. He stopped to listen.

'. . . we believe that Parliament is the ally of the working man, not his foe . . . it is upon the floor of the House of Commons that we should set forth our grievances for just men to hear . . . I'm not standing here, in the teeth of the winter, to talk about revolution. I'll make you no promises, I'll tell you only that I'm not a humble man, my wants are not humble. I will tell you what I will ask for, in that House. I will ask for an end of free trade. I will ask for the introduction of tariff reform. I will ask for the end of capitalist domination. I will tell whoever will listen that the workers must own the means of production, and the workers must benefit from the fruits of production. I will help to wrest from fools and fops the control of this country, and I will seek to place it in more competent hands . . .'

Rennie asked the man next to him who the speaker was.

'One of Keir Hardie's lads, I suppose.'

'What party is that?'

'Independent Labour Party.' The man tipped his fawn bowler to the back of his head.

166

'They've come up fast. Near fifty seats they won in the 1906 election, and that was the turning-point. You won't stop them now.'

'Will you vote for him?'

'No!' The other laughed. 'I'm for the Liberals, like most hereabouts. But I like the cut of his jib.'

Not all of the hundred or more people on the site seemed to share that liking. A vociferous and somewhat beery group had begun to heckle the speaker.

'What's your tariffs goin' to do to the ship building?' 'What about the cotton-mill workers, you'll do 'em out 'v their livin'.'

The speaker answered cheerfully enough. Then, in a pause, came a voice from the back of the crowd. 'What about women's suffrage?'

The speaker's eyes searched for the questioner. His hearers guffawed, jostled and craned their necks. A huge navvy called out, 'Here she is, lads, here's Mrs Bloody Pank'urst 'erself.'

Rennie saw Alice lifted shoulder-high in the beefy man's grip. He was evidently half-drunk, roaring with laughter and swaying on his feet. Rennie began to push his way through the press. But Alice seemed unconcerned about the indignity of her position. She braced an elbow on the navvy's head and raised her voice. 'Yes, Mr Lloyd. What about a vote for me?'

The speaker straightened up. He lifted his hand in a half-salute. 'Madam, you shall have it.'

'When?'

'As soon as enough men will see the light, and vote my Party to power.'

'Good. Then I support your candidacy.'

Someone bellowed. 'Go home to your husband and kids, lass, you haven't a vote.' Surprisingly, the navvy rounded on this wit and floored him with a sweep of the forearm.

'The maidie 'ave no vote, but I 'ave. An I'm for yeu, Mr Lloyd, even if it means votes for the ladies.' He swung Alice down to the ground with a flourish. Rennie, now beside her, grabbed her hand and towed her into the roadway. She was giggling like a schoolgirl.

'Well, at least I have the support of the town toper.'

Rennie was urging her along the road. 'And of Mr Lloyd, it seems.'

'And how about you?'

'What?'

'Do you think I merit a share in government?'

'I've never thought much about it.'

'Well think now! That drunkard has a vote. I don't. Do you think me less capable of making a cross than he is?'

'No. I think you're capable of anything.'

'Thank you. And thank you for forging through that mob to save me. Were you meaning to punch that huge creature?'

'I suppose, being conservative, I would have tried. It's expected of one.'

'Poor Philip! I'm afraid I'm not a very restful companion.'

'Who wants rest? I've been enjoying myself today as never before.'

'Well, now we will do something restful. Shall we drive out along the shore, and watch the sea?'

They drove south and west towards St Alban's Head, and at about three o'clock reached the brink of the downs. The sun was already westering, and cast upon the water far below them a sinuous pattern that seemed not to move, but was yet marked with pale green currents and threads of brilliant foam. As they stood there, a warship came into view, travelling unusually fast, and they saw by the dip and lift of her massive bows that the sea was far from calm.

'She's huge,' said Philip.

'One of the new Dreadnoughts, do you think?'

'Perhaps. But I think they're heavier amidships.'

'You like the sea, don't you?'

'I was born in a port. Durban's built on a steep hill, you know, and everyone has a sea-view.'

'Is it a pretty town?'

'Very. There's a big harbour, shallow, but they're deepening it. There's an Island in the centre of the Bay and, on the southern side, a long promontory called the Bluff.' He went on to tell her about his town; the steamy summers which brought a profusion of flowers and insects; the exotic fruits, mangoes and grenadillas, lemons and pawpaws, lichis and quinces. He told her of the developing town buildings; the Town Hall where Union had been signed a year earlier, the Pavilion on the Beach, the new hospital on the Front. He told her of the people who lived in Durban; Zulus, still strangers to urban life, but coming in to seek work; Indians, Tamil and Gujerati, indented at the end of the nineteenth century as labour for the sugarfields of Natal, and working now as craftsmen, wash-dhobis and market-gardeners of the Province; the Dutch settlers and the English, the Germans and Scots, the French from Mauritius, and the many-hued offspring of all these races. Alice said at the end, 'It sounds like Paradise.'

'Well, it's not. It's parochial, snobbish, and lacking in many of the things you're used to.'

'And the country round about?'

'The most beautiful in the world. Hills and grassland, natural bush. The whole of Natal is green, and it rises to the Drakensberg escarpment, which is really the edge of a plateau one thousand miles long. There are rivers and streams everywhere. Fish and birds.'

She was watching him with a dreamy, half-smiling expression, and then suddenly she jumped to her feet. 'Heavens, look at the time! Come on.'

They drove back along the powdery white road. The evening sun turned the dust to rose and amber, and Corfe Castle looked as if it were ablaze with the flames of a siege. When the sun dipped it became very cold, and Rennie dragged a fur rug from the recess behind his seat, and tucked it round Alice.

'Keep some for yourself.'

He did as he was bid. 'You're not tired of driving?'

'Not a bit.'

He lapsed into that half-entranced state that night travel brings, vaguely aware of dark fields and hedgerows, of lights that spun into sight and fell away. Yet he was intensely conscious of happiness. He felt more vibrantly alive than ever before.

From time to time he glanced at the woman beside him. Her profile with its fine nose and slightly pouting lips showed only concentration on the road ahead, yet he would have sworn that she shared his excitement.

When they reached Wrendale, Beth Pottergill ran down the front steps, a shawl in her hands.

'Miss Alice, thank God you're back. Why are you so late? Here, put this round you. We were so worried. The thermometer's dropping right down, we feared you'd be frozen.'

She took no notice of Rennie, but bundled Alice into the house, helped her off with her coat, and even sought to chafe her cold hands. Alice pulled away, smiling.

'For heaven's sake, Beth, I'm not porcelain.'

'You'll take a chill.'

'Not I. What we need is whisky and hot food. Be a dear and fix it, will you?'

The woman shot Rennie one lowering look before she went off.

He said apologetically, 'I should have brought you back sooner.' And received his reward when she gave him her wide smile.

'I wouldn't have come. It's been a lovely day. Now let's find something to eat, you must be starving.'

*　　*　　*

The next morning Rennie woke to a silence so

total he thought he'd gone deaf. He got out of bed and went to the window, expecting to see snow. The country was indeed white, but with frost, the mill-stream barely moving, the big wheel hung with icicles. A feeble sun struck rainbows of blue, rose and emerald from every surface.

Rennie found himself thinking that a wise man would leave quickly, since by nightfall the roads might well be impassable. He dismissed the idea at once. He had no intention of leaving.

After breakfast Muirhead, Alice, Beth Pottergill and Philip tramped across the fields to Appley church. The little Saxon building was packed. They hung their top-coats on pegs near the door and went to the family pew near the front. Philip sat next to Beth. She followed the service from memory and during the hymns took the contralto part with a natural sense of harmony that he guessed was born in her. Her body swayed a little to the rhythm of the music, her eyes half-closed as she sang. He had seen black women at home sing so, expressing in song their passion, pain or joy.

After the service, Philip noticed that while a number of people greeted Alice and her father, others sidled away without doing so.

The party walked home into a stiffening

wind that curled round their ankles like an unfriendly dog. By lunch time it was blowing hard from the north. The meal over, Alice announced that she had some work to do, Muirhead retired to his bedroom to sleep, and Philip settled down in the library, intending to write to Walter.

He had barely begun when there came a tap on the door. He went to open it and found Mrs Pottergill on the threshold.

'Could I talk to you, please sir?'

'Of course. Come in.'

The woman followed him towards the fire, but when he gestured to her to sit down, she refused. This was not, her manner inferred, to be a friendly chat. Folding her hands before her she began abruptly:

'Mr Rennie, you mustn't take her to that place!'

'I? I have nothing to say in the matter.'

'Oh yes, you have. She's asked you what you think, she told me.'

He was tempted to snub what seemed to him to be impertinence but he remembered the strain put upon her in recent weeks, and said mildly, 'Durban is a very pleasant place for a holiday, Mrs Pottergill.'

'The place doesn't count. It's the people that count. Those people will be bad for her.'

'If you mean the Frobishers, then you are

174

wrong. I am better acquainted with them than you are, and I assure you they will do all they can to make Alice happy.'

'There's hatred in them against her.'

'Not now. That's all past.'

'It's present, and to come.' She moved towards him, her voice urgent. 'I know. I've had a warning.'

'What sort of warning? A letter? You mean someone has written to you?'

'No. In my mind, in my thoughts.' She pressed her hands to her temples. 'I knew Mr Hugh, and they're his kin, aren't they. What good can come of her going among them?'

'Reconciliation, perhaps.'

She shook her head wildly. 'It won't happen that way.'

His anger rose. 'You are not in a position to judge that. I repeat, Miss Alice will have a happy holiday, and return to you all the better for it.'

She stared at him in surprise. 'If she goes, I go.'

'That is hardly for you to decide.'

She was silent for a moment, then smiled as if at a foolish child.

'You don't understand, sir,' she said gently. 'You don't know anything about it. Mrs Frobisher would never leave me behind, not after what's happened. I mean no disrespect,

Mr Rennie. I know you feel kindly to Mrs Frobisher, but I know things about her that you don't. If you persuade her to go, then I'll not allow her to go alone.'

And with a bow of the head half-apologetic, half-defiant, she turned and walked out of the room.

★　　　★　　　★

Rennie went back to the desk and sat for some time trying to arrange his thoughts. Not only was he furious at being put in his place by a woman who was, after all, a servant in the house. He was also fighting a new and horrible dread.

What did Beth Pottergill know that made her so sure of her hold on Alice?

His mind went back to the day of the inquest. He saw the mulatto woman on the witness stand, radiating honesty. Her evidence, more than any other, had convinced the jury that Alice had no part in the death of her husband. Her statement that she had finished the coffee left in the coffee-pot, had brought them to conclude Hugh had taken the morphine of his own will.

But what if she had lied about that one thing? What if she had not tasted the coffee? Then, surely, it became a possible vehicle for murder? The journalist, Keech, had hinted as much, hadn't he?

Rennie picked up the letter he had started to Walter, and folded it away in his breast pocket. He went over to the fireplace and pulled the bell-rope. A youthful maid came to answer it.

'Can you tell me if Mrs Frobisher is resting?'

'Oh no, sir. She'm up in the attic, turnin' things out.'

'Could you show me the way there, please?'

They climbed several flights of stairs, and came at last to a landing under the rafters. The 'tweeny vanished. Rennie pushed open a door and stepped past sloping beams to a central loft where Alice knelt, surrounded by trunks and packing-cases.

'Hullo, Philip.' She looked up with a smile. She was wearing an overall over her dress, and had tied a kerchief round her head. 'Be careful what you touch, the dust is dreadful. Here, this is clean.' She pushed a chair towards him. Philip rested his hands on its back, but did not sit down.

'I'm going through Hugh's clothes,' she said. 'I've been putting it off, and it won't do. You know, the night he died I sat until dawn, holding one of his jackets. It had the smell of him. But the next day, Dr Bell came and told me my neighbours thought I'd poisoned

177

Hugh. Then the police searched my house. They went through every drawer, every cupboard, every pocket of these clothes. I helped them. There was no poison, but when we'd finished there was nothing at White Lodge I wanted to remember.'

Philip spoke carefully. 'Alice, I want to ask you something. Did you ever suspect that Hugh was taking drugs?'

'Never. I suppose I was stupid. But he was so often drunk . . .'

'When did they tell you he died of morphine poisoning?'

'After the post-mortem, they told me they'd found it in him.'

'And when did you first hear about the party at St Joseph's, the one where Hugh handed round morphine?'

'The day Father went to see that old fool of a Professor Wendell.'

'Just before the inquest, in fact?'

'Yes.'

'So it didn't come as a surprise to you, when it was mentioned in court?'

'No.'

'Yet you broke down. Why?'

'I was so angry . . . that old goat . . . if he'd been sorry for letting Hugh go on taking the stuff, for not warning me . . . I wouldn't have minded so much. But he didn't care. All he thought of was the reputation of his dreary old College.' She folded a coat and dropped it into a trunk in front of her. 'I don't suppose the family will want Hugh's clothes. I thought I'd send them some of his books, and his signet ring and pipes, things like that.'

'Don't you want them yourself?'

'No. I told you. But this, I'll keep.' She had picked up a small blue velvet locket framed in gold and seed pearls. It contained a photograph of Hugh as a child. She held it up for Rennie to look at, but he waved it aside.

'Alice, did you actually see Beth Pottergill drink the coffee that Hugh left in the pot?'

'If she says she drank it, she drank it. She's incurably truthful.' Alice was getting slowly to her feet. 'What is all this, Philip? Why are you asking these questions?'

'I must tell you that a short while ago Mrs Pottergill tackled me and told me she was against your going to Africa.'

'Yes, that's true. But I don't see . . .'

'She also suggested that if you went, she would accompany you. That you would be . . . in some way . . . bound to take her.'

'If she wanted to go . . . I owe her a great deal. She's given me loyalty I can never repay.'

'Would she lie for you?'

'I . . . don't know.'

'If she thought you had poisoned Hugh by

putting morphine in the coffee-pot, would she have trumped up a tale to protect you?'

There was silence in the attic. Rennie gazed at Alice with a strange feeling of detachment. The light falling through the dusty windows gave her skin a greenish glow, like ice in a forest. Her mouth was a little open, her eyes wide. It was an expression of challenge, not of fear.

'She might have done. But I did not kill my husband.' She put out a hand and lightly touched his wrist. 'Do you believe me?'

'Yes. Yes, I believe you.'

She nodded, reached up a hand and pulled the scarf from her head, dropped it on the chair.

'I'm tired. Shall we go downstairs for tea?'

He followed her down through the house, knowing that now he had cast in his lot with hers, and would follow her anywhere. As they passed the big window on the main stairway he saw that the wind had dropped and thin flakes of snow were whirling down.

The snowfall lasted for three days, the thaw for two. By Friday, when Philip left for London, it had been agreed that Alice would travel with him aboard the *Falstaff*, and that Beth Pottergill would accompany her as her maid.

★   ★   ★

Three members of the Frobisher family wrote to him about these arrangements.

Delia Frobisher asked Philip to 'go to Asprey's and choose some little gift for Alice. Arrange payment through my London bank, if you will? I want her to know I'm thinking of her, and looking forward to her visit. We've had the guest-rooms re-done for her, and I'm glad to say the Winter Programme will be a very good one this year, some splendid concerts and plays, and of course the Coronation celebrations. Dear Philip, it is so kind of you to do so much for us. You are a tower of strength . . .'

Walter's letter was couched in more anxious terms. 'Sorry to add to your burdens, old man, but there's nothing for it but to ask you to help Alice with her travel plans. It's the damnedest rush here, painters everywhere, cleaning, gardens re-furbished, stables whitewashed, and all for Alice. I've arranged for £300 to be transferred to your account at Barclays. That will cover the steamship tickets for Alice and Mrs Pottergill. On no account must A. be allowed to foot the bill, both Mother and I are firm on this. I've told Beryl, Eve and Molly they must pull in their belts a bit. None of them has any idea of economy and they are

181

demanding money all the time ... also, of course, because Alice is coming. I'll have to talk finances with you when you get back. In the meantime, thank God you're in London and can see to things for us.'

The last letter was from Molly and caused Philip some alarm. Her large writing, looped across seven sheets of rather blotchy paper, called her sharply to mind. He could see her, crouched over the old table in the study, hair coming down at the back, fingers stained with the medicines she'd been packing at the Mission. She had no guile, Molly, she was like a child in her gaucherie, and like a child she was sharply observant. She wrote bluntly that she thought Alice should not come to Durban.

'They think it will be all right, Phil, but it won't. Because no-one really wants her. I don't. Walter says we have a duty to have her. I don't think she'll be happy, being a duty to us. I don't think she'll like it here at all. Frank Reppley agrees with me. He says it's all self-deception arising from a bad conscience, and when I talk to Mother I know just what Frank means. She wants to get back in God's good books. Well, that won't bring Hugh back, will it?

'Eve doesn't care much, either way. Since her illness she doesn't take much interest in anything. When I said it would make trouble, having Alice I mean, she just shrugged. I don't think Eve realises people are already talking. Cissie Lambton asked me a lot of questions about the inquest yesterday. I told her it was a verdict of accidental death, but you know Cissie, she'd much rather believe it wasn't. She just loves thinking the worst.

'And Beryl is sure Alice gave Hugh poison. She doesn't actually say so, because Walter would be so angry, but I know she thinks it. She's pregnant, you know, and that makes her sillier than ever about her nerves. She's scared out of the few wits she has.

'Can't you speak to Alice, Phil, and warn her not to come? She'd much better not. I feel it in my bones.'

This warning annoyed Rennie the more because it echoed doubts in his own mind. He knew his judgement was not clear on the subject of Alice. He wanted more than anything that she should come to Africa. He could dream up any number of reasons why it was too late to change the plans now. But was he perhaps risking fresh humiliations for her, more rumours, more problems?

Having worried about this for several days, he made a half-hearted attempt to talk to Alice. She made it clear he was wasting her time. She had made up her mind to go, and nothing would change her decision.

183

They sailed in mid-February as planned.

*   *   *

In early March, the *Falstaff* edged across the harbour bar at Durban, between the wedge of the Point on the right and the embracing arm of the Bluff on the left. Long sandbanks rose from the undredged shallows at the Bayhead, and on them mists curled and flamingoes basked. Closer at hand, in deep water, lay the ships; liners and trawlers, a British warship, a grain barque with sails furled.

Rennie stood at the rail with Alice, pointing out aspects of the town.

'This anchorage is new. The first settlers landed near the harbour-mouth. If you'd come ten years ago, even less, they'd have swung you ashore in a basket, over the ship's side.'

'I'd have enjoyed that!' She was looking very pretty in a lavender-coloured dress with wide sleeves to the elbow, and a big straw hat trimmed with lilac. Her excitement and pleasure in arriving were infectious.

'It's bigger than I thought.'

'About seventy thousand souls, thirty thousand of them white.'

'I've been wondering,' she said, 'how Beth will fit in. Hearing some of the people aboard

184

talk about coloured folk ... Beth has never lived out of England ... she thinks of herself as English.'

'It will be all right. Delia will give her whatever standing you ask for her, which I suppose will be the standing you gave her in England. She'll have her own rooms in the house. If she wants to help Aunt D. with a bit of stitchery, or whatever, that'll be for her ... and you ... to decide.'

The *Falstaff* was now close inshore, and they could discern the main town area, the jumble of brick, stone and trees, the wide streets, many still sandy, the wood-and-iron houses at the Bayhead, and to the east the handsome cupola of the New Town Hall.

'Where is Yellow-wood? Can you show me?'

Rennie moved closer to her and pointed over her shoulder. 'You see the road that runs up the hill? That's Berea Road. About three-quarters of the way up there's a large space cleared. Let your eye run past that to the right, until you come to a very tall fir tree. Yellow-wood is next door but one.'

The band on the deck behind them suddenly struck up a dashing tune. Down on the quay, a large crowd waited. Handkerchiefs began to flutter.

'Are they there? Can you see them?' Alice

lifted her face to him, eager and smiling, and at that moment he forgot all his good resolutions not to speak clumsily, not to muff things.

Like a schoolboy he blurted out the first words that came to him, shouting them against the thump of the band. 'Alice! Will you marry me? I said, will you marry me?'

She shook her head, laughing. He couldn't tell whether she meant, 'No, don't be silly,' or, 'I can't hear what you're saying.' Other passengers were pressing towards the rail. There was only a narrow passage of water between the ship and the dock. Rennie heard his name shouted, and saw Walter move clear of the waiting throng, arms raised in welcome.

CHAPTER TWO

DURBAN

SOMEONE WAS BANGING at the door.

Philip Rennie, slowly becoming aware of the noise, tried to drag his mind from 1911 to 1958. He felt disembodied, as one does after a long air flight. Who could have imagined that resurrecting the past would be so exhausting? He had thought it buried for good, a whole lifetime piled on the grave, and yet a single letter had revived it.

He looked down at his hands, the brown-splotched hands of an old man; between them lay Toby Rourke's manuscript, open still at the third page.

He lifted his head and stared at the door. 'Come in!'

His housekeeper stuck her head into the room. 'Mr Philip, your tea's going cold. Didn't you hear the bell?'

'Oh . . . let it be.'

'Aren't you well, Mr Philip?'

'Yes, yes, quite all right.' He eased his body, realising he had sat brooding here for three hours. 'Bring me a cup in here, will you Mrs Riggs?'

'And some cake?'

'Anything you like.'

'Love,' he thought, 'and hate, avarice and lust. I was never meant to withstand the force of the passions. My instinct told me to avoid them, and it was right. That very first day I saw her, in Thameside, I knew I should get away. But I didn't. She bewitched me, and we all suffered.'

Mrs Riggs returned with the tea-tray, set it down and fussed over it. Rennie hardly noticed. He was gazing round him like a somnambulist, and suddenly he burst out, 'But I was alive then, alive! Isn't that more important. . . ?'

'Pardon, Mr Philip?' His housekeeper was staring at him in concern. He dismissed her with an impatient movement of the head.

Before she was out of the room he had turned back to the manuscript, to that point where the Frobishers received his letter, telling them Alice would accept their invitation.

*　　　*　　　*

February 18th. Molly had a letter from Phil Rennie and brought it down to the Cottage. Eve, who was resting on the ottoman, said she couldn't be bothered with Phil's scrawl, and

188

asked Molly to give us the gist of it.

'Phil says she's coming and he can't prevent it.'

'Whyever should he try, goose?'

Molly wore her guilty look. It was clear she'd tried to get Phil to head Alice off. She does extraordinary things, sometimes. Eve said, 'Does Phil like her?'

'I think he's head over heels in love with her.'

Eve and I both laughed at that, the idea of old Phil losing his head over any woman. But Molly said obstinately, 'He's in love with her. You'll see.'

I talked to Eve when we were alone. She didn't particularly want to discuss Alice. A friend of hers had taken her to see their new house, up near Mr Stellar's old property on the top of the Ridge, and she was on fire for us to start building our own home. It was an old tussle, and I gave her the answers I'd given so often, that although we had the land we didn't have the capital to build, and the firm couldn't fork out until the new Port Elizabeth branch got going. Then Eve flared up and said she was sick of living in the family's back yard, and I lost my temper and said if she spent less on clothes and parties we'd be able to build a bit quicker, and she burst into tears. Then, great reconciliation, I told her I enjoyed tricking out

189

my wife in finery, and I was proud of being married to the most beautiful woman in Natal. She said she was sorry for being beastly, her nerves were all to pieces; and I put my foot in it by suggesting she see another doctor.

'Why should I? Frank's been our doctor for ever. Why should I change?'

'A new opinion might help.'

'Why are you so against Frank? You're always criticising him.'

'Well, if you must know, I think it would be better if Frank wasn't always at Yellow-wood.'

'Better for whom?'

'For Molly.'

'Oh, don't be ridiculous! The only thing she thinks about is that old Mission Hospital. She'd spend her life there if she could.'

'Because she sees Frank there. For God's sake, Evelyn, can't you see that Molly has a colossal crush on the man?'

Eve swung herself off the ottoman and came over to me. 'What are you talking about, Toby? Has something happened? Have you seen something. . . ?'

'I've seen the way Molly looks at Frank. She worships the ground he treads on, and he's not worth it. I grant you he's a competent doctor, and a bloody good polo-player, but he can't keep his hands off a woman.'

190

'That's not so. He flirts a little. Quite harmlessly.'

'It's not harmless when he flirts with Molly. She takes him seriously. You know she's damn near simple in such things. It would give me a great deal of pleasure to kick Reppley's backside, but short of that, I'd like you to find another doctor.'

'Well, I won't. I'm not going to hurt Frank's feelings because you have a ridiculous prejudice. You're so earthy you think everyone else is like you.'

We were close to dangerous ground. Luckily Eve remembered we had tickets for the Town Hall Concert, and rushed off to change.

I couldn't help thinking that Molly was right. It wasn't going to be much fun for Alice, to live at Yellow-wood.

*　　*　　*

The arrival went well.

The whole family had an early lunch at Aunt Delia's, and then drove down to the docks.

Phil Rennie got Alice and her maid ashore very quickly. There was the usual free-for-all on the quay, and we couldn't do more than exchange commonplaces. Alice looked pretty, and thanked old Seymour Rennie for 'all Phil had done for me', which pleased him. I heard him tell Walter she seemed a well-brought-up gel. Her maid, on the other hand, was both ugly and surly. When I remarked on it to Phil, he said an odd thing, 'Don't underestimate Beth.'

We settled Customs, arranged for Portman's Services to bring the baggage up later, and made for Yellow-wood. Had tea there, and then left our guest to settle in.

Back at the Cottage, I asked Eve what she thought.

'She's very chic. She wasn't wearing corsets.'

'Good God! How shocking!'

'I thought you'd noticed yourself.'

'Staring, was I?'

'Goggling.' Eve stood aside to let me unlock the front door. 'I wouldn't call her beautiful.'

'Nor would I.'

'So why the goggling?'

'She's attractive. Umh . . . sort of mettlesome.'

'Like a thoroughbred horse, you mean?'

'Yes,' I said, meaning nothing of the sort.

At eight that night we presented ourselves at Yellow-wood once more. We had a quiet evening. Aunt Delia tossed us neatly about so we all had a chance to chat to Alice, who responded as neatly to our gambits. I noticed she adapted her manner to each of us—feathery with Beryl, gentle with Walter, and serious as a judge with Molly. During dinner, the talk was mostly of the voyage. The *Falstaff* had called at Teneriffe, missed Madeira because of cholera. Alice gave us some amusing anecdotes of her fellow-passengers. I got the impression she was choosing her subjects carefully, waiting to guess our tastes before displaying her own.

When we went through to the drawing-room, something happened that might have destroyed the whole visit.

Aunt Delia doesn't pour coffee herself, but sends the tray round so that every guest can help himself. Walter, acting as butler, naturally took the tray first to Alice. It turned out that as she picked up the coffee-pot there was a lull in the conversation, and everyone watched her fill her cup. Seeing her busy over the silver tray, her small face intent, struck an inevitable chord. Hugh's death, the poisoned coffee. I felt a coldness down the spine, and that fool Beryl actually gave a loud gasp, and pressed her hand over her mouth like the heroine in a Bio melodrama. Then everyone began to talk, too loudly.

Only Alice kept her head. She gave Beryl a half-quizzical smile, and said quietly, 'I don't think, you know, we should let things haunt us. After the inquest, I felt I could never touch coffee again. Then I saw that if I allowed ordinary things to become symbols, I should go mad.'

Aunt Delia grabbed hold of the lifeline. 'You're quite right, my dear. We can't avoid the facts of Hugh's death, nor pretend we don't care about them, but we must be sensible. Life has to go on. We have to draw a firm line between what is decent grief, and what is morbid. We have to come to terms.'

Alice was watching Aunt Delia thoughtfully. 'I wonder whether you wouldn't like to talk about Hugh tonight? While we're alone, as a family?'

'It would be a comfort to do so.'

So Alice told us about how she'd met Hugh, their courtship and marriage. Their happiness and unhappiness. The circumstances of the last few months. She spoke of the inquest, and of Phil Rennie's kindness to her.

'Phil thinks that the Sopwiths use the Bargee as a clearing house for drugs. He said as much to an Inspector of Police who attended the inquest, and the Inspector hinted they were watching the Sopwiths.'

'And they attempted to avert suspicion from themselves, by blaming you?' Walter

194

was very much upset by what he'd heard. He kept pulling off his glasses and polishing them, a sure sign he's distressed. 'What a devilish thing for you . . . and for your father.'

'He was wonderful. He's sent a letter to you, Mother. I have it in my case. I'll give it to you tonight.'

That 'Mother' did the trick. Aunt Delia had tears in her eyes, and Walter made a little speech about how badly we'd all behaved in the past, and how we wanted to make a fresh start. And Alice smiled and said, yes, that was exactly how she felt, and she was so glad to be here, with Hugh's people at last.

In short, Alice turned a blunder into a lucky chance. I thought it showed generosity in her.

But when Eve and I left Yellow-wood to go back home, Molly saw us to the door. I asked what she thought of our guest, and she gave a typically Mollyish answer.

'Which guest?' she said. 'Alice, or Mrs Pottergill?'

'Well, Alice. You can hardly have had time to form an opinion of the maid.'

'I talked to her this evening.'

'And what did you make of her?'

Molly thought for a while. 'She's frightened.'

'What of?'

'Us. She's frightened, and she's clever.

195

They're both clever. Don't you think?'

★ ★ ★

On March 24th, Walter and I went out to Mount Edgecombe to discuss new crushers for the sugar-mill. We were to import and install the machines, and we wanted to discuss siting problems with the mill-owners. By three we'd done talking and started for home. We gave a lift to a Zulu woman with a sick child, the wife of the induna at the mill. She was a beautiful creature, wearing the smoky blanket and mud-packed hair like royal regalia, but she had never visited town before, and was plainly terrified. Walter took her straight back to Yellow-wood, where the baby could be seen by Frank Reppley, and cared for properly.

When we'd seen her settled we went in for tea. Beryl looked charming, playing hostess in a pale yellow gown with a good deal of lace about it. Clearly, Walter had read her the riot act about her gaffe of the previous evening. She hastened to tell me that Phil Rennie had called round and told them about Alice, how she'd suffered, how sensitive she was, how we must all help her to rebuild her life, etcetera.

I said that while this might be true, Alice didn't strike me as a helpless woman but as one who could fight her own battles.

Walter said he agreed. 'She has plenty of courage, and I admire her frankness. She asked Mother this morning to allocate some household tasks to her, while she's here. Said she needs to be occupied. I think Molly would have had her rolling bandages before breakfast if Mother hadn't intervened. I must say, I'm very impressed with her spirit.' Walter didn't notice the look of impatience that crossed Beryl's face.

After tea I found Eve arranging arum lilies in a big urn in the hall.

'R.I.P.' I said.

'Too funereal?'

'In view of all circumstances, yes.'

'I'll add roses.' There were dark circles under her eyes. I told her not to tire herself, and she shook her head.

'I'm not tired. These first few days of her stay are important.' She began to take pink and cream roses from the basket at her feet and arrange them in the urn.

'Who's coming tonight?'

'Family. The Cunninghams, with Malcolm. The Reppleys. Phil and Seymour.'

'Aunt Dee's grasping the nettle.' I was thinking of Mrs Bartley Cunningham. She's one of those wispy, willowy ladies whose quiet word in someone's ear can send you to the guillotine. An old friend of Aunt Dee's, she

197

married a judge, now retired, and their son Malcolm was a subaltern in the Royal Scots Fusiliers, at present on leave in Durban.

We gathered at Yellow-wood at seven-thirty. Aunt Delia and Alice were in black, Aunt Dee's monumental and Alice's ethereal. The other women had chosen those anaemic pastels suitable to half-mourning, except for poor Faith Reppley, whose mulberry ruffles accentuated her lined and yellow skin. She looked twenty years older than her husband, and so ill that Eve drew her aside and made her sit down. I gave her a glass of dry sherry. She touched it once to her lips and set it aside.

'Asthma troubling you again?' I said, and she nodded.

'It's the pepper tree. Too close to my bedroom. Smells.'

'Get the damned thing cut down. Say the word, and I'll send a couple of chaps over tomorrow to do it.'

'Thank you, Toby. I'll speak to Frank.' Like hell she would. He was busy talking to Molly on the far side of the room. I stayed with Faith, partly because I liked her, and partly because I wanted to watch how the party was going.

The Cunninghams and Rennies arrived together, young Malcolm resplendent in his regimentals, having come straight from some official do. We all knew one another well, and the conversation was general, so it was only at dinner that one could gauge what sort of impression Alice was making.

Aunt Delia's parties were seldom over-formal. That night she took one end of the table and Walter the other, the younger and older guests being jumbled together. Alice sat on Walter's right, with Phil next to her, and Mrs Cunningham next to Phil. I had the watershed position at the centre of the board.

From time to time I glanced at Alice, who was chatting easily to her neighbours and to Eve and Malcolm who were opposite her. I could see Mrs Cunningham paying attention to what was being said, but her face showed no emotion beyond a polite interest. Then Frank Reppley began to tell us what was being done to clear the malarial swamps on the North Coast. It was a dreary topic to accompany champagne, and my attention wandered. I noticed that Walter's end of the table was working towards one of those teasing and noisy arguments that indicate a controversial subject, and suddenly a real chorus of derision made everyone else break off their talk and look at Walter.

'What is it?' smiled Aunt Delia.

'Merely that I saw the lady in the harem-skirt yesterday.'

'You didn't!'

This bold lady had appeared on the Back Beach Promenade wearing a balloon-like garment, neither trews nor skirt, which the journals described as the avant-garde wear in London. She had attracted a large crowd which followed her with hoots and jeers until she took to her heels in panic.

'It was highly exciting,' said Walter. 'The wind kept filling them, you see, and there seemed a good chance she'd blow clean out to sea.'

Judge Cunningham, who has a robust Victorian humour, guffawed. 'No chance at all, dear boy. Too much ballast in the female rump.'

'Which for me,' said Frank Reppley, 'is a contra-indication to a woman's wearing trousers ... physically or metaphorically. A woman's power lies in her femininity. Anything that detracts from that detracts from her real power to shape her destiny ... and mankind's. The Suffragettes, for instance. What have they achieved? Nothing. Nor will they. G. K. Chesterton, whom I admire, is clear on that point.'

I saw Phil Rennie glance quickly at Alice, and away again. She sat with her head a little tilted, smiling at Frank.

'They've gained some ground in Britain,' I

said. 'Winston Churchill has warned the Police to go easy on the Suffragettes, I believe. How do you rate their chances here, Judge?'

'Oh, dear man, don't bring me into it. Unlike Frank, I have a strong sense of self-preservation.'

Mrs Cunningham said in her soft voice, 'I was talking to Advocate Dimble. He says that if we enfranchise women in the Union, we'll give an advantage to the Dutch. Increase their supremacy in voting numbers still further. I don't know if that is a moral argument against female suffrage.'

'Anything is an argument that affects Natal's cause,' said Frank. He glanced round the table. 'In my experience, women themselves don't want the vote. Give them dominion in the home, and over their children; security and fulfilment in the supreme rôle of wife and mother, and they don't ask more.'

Faith Reppley sighed and looked at her plate. Mrs Cunningham ignored Frank and looked straight at Alice.

'What do you think, my dear? You must know more of the Suffragette movement than we do.'

Alice hesitated a moment. Then she gave a small shrug. 'I support the enfranchisement of women.'

Every eye turned upon her. 'Honestly?' said Eve. 'All that chaining to railings, and picketing M.P.s?'

'That's nearly over,' said Alice calmly. 'Recognition is growing in Parliament. There's a big lobby.'

'A threat to the home, in my view,' said Reppley. 'How can domestic peace not suffer if the wife is at loggerheads with the husband, the daughter with the father?'

'There are many homes in Britain where women would disagree with you. There are children who are neglected and starved, and would be glad of women to speak for Reform. We're capable of giving more to society than just the tasks about the house. We must be free to meet our own needs and the needs of the world.' She turned to Mrs Cunningham. 'I'm a stranger in this country. But if I were you, I'd tell Advocate Dimble that if the Dutch women could stand and load the guns for their men, and take their chance with them in battle, then they should be given a chance to decide who shall govern them.' She leaned back in her chair a little. 'But I may be quite wrong.'

The Judge gave his throaty chuckle. 'Damned if you wouldn't make a better speaker in the House than most of the thunderclucks we've sent there. Eh?'

After dinner, Eve played the piano, which she does very well, and later Molly and Frank Reppley sang a couple of duets. Seymour Rennie was beside me during the recital. He looked worried, I thought, and I guessed it was on Phil's behalf. Anyone could see Phil had gone a mile for Alice, he couldn't take his eyes off her. While she treated him with friendliness, nothing more.

She seemed to enjoy the music, listened attentively, and when it was over, went across and complimented Frank in a way that took the sting out of the argument at dinner. I was ready to agree with Molly that Alice was a clever woman.

We left the party at about eleven o'clock. Malcolm Cunningham walked down the drive with us.

'A grand evening. I admire your sister-in-law. Stood up to m'mother. Takes some doing. Phil says she's a crackerjack horsewoman, too. Only sorry I leave for the Cape tomorrow, or I'd offer to take her riding.'

'She has every manjack of us on her side!' I said, and didn't add that it was the women she'd have to win over to be happy in a small town like Durban. The Judge and Malcolm might say what they liked, but I'd no doubt that in the Cunningham household, Mrs C.

wore the trousers, harem-style or not.

Later, Eve asked how I'd enjoyed the evening.

'Entertaining.'

'You like her, don't you?'

'She's interesting. It's early days to pass opinions. I might quite easily want to wring her neck, some day.'

'She's too radical for this town.'

'You're probably right. She enjoyed your music. I thought you played well tonight, love. What was the name of it?'

'It's a bit of Vivaldi.' Eve broke off a spray of fuschia that was tapping our window, and held it against her mouth. 'I thought she'd recognise it. It was a great favourite of Hugh's.'

★　　　★　　　★

Next day after work I went to the servants' quarters, to enquire about the woman and the sick child. The poor mite had been burned by boiling porridge, on its right leg, and I found Molly and Alice showing the woman how to dress the burn. Molly asked me to speak to her in Zulu, as she didn't understand the pidgin tongue used in town, and I explained how the 'muti' must be applied, and then talked to her for a bit, just for the pleasure of it. She had all the virtues of her people, grace, humour and courage. Her skin was scrubbed with cold water and polished so that it shone, and she smelled cleanly of smoke and earth and sweet grass mats.

Old Mlaas came out of his kitchen and stood watching the baby. After a while he asked me, in Zulu, please to tell the 'nkosikaas from far away that he was sad that she had lost her husband.

I did so, and Alice at once asked what Mlaas was called, and a conversation began, with me as interpreter, which went on for almost half an hour.

When we returned to the house, she said, 'What a beautiful language Zulu is. Do you think I could learn to speak it?'

'Yes, but it would take time. It's a difficult thing to do well.'

'Will you teach me?'

'If I can.'

From that day on, Mlaas, who had loved Hugh, was devoted to Alice. He came to me and said that his youngest son would come into town soon, to seek work, and when that happened he would apply first to Alice.

It's difficult to say when I first noticed the dangerous drift of events. Certainly not in the first three months Alice was in Durban. Almost from the first she won a coterie of supporters to her side. Aunt Delia was one of them, Phil Rennie and Seymour, Faith Reppley and Mlaas.

But she also had her detractors. The first week showed that she was a woman who was born to cause controversy. People seemed to be attracted or repelled by her. She was intelligent and very determined and she meant to make a success of her venture. I watched her work, at first with detachment, then amusement, and finally fear; but the fear came only when I understood the depth of the emotions she had let loose among us.

The incidents and conversations I record are given with hindsight, in an attempt to show how Alice Frobisher took up a position at the very centre of our lives.

There were no dramatic events. Alice was in half-mourning. Although she did not wear black, nor shun society, she kept away from parties and was entertained only in the homes of our close friends. She went with us to concerts and theatres. She explored the town and the country round about, went to church, read, rode and chatted.

Sometimes she would disappear and we'd know she was with Beth Pottergill, or writing a long letter to her father. She was the ideal guest, easy company, sharing in the household work and anxieties to exactly the right degree, quick to withdraw when people wanted privacy.

Aunt Delia was delighted with her. They used to talk about Hugh a great deal, and from that they went on to discussing themselves. (What more pleasant subject is there?) Alice, it seemed, was keen on medical topics, particularly the work being done in Vienna on the human mind. Aunt Dee was always regaling us with 'Alice says . . .'

'Alice says the science of the psyche is in its infancy, but will change all our attitudes in time.' Alice said this, that and the other about everything under the sun, even sex, which Aunt Dee referred to as 'private matters'. It had never occurred to me that she, who was the epitome of Victorian rectitude, should be anxious to talk to anyone about her sexual experiences. Bernard, her husband, had been a mean man, never known to caress one of his own children, let alone grab a passing bosom, or laugh at a bar-room joke. But I learned, to my fascination, that it was precisely this haddocky nature that made him interesting to the chaps in Vienna. Bernard, it seemed, was responsible for practically all the unpleasant things that had ever happened at Yellow-wood, and certainly for the destruction of Hugh.

Suddenly all the pictures of Bernard which

had cluttered Aunt Delia's walls were removed, a great improvement aesthetically. And Aunt Delia, helped to shed a load of guilt, looked ten years younger.

Alice seemed to like everything we planned for her. Her tastes were catholic. She would lay aside the short stories of Dostoevsky to go with Phil to hear John Philip Sousa and his band playing in the Town Hall. She would spend the morning romping in the mud with the neighbourhood kids, and the afternoon arguing philosophy with old Judge Cunningham. She loved fashion but was never the victim of its extremes.

I took her to one of the first full-length films to be shown in the Town Hall . . . Sir Herbert Beerbohm Tree's *Henry VIII*. It was quite an epic, lasting one and a half hours, with the Durban Orchestra hammering away at German's music as background.

During the drive home she confessed she'd never liked the play. 'Perhaps because I dislike Henry himself. A power-mad syphilitic bully, who murdered two wives and several of his friends.'

'Perhaps his trouble was hereditary. His father was a killer, I'm sure. Just think how all those fine, blond, upstanding Plantagenets disappeared to be replaced by horrid, grasping Tudors. Your friend Freud would find interesting material there.'

'Have you read Freud?'

'No. I'd be afraid to. Too close to home.'

I was only half-joking. There was enough wrong with my own life to make me sensitive. I knew that Eve and I weren't just 'going through a bad patch'. We hadn't made love for more than three months. She wouldn't even discuss the situation, let alone share her bed. If she'd been a cold woman I suppose I'd have accepted the fact and looked elsewhere for company, but she'd been eager enough in the first year of our marriage.

Reppley said her depression was a result of the miscarriage, and would pass. I couldn't help feeling that the causes must lie deeper. I'd sit and brood, trying to think where I'd gone wrong. And lately I'd begun to wonder whether Hugh's death hadn't hit her harder than we guessed. They'd been very close, as children, in age and character.

As a second cousin of the Frobishers I'd known Eve a very long time. I'd married her with my eyes open.

Brought up in a home where male dominance went unquestioned, she disliked anyone to challenge that authority. She wanted to be respectable rather than free, she was extremely conventional. To make social calls with a card-case in her hand; to sit in the right pew at church; to meet her friends at the right places and to be dressed, if possible, just a little better than they were; these were the norms she approved and enjoyed.

Our home was well-run, hospitable, and charmingly appointed. She despised bad housekeepers, but also despised women who were efficient at the expense of charm. Meals must be good, but they must not be brought to the table by a sweaty wife. We had servants, but if we were deprived of them, she would see to it that things ran smoothly.

In return for these virtues she expected to be protected . . . spoiled, if you like . . . by the men of her circle. Her beauty was very great, the wheaten blonde good looks shared by all the Frobishers except Walter; but she herself over-valued it. She believed that the beautiful should inherit the earth. She took it as a personal injury when Walter or I told her she must economise. She had done her part, she was a credit to us, and we were cheating her of her rightful reward.

I'd been idiot enough, when I fell for her, to think I could change her. In order to win her I gave up being an unsuccessful painter and became a successful business-man. I expected her to make a like sacrifice, which is another way of saying I expected my pound of flesh. I don't think I was being malicious when I told

Eve we couldn't afford the new house yet, or the clothes and jewels she wanted; but perhaps, deep down in me, there was an element of revengefulness. Perhaps she sensed it. Perhaps that's why we quarrelled so often.

All this went through my head as I drove Alice home. I looked at her and saw that she had slid down in her seat and was watching the blaze of autumn stars with a dreamy expression. She was lost in some realm of her own. I held my tongue, not wishing to drag her back across the gulf. We are all two people; what we are, and what we imagine ourselves to be.

When I turned through the gates of Yellowwood, I saw a figure move along the darkened upper verandah. It was a woman in black, Beth Pottergill I thought. She vanished as we reached the front door. I had the feeling she'd been waiting up for Alice.

*　　*　　*

With April came the cool weather, and Alice began to join Walter, Phil and me on early morning rides. The Rennies and Frobishers owned a number of horses, and we soon found that she could handle any of them, and be trusted not to ruin their mouths.

We usually went out at five o'clock. Often

we went over the back of the Ridge, to the old saw mill, from which point a number of soft sand tracks radiated towards the Umgeni River. The bush there was full of indigenous flowers, birds and beasts. Phil Rennie, who was something of an expert on these, made them an excuse to dawdle behind with Alice. But when not dawdling, she liked to race. She loved speed and, I think, danger, and was only kept within limits by consideration for the ponies.

Sometimes we rode down to the Beach and galloped from the last of the night to the first of the day, the town behind us filling with cloudy colour. And after the gallop we would let our mounts stand in the waves to strengthen their legs, while the sun burst from the horizon, dripping fire.

For formal riding Alice wore khaki skirt and jacket and pith helmet like other women, but when we went off the beaten track she wore her own quaint gear, trousers, shirt and pullover, like a boy.

She was an original in dress, but not eccentric. She never wore corsets, or lace collars, or long sleeves, or trains, but soft lines and fabrics that showed off her slender figure.

I never thought her pretty. Her nose was too sharp, her forehead too broad, the planes of her face too pronounced for that anaemic word. What she did have was a sexuality that one couldn't miss. Phil was no different from the rest of us. He wanted to get her into his bed, but being Phil he had to call it something romantic. The womenfolk, of course, weren't fooled for a moment. They knew what men saw in Alice, and were annoyed or amused in direct proportion to their own powers in that direction.

Beryl said to me once, 'She's no better than a street-woman. She lives to catch men.'

'Do you think so? I don't believe she's even conscious of her effect.'

'Nonsense, she makes up to every man, even Walter. He's clay in her hands, don't pretend you haven't noticed.'

This was nonsense. Walter wasn't clay in anyone's hands. He was shy and awkward, but no weakling. He had liked Alice from the start, and he trusted her. He'd made the mistake of marrying a pretty little featherhead, and found in Alice a sharp mind and a sense of humour, something Beryl entirely lacked.

He used to talk to Alice about business matters. I was surprised once to find them at Yellow-wood, sitting on a bench in the orchard, with the small of lime-trees all round them, and the balance-sheet of Frobisher Fitments and Company spread between them.

They were discussing whether or not it was time to float a new subsidiary. When I joined in, I saw Alice had a good idea of what was entailed, and had grasped a fact that many men missed ... that Durban was going to become one of the great cities of the southern hemisphere.

'Look, Walter,' she said, 'it's the outlet for the gold mines, it's a repair port for shipping. It must expand. So should your firm.'

'Expansion takes capital.'

'And confidence attracts capital. My father told me that. One must use money, not be used by it. Money is only a power in the hands of someone with the will to direct it.'

She made an oddly expressive movement of her hands, as if she had an enemy by the neck and would force him to his knees. I saw how strong her will and ambition might be. The next moment, she was smiling.

'It's really none of my affair. I get carried away by this country, so new, so full of marvellous opportunity.'

I noticed that Walter went ahead with the flotation plans, although it meant certain economies in the Frobisher household ... economies which annoyed the girls very much.

And finally, Alice shared with Walter an interest in medicine. While her concern was

214

academic, his was personal. He had suffered all his life from gastric ailments, and was always trying new remedies. His cupboards at Yellow-wood were crowded with patent draughts and pills, which he was all too ready to share with the rest of us. He fussed over the health of his family, his friends and his animals. Alice tried to persuade him that diet was the right way to mend his stomach. She was wasting her time.

I saw them once, arguing in the stable-yard over whether or not antimony was good for conditioning horses.

'We've always used it at Yellow-wood,' said Walter.

'I know. Hugh used to give it to the carriage-horses, but I hate the idea. Oats and exercise are the way to put on condition. Antimony is dangerous.'

'My dear girl, one uses a minute quantity. There's no danger.'

'I've seen enough of poisons to last me a lifetime!' Alice spoke vehemently. She was shivering. I was to remember this conversation later.

Of course, the better Alice got on with Walter, the less Beryl liked it. At first she confined her resentment to wearing an injured expression. Then she started nagging Eve, me, or Molly about it . . . she was just smart enough not to tackle Walter.

Alice, she said, was a flirt. A hypocrite. She was after what she could get.

I told her not to be an ass. Towards the end of April she made a more specific accusation. She told me that Walter had altered his will, so that Alice would inherit what would have been Hugh's share of the Estate.

'Well, that may be so, Beryl. But you've no business to tell me. A will is a private document.'

'Well, I suppose you don't care if that woman gets our money.'

'It's nothing to do with me.'

*   *   *

Molly, who had had the most misgivings about Alice, now seemed to have none. Her doubts had faded as soon as she understood that Alice had suffered and been victimised. From then on, she claimed Molly's pity and, therefore, her active help.

'She needs an interest, Toby. Something to do.'

'She seems busy enough, to me.'

'I mean something worthwhile. A life's work.' Molly looked at me anxiously, to see if I was going to laugh at her, as people often did. 'I mean, she has so much energy, and it's all bottled up. That's not good for a person. It makes them destructive. Like when you gave up painting . . .'

'. . . Molly, I've told you . . .'

'. . . all right, we won't argue about that. But you know what it's like to be frustrated.'

I did, and not because of painting, but I could hardly discuss that with Molly.

'Don't you think Alice will find what she wants to do, in her own way?'

'We could give her a shove in the right direction.'

'What's that?'

'The Mission. She likes medical things. She told me once she'd like to be a doctor. She can help us at the Mission.'

'Bit grim, isn't it?'

Molly stared at me almost wonderingly. 'It's a wonderful place, Toby. Father Maurice has such plans.'

'Well, you could ask her.'

The following week, Alice drove out to the Mission with Frank Reppley and Molly. Aunt Delia was furious.

'Molly has no right to take a guest to that place. Because she likes it doesn't mean she should inflict it on others.'

'Why don't you let Molly go nursing?'

'It's no occupation for a woman of breeding.'

217

'But she is already nursing, Aunt Dee. Why don't you make an honest nurse of her, pay for her training? Better for her patients, and she'd have a source of income.'

'Molly doesn't need money. I can provide for her.'

When the party returned to Yellow-wood, Aunt Delia awaited them on the front steps like Fate with her shears. Frank sprang down from the trap and helped the girls to alight. They were all in high spirits.

'You must be exhausted,' said Aunt Dee, frowning heavily at Molly.

'Not a bit,' said Alice. I asked her what she'd thought of the Hospital, and she gave me one of those cool, bright looks that tell you she knows exactly what's in your mind.

'At first I thought it was pathetic. They have nothing, compared with any cottage hospital I've seen. But as we went round, I began to see that it's what the people need. A place where they won't be frightened, where the witchdoctor can come as well as the white doctors. I think Father Maurice is one of the most wonderful people I've ever met. A surgeon who plants cabbages and conducts communion services and doses the cattle. I think . . . out there . . . the rule of poverty means something. Everyone shares it, it's the bridge between our world and theirs.'

'Could you work there?'

'No. I don't think so. I'm too impatient.'

'And too rich?'

Her sharp look probed me, as if she asked why I was taunting her. 'Perhaps,' she said.

I saw I'd hurt her, and I was obscurely glad.

Molly came up to us. 'Let's have tea. You'll stay, won't you, Frank?' She was looking at Reppley with that dumb, hopeful expression I'd seen all too often ... in my shaving-mirror. Reppley dropped a casual arm round her shoulders. Aunt Delia led them inside. I didn't join them, but walked slowly down to the stables.

I was feeling ashamed of myself.

I mooched round the yard for a while, and then climbed up to the loft, where I'd stored all my painting gear. I looked over the canvasses stacked against the wall, and decided they were rotten bad, anyway, and I'd done well to go into business instead.

It was only when I got back to the Cottage that I realised I'd brought my box of pastels home with me. I looked at them awhile and then locked them away in the bottom drawer of my desk.

*　　　*　　　*

I noticed that after the visit to the Mission

Frank Reppley stopped criticising Alice. He dropped his pompous line about female suffrage, and adopted a new one, about Womanly Independence.

One afternoon late, he called at the Cottage and asked if Eve and I would like to go and watched the Nongoma dancers rehearsing for the Coronation. 'Alice is keen to see them. Thought you might join us?'

So down we went to the polo-ground, where some thousand of the best Zulu dancers from scores of kraals were waiting. Some of them had come straight from the country and had brought their traditional finery with them . . . ostrich plume and oxhide shield, leather kilt and beads, the tuft of white fur at the knee and the knob-kerrie in the hand. Others, who lived and worked in town, had simply stripped off the trappings of civilisation and donned the bechu.

Getting the dancing under way did not happen quickly. There was the usual delay, and shepherding-about. But, at last, they began. The plumes advanced, leaped, retreated in perfect unison. The feet lifted and stamped, so that the ground shook. The splendid bodies, streaming sweat, proclaimed the fundamental emotions of courage and rage, loyalty and triumph. It was pitch dark when we left, and they were still dancing.

This spectacle, while it pleased us, had a tragic result. Such a large crowd of men, drinking from old and unsafe wells, and eating what food was offered them, was a hazard to itself. The result was an outbreak of gastro-enteritis, which was spread all over the Province in no time. The illness was particularly dangerous to children, many of whom died. Molly and Alice were out at the Mission almost every day, helping to nurse the sick.

The epidemic hit whites as well as blacks, and several of Frobisher's staff were away from work.

Eve chose this unsuitable time to have a fight with Walter. As usual, about money.

I was not home when it happened, but arrived to find Eve in bed, and hysterical, while poor Walter marched up and down outside the Cottage, waiting to talk to me.

'I'm sorry Toby. Perhaps I was too rough with her. But honestly, I can't find the money this month. Next month, perhaps . . .'

I got the story pieced together. Eve wanted to borrow enough to start building the house. I told Walter I'd forbidden her to mention it to him, and he wasn't to worry. Then I went in to Eve.

It was no use trying to talk to her. She was screaming and throwing herself about the bed.

221

I telephoned Frank, and was told by Faith that he was out. I asked her to suggest another doctor, and she gave me the name of Anton Leiper, who duly came to see Eve, gave her a sedative, and waited until it had taken effect.

Leiper was a very ugly, hairy little man with a beautiful voice and shrewd eyes. I told him I wasn't happy about my wife's health, and asked if he would allow himself to be called as a second opinion.

The net result was that a few days later, Eve and I were in Leiper's consulting rooms in town. He gave her a thorough examination, did blood tests and other tests that showed up no dread diseases, and told us more or less what Frank Reppley had done, that it was a depression triggered by an aborted pregnancy, and it would pass.

In one way, though, Leiper differed from Frank, and that was in his dealings with me. He got me along to see him without Eve's knowledge, and he asked me what seemed like impertinent questions about our marriage, my work, my plans for the future. At first I resented this, and then I found myself saying to him, what I hadn't even said to myself, that our marriage was a dead failure, and I didn't know what the hell to do about it.

'Maybe you should give her what she wants.'

222

I started to say I gave her everything I could, and he held up his thin little hand. 'Oh yes . . . please . . . I'm not criticising you, Mr Rourke. Your wife is demanding, I've no doubt. She's told me about her early life. She was brought up in a very materialistic home, where it was considered admirable to strive and grasp . . .'

'That's a fair description of her father's attitude.'

'She admired her father.'

'She detested him!'

'Not entirely. I think she admired him also. Because he knew how to get what he wanted, and did so.'

'I don't see what this has to do with our marriage.'

'It may have a great deal to do with it.' He paused, and then took a different tack. 'How close was she to the brother who died in England? His death must have been a great shock to her?'

'Yes, it was. But Eve gets over things quickly. I mean . . . I don't think she's grieving for Hugh . . .'

'He died in January, soon after she had suffered her miscarriage?'

'Yes.'

'So perhaps there is a double reason for her depression. Some people mourn by weeping,

223

others don't eat, quarrel with their husbands
. . . umh?'

'Perhaps.'

He began to cross-examine me about my sex
life, its quality and quantity, and when I
showed resentment he smiled at me so
placatingly that once again I told him more
than I meant to. I described the whole tattered
fabric of my life, in fact. I was damn near to
tears.

Suddenly he stopped me. 'Mr Rourke.
Your wife wants something quite simple. She
wants her own house. Why don't you get it for
her?'

'I told you! I can't afford it!'

'No? How many horses do you keep, for
your own use? Is it really impossible to find
the money, or are you telling yourself it's
impossible, because you like things as they
are?'

'Now wait . . .' I was ready to ring a peal
over him, and then some words popped into
my mind, and I spoke them. 'I gave up
painting, isn't that enough?'

He studied me quietly. 'Evidently not.'

For a moment I couldn't say anything, there
was so much anger in me, and a queer sort of
pain at having said something I'd never meant
to say to anyone.

'You married a Frobisher,' Leiper said,

'and people who marry into that sort of family often have to give up a great deal. More than they can afford to. Then the marriage breaks up. I don't know if you've been asked to give more than you can afford. That's something only you can decide.'

He was right, there.

I spent some time thinking about Eve and me. I remembered the happy times. I didn't like the idea that all that could vanish into dust. I went to see Seymour Rennie and talked about my investments. I sold two ponies. Putting everything together, I was still short of the sort of money we'd need to complete the house.

But I told Eve she could start building.

How I found the rest of the money was my problem.

★   ★   ★

At the end of June, came an occasion when no man in his right mind could have refused extra money to his wife. It was the week of the Coronation, and every last woman in town wanted a new dress, a new hat, and a household kickshaw with a picture of George and Mary on it.

The town fathers had been plotting away for months to meet the occasion. The Pictorial of

May 25th had shown us pictures of the ninety men of militia and police chosen to go to London for the Crowning, and by mid-June we'd committed ourselves to any number of true-blue activities.

Aunt Delia belonged to a group called the Loyal Women's Guild, which in the third week of June held a ball in the Town Hall. Naturally, we attended. At some point in this endurance test, I asked Mrs Cunningham if she would like to dance, and she said, 'No, but I want to sit somewhere quiet and talk to you. You may fetch me a glass of lemonade.'

I found her a seat behind some palms, and fetched her a drink. She sipped it silently for a while, and then said:

'I want to talk about Alice.'

I knew Alice had been invited several times to the Cunninghams' home, a mark of courtesy but not necessarily of patronage. Mrs Cunningham's rather cold blue eyes were fixed on the crowd swirling on the floor of the hall, and I couldn't read their expression. I could see Alice and Phil Rennie dancing together. They were both laughing. Mrs Cunningham turned to me.

'Alice is not the right woman for Phil, do you think?'

I was silent. I agreed with her, but I disliked talking about Phil's affairs with anyone. My companion gave her frosty smile.

'You'd like to tell me to mind my own business, Toby. Well, I can't. Seymour Rennie came to see me yesterday, in great distress. He's been getting anonymous letters about Alice.'

'Saying what?'

'That she killed Hugh, and that Phil will be next. The newspaper cuttings about the inquest were pinned to the first letter.' She reached out and put a hand on my arm. 'Now it's no use getting angry, Toby. I know quite well that anonymous letters are untruthful as well as contemptible. My husband is a Judge and gets his share of the trash, and throws it straight into the waste-paper basket. But Seymour is worried because the letters seem to show ... well ... an inside knowledge of Hugh's death, and of the inquest.'

'Anyone could have read the English newspapers. There were screeds in them, according to Phil. Plenty of people here get the overseas rags.'

'Yes, that's true.' Mrs Cunningham spread out her ostrich fan and stroked it, as if ordering her thoughts. 'But there's already been a lot of talk about Alice, which your family naturally won't have heard. You can't avoid gossip in a town this size. If someone starts to spread vicious rumours, to hint that

Alice murdered Hugh, then it would be hideous for everyone. Bart says it is always difficult to trace a poison-pen.'

'Seymour didn't recognise the writing?'

'It was printing, and he thinks disguised. There were three notes in all, very short ones.'

'Has Seymour kept them?'

'The first two he destroyed. The third he showed me, I think because he needed to talk to someone. You know how much Phil means to him.'

'Yes. Why doesn't he go to the police?'

'I asked Bart about that. He says they would naturally have to ask a lot of questions, and perhaps bring the whole matter into the public glare. That would be shattering for Delia and Alice.'

'I certainly don't relish the idea of the police . . .'

'And if there are no more letters, then the whole thing may blow over, mayn't it?'

'A big "if".'

Again her hand stroked the feathers. 'I think it's worth a try . . . letting things lie for a while. There have been no letters for over a fortnight. If they begin again, Seymour will have to consider calling in the law.'

'What about Alice? Isn't it possible she's been sent letters too?'

'That may be. Is there anyone one could

ask? One can't approach Alice herself, in case she knows nothing about it.'

'I might talk to Mrs Pottergill.'

'Good. Do that. In the mean time, I shall put it about that Alice is my friend, and protégée.' She gave me a brisk nod. 'I intend to join the Durban Enfranchisement League, what do you think of that? I read a most stirring account recently of the Suffragettes' march in London. Forty thousand women parading from the Embankment to the Albert Hall, with purple white and green banners! I hope I shall not be asked to march anywhere.'

She rose and took my arm as we made our way back to the main hall. The music was swelling to patriotic heights. Mrs Cunningham bent close to my ear.

'I rely on you, Toby. You're the only man in that family with his feet on the ground.'

I didn't return to my party. I needed a drink, and went and bought one at the Royal Bar across the street.

I was both angry and perturbed, because it was pretty darned clear what message Mrs Cunningham was trying to get across to me.

The people who had inside knowledge of the Frobisher tragedy were the Frobishers themselves. Any police enquiry into anonymous letters would undoubtedly begin at Yellow-wood.

                    ★   ★   ★

For a day or two I tried to make discreet
enquiries about the letters. I told Walter about
them, and asked him whether there were any
cuttings about the inquest at the big house. He
told me he'd seen some soon after Hugh's
death, but didn't know where they'd got to.
He was very upset about the whole nasty
business.

'Whoever sent them must be off his rocker.'

'Her rocker. It's usually a woman.'

'Well, keep it to yourself until I've looked
for those cuttings.'

'I've been wondering whether to speak to
Phil.'

'You can't, if Seymour hasn't done so.'

In the event, Phil solved this difficulty by
speaking to me. He erupted into the Cottage
while Eve and I were eating dinner and waved
a sheet of paper under my nose. 'Read that!'

It was a letter, addressed to his father, and
unsigned. The text, printed in block capitals,
said, 'If you love your son, keep him away
from Alice Frobisher.' Pinned to the letter was
a cutting from the London *Times*, referring to
the inquest.

Philip was white with fury. 'It came in the
afternoon post. Luckily I was there when Dad

opened it, and I saw his face. Made him show me the filthy thing. He's had three others.'

Eve got up and took his arm. 'Sit down, Phil. And Toby, let's have some brandy with the coffee, shall we?' She went off to the kitchen. I said at once:

'I've heard about the letters. Mrs Cunningham told me.'

'It's unspeakable. Do you think Alice has been sent this muck?'

'Not to my knowledge.'

'And why write to my father?'

'Presumably in the hopes he could put you off marrying Alice.'

'As to that, she won't have me.' Phil was so distressed he was talking more wildly than I'd ever known him to. 'But I shall certainly keep trying. As if I'd be put off by this horrible stuff.'

Eve came back with the coffee, and I poured brandies all round. The liquor seemed to calm Phil.

'What's so beastly is knowing someone feels this way . . . so rotten with malice . . .'

'Can you think of anyone with cause to hate you?'

He gave a lop-sided grin. 'Not this much.'

'A business rival? Anyone you've crossed? An employee you've sacked?'

'No.'

231

Eve asked to see the letter and read it, and the cutting. 'It's not even as if the newspaper said anything nasty about Alice. It makes it clear Hugh's death was accidental.'

'Put together with the note, though,' I said, 'one gets the impression that Alice did for him, and will do for Phil if he marries her.'

She turned to Phil. 'Is there anyone else who wants to marry her? Someone who might feel that if you were out of the way. . .?'

'I don't know of anyone who would write such a letter for any reason whatever. I simply . . .' He stopped and stared at me.

'Thought of someone?'

'There's one person who might be pleased if I kept away from Alice. But she's devoted to Alice. She'd never accuse her of murder.'

'You mean Beth Pottergill?'

'Yes.' Phil now looked unhappy. 'But I don't think . . . she's a very loyal woman, even if we don't always see eye to eye.'

'Has she shown you any ill-will?'

'Not exactly. She's a bit prickly. Sensitive. She had a dreadful childhood in the Cardiff slums, she lost her husband and kids, she's been through hell, really. When Alice found her she was practically down and out. Alice offered her a job and a home. They've become friends . . . allies . . . I don't know how to describe it. But I do know Beth is utterly devoted.'

'How does she behave towards you?'

'All right. She doesn't think I'm good enough for Alice, but I've never felt she disliked me.'

'Might feel that if you marry she'll lose her job?'

'I don't think that's crossed her mind. She is convinced Alice will never abandon her. It was her testimony, you know, that convinced the coroner's jury that Hugh took too much morphine by accident. No, I can't think of any reason for her to send those letters.'

'What are you going to do about them?'

'Well, I don't want to go to the Police. Father and I had a chat, and we agree the first thing is to make it clear to the world that the letters aren't having any effect. We're taking Alice to the Coronation Concert, day after tomorrow, and Father will sponsor her for the Governor-General's At Home. Show of force, eh?'

Phil stayed talking for about an hour. When he'd left, Eve and I took the brandy and coffee things out to the kitchen and washed them. As she returned the cups to the shelf, she said,

'Something's troubling you about Mrs Pottergill, isn't it?'

'Not really. I agree that she wouldn't harm Alice.'

'There's one thing.' Eve came towards me, and the kitchen light shone on the pile of her hair. 'One thing that frightens me. Mightn't Mrs Pottergill have sent those letters because she likes Phil? Because she wants to protect him?'

I knew what she was thinking. It was in my mind too, but I thrust it aside. 'He doesn't need protection.'

Eve caught hold of my hand. Her own was ice-cold. 'Not if Alice is innocent. But what if Mrs Pottergill knows she's guilty?''

*　　　*　　　*

That night, Eve slept with me.

The happiness of having her back in my arms made everything else unimportant.

Next morning, when Eve went to draw the bedroom curtains, the sharp June air flowed in loaded with the smell of woodsmoke. I got up and went to stand beside her at the window. On the far side of the orchard, the garden-boy was raking leaves and throwing them onto a bonfire. The sound of his chanting reached us in irregular snatches.

'Those letters seem ridiculous in the light of day.'

'They are ridiculous,' I said. 'Seymour should throw them on the fire and forget them.'

'I think they're right about showing the world. We must show people that Alice is one of the family, and we won't have her bullied. We must give her a good time. Now the Season's begun, there'll be plenty of fun.'

'And new dresses,' I said.

Eve giggled. She pulled the thick gold braid of hair over her shoulder and squinted at it. 'Shall I have it cut short, like hers?'

'You dare,' I said.

I knew we'd a long way to go, to make up what we'd lost. But that morning, everything seemed possible, and the smoke curling up from the orchard represented the death agonies of the dragon Despond.

★   ★   ★

The Durban Season was on.

From June 1st until the end of July, the visitors crowded in, escaping from the cold of the Cape and the Transvaal. Every hotelier, trader and entertainer in town concentrated on skinning them of as much cash as possible.

In July the Governor-General came to King's House, and was paraded at every social and sporting event on the programme. He attended the Polo Club Tournament, which he seemed to enjoy. We had some good up-

235

country teams playing, and all of us knew one another pretty well.

I played in the same four as Phil Rennie and Frank Reppley. Frank was one of the best men at back in the Union. When he played polo he forgot about being a society physician and his pompous manner vanished. He never played to the gallery, either, although he attracted attention by his fine horsemanship, and his beautiful range of strokes.

We won our first match and, after the final chukka, cantered down to the horse-lines under the gums at the far end of the field. A number of players were there, with grooms, and friends anxious to buy or sell ponies. To my surprise we found Eve and Alice there too. Eve came forward as I dismounted.

'Well done, darling.' She looked delicious in a cream suit and hat, and her skin had a cool glow in the dappled shade. I picked up a towel from the tethering-rail, and wiped some of the dust and sweat off myself.

'It was Frank's match,' I said.

She glanced over to where Frank and Phil were chatting to Alice. 'You all played well. Here, give me that.' She took the soiled towel from me, and gave it to a groom, telling him to fetch the bag with my clean duds in it and take it to the bath-house at the back of the Club. Then she tucked her arm through mine and we walked over to join the others.

Alice was admiring Frank's pony, a sturdy little black with the quickness and strength to match Frank's skill. 'With you all the way, isn't he?' she said, stroking the horse's nose.

'Before me, often as not,' he answered. 'He loves the game. He knows.'

'Did you train him yourself?'

'Mostly, yes. But I haven't time to do all I'd like.'

'Walter says you've been invited to tour Argentina.'

'Oh . . . well . . . it was suggested, but it's out of the question, I'm afraid.'

'Would it have been a long tour?'

'Long, and expensive.' Frank spoke abruptly. He turned away and set his saddle down on the ground. The expression on his face surprised me. Longing, and a sullen anger. He raised his head and saw me watching him, and at once laughed.

'Family doctors shouldn't hope to play polo. It's a game for the idle rich. That is, if you want to take it beyond Club level. And after all, that's a pretty good place to stick. Grand chaps to play with, and pretty girls to cheer one along.'

That chance discussion made me see Frank in a new light. For a moment he'd looked as if he hated the lot of us. I knew he'd come up the

237

hard way. His father was said to have been a herbalist in Kimberley, who'd made enough out of dosing the miners to put his son through medical school. Not that anyone held that against him. Most of us came from settler stock, with empty pockets. The thing was, we were proud of it, while Frank never spoke of his beginnings. It was common knowledge he'd married poor Faith because she was a Tomasey who could trace their family way back, and frequently did. Faith was older than Frank, and plain, and asthmatic. She'd no money, but she had social standing. No doubt that advantage had worn thin in ten years of childless marriage. But I must admit that Frank always treated Faith with great courtesy, and she plainly adored him.

She ignored his flirtations with other women. No-one could even tell if she noticed them, but I think she did. I think, in her quiet way, she noticed far more than the rest of us.

★　　★　　★

Our Season gathered momentum.

While in Europe the talk was of the new dirigibles, and in the Antarctic Amundsen was getting ready to search for the South Pole, in Durban we were busy with the Agricultural

Show and the At Home held by Viscount Gladstone. The winter race-meetings began, Nobleman won the July Handicap from Madsan, and at the Mechanical Exhibition our exhibit won an award. It was at this display that Alice bought one of the new type-writing machines.

When I lugged this brute from the car to Yellow-wood, I asked what she meant to do with it.

'Learn to use it.' She did, too, taking lessons from a young man with waxed moustachios. By the end of the month she'd progressed to typing lists of orders from our stall, and was doing some of Walter's business letters.

She was now treated as one of the family. She had a circle of friends, played tennis, rode, went to the theatre and the Mission, and was on the committee of the Women's Enfranchisement League. It was quite clear that her holiday had become something more, and early in July she told me that she wanted to settle in Durban.

We were out on our pre-breakfast ride. It was bitterly cold, and we galloped through Stellar Bush to warm up. When we slowed the horses we were right on top of the Ridge, and could see the ocean on one hand, and the empty inland hills on the other. Alice said, 'I should like to build a house here.'

'It's a splendid position.'

'Who owns the land?'

I told her it was part of a farm property, and she asked if I thought the owner would sell her a couple of acres.

'You're serious?'

'Yes. I've been so happy in Durban I'd like to stay, but I can't impose on Aunt Delia. I thought I'd rent a little house, and live there till I can build.'

She was quite decided. A lot of thoughts tumbled through my head, about what her father might feel, and whether she really wanted to uproot her life, but I remembered that Phil might be part of her reason for staying. So I told her I'd make enquiries about houses to rent, and the Ridge land.

I don't know if she even bothered to find out whether the family would welcome her as a permanent fixture. Alice didn't agonise, she acted.

In this venture she found an ally in Eve, who was only too happy to help Alice look at houses. They found a little bungalow, at last, about a quarter of a mile up the hill from Yellow-wood. It was a boxy place, built in the old settler style with a narrow front verandah and grey calico ceilings. The garden was well-established, and flat, a rarity in Durban. Alice signed a six months' lease.

The house was painted and spruced up in record time. That same week a delighted Aunt Delia took Alice through the stable-lofts of Yellow-wood, and told her to take any furniture she needed from that stored there. There was a lot of solid Victorian stuff, among it pieces of the serpentine suite that had belonged to Bernard Frobisher's mother. It was over-ornate walnut, but very enduring, and every Frobisher bride started married life with at least one serpentine, chair, desk or cupboard. Alice chose a tall-boy, and put it in the sitting-room of her new home. So from the start Greyling (the house was named after its original owner) had a Frobisher look about it.

Alice moved in at the end of July, with a tribe of family and friends to help her.

       ★   ★   ★

Everything seemed set fair at this time.

Eve's health was improving daily. Leiper had been right about allowing her to build her house. She threw herself into such a round of visits to architects, plumbers and bricklayers that she had to cancel a large part of her social diary.

We hadn't regained happiness, but at least it seemed within reach. Eve didn't quarrel

241

with me. She allowed me to make love to her, though not as often as I wanted. When I came home from work she was charming and attentive, told me about her day and asked about mine. Our relationship was like a very delicate vase that has been broken, and skilfully mended, and will set firm if you do not handle it too soon. It was too early to know whether it would hold water.

*   *   *

Alice's move to Greyling affected our lives in many ways, one of the strangest being that I started painting again.

When Alice searched the Yellow-wood lofts for furniture, she found the stacks of my old canvasses. She came and asked me if I'd let her hang a couple of them.

'Of course. Take what you like.'

She looked at me thoughtfully. 'Have you ever tried to sell your work?'

'Yes. Disaster. People don't want modern stuff. They want autumn tints and bluebell woods.'

'Not everyone.'

She chose three of my landscapes and hung them about her walls. They made me realise I was pretty bad. One evening when Eve and I dined at Greyling, I asked her if she'd mind if I did a bit more work on one of the oils, a view of the orchard at the Cottage. When she asked why, I pointed out several defects of light, and she let me cart it away.

That Saturday I tried to fix it and failed. On Sunday I took a fresh canvas, set it up and painted the orchard again. I worked faster than I'd ever done. I was so interested that I forgot to eat or rest and when I stopped at four in the afternoon I was stiff, clear down to my heels. I took the picture, still wet, up to Greyling and showed it to Alice.

'It's splendid,' she said. 'I can smell the lemons.'

'I'll get it framed for you.'

'But Toby, you could sell this.'

'Don't want to.'

'You need the money for your house.'

'Argue, argue. The picture's not for sale. It's yours.'

She hung it over the fireplace. It was not bad. It made me want to work again, so I did. I painted like a secret drinker, not telling Eve, getting up early on the pretence of going riding. Alice encouraged me. She had a natural eye for colour, and she'd seen a lot of good stuff in Europe.

I used to drop in at Greyling after work, while Eve was busy with plumbers and glaziers, and I'd talk to Alice, sitting on the poky little back verandah while the sun rolled down into the inland valley. Sometimes Beth Pottergill would join us, her crochet-work on her lap. She seldom spoke, but I never got the feeling that she disapproved of my visits. On the contrary, there was an air of peace about her. I was ashamed I'd ever suspected her of sending the anonymous letters.

We heard no more of these, and though I watched Beth's reactions to Phil I never saw her display any hostility towards him. I decided they'd been sent by someone with a sick mind, and the best thing to do was forget them.

Particularly as Alice was apparently established in Durban. She had a growing circle of friends. Phil was often at Greyling, so were Faith and Frank Reppley, and you could be sure that on most evenings you'd find friends there, or interesting strangers. With each week that passed, Alice became less vulnerable to attack.

She and Beth shared the housework and cooking, but they needed someone to look after the garden. Alice spoke to old Mlaas, and his youngest son was brought from the kraal at Ndwedwe, to fill this bill. He was a bright, likeable boy called Sipho, and under the stern eye of his father he learned to make himself useful at Greyling.

244

At this time, Alice owned no horses. She asked me to take her to the sales at the Old Market Square, but we saw nothing worth buying. Walter therefore suggested that she should stable a couple of his horses. His own boxes were filled by the mounts of visiting polo-players, and he offered to lend her Rollo and Slyboots, two ponies that weren't up to his weight but were very good rides. The understanding was that if Frank Reppley was short of a mount for any game, then he'd have first call on them, but otherwise they were for Alice to use.

It often happened that she called on me to help exercise them. She also found that young Sipho was better with horses than with plants, and gave him the job of groom.

★   ★   ★

It was during this winter that Faith Reppley's health deteriorated sharply. I noticed the change on the night that Eve and I took her to hear the 320-voice Sheffield Choir that was visiting Durban.

I'd always liked Faith. I liked the way she enjoyed music; without theorising, like a child tucking into a good meal. That night, though, she was clearly exhausted by her asthma. Her arms and legs were like thin little twigs, and her eyes had a bluish film.

At the Interval, when Eve moved into the foyer to talk to friends, Faith and I stayed inside the huge and empty hall and talked.

'Toby,' she said suddenly. 'I want to tell you something. I know you don't approve of Frank, but I want you to know that I count myself lucky to have married him. No-one knows how wonderful he has been to me, how kind and attentive. I thank God for him daily.'

As I was silent, she smiled and put her hand over mine. 'I know what you're thinking. That he deceives me. Perhaps he does, but it doesn't matter. Frank will never leave me. He loves me. Believe it.'

Looking at her face, so tired and yet so serene, I did believe it, and was enough moved to tell Eve about it when we got home.

Eve shrugged. 'Why tell me about it?'

'It seemed to me . . . important.'

'Important? Why should Faith's affairs concern me? I can't understand how anyone could discuss such a thing with an outsider. I hope you didn't talk about me!'

'Of course not.'

'I can't bear heart-to-hearts. They're bad form.'

Anger made me say, 'There's no such thing as form, when you're dying, as Faith seems to be.'

246

It hadn't occurred to me that my visits to Greyling might be misconstrued. So it was a shock when Phil Rennie buttonholed me in the bar of the Theatre Royal, in the second interval of Matheson Lang's production of *Romeo and Juliet*, and told me I was giving Alice a bad reputation.

'My dear man, you've been seeing too much Shakespeare!' I said.

'No. People are starting to talk. Those two old biddies who live opposite Greyling told me yesterday, most pointedly, that Mr Rourke was "a frequent caller on Mrs Frobisher".'

'So I am.'

'Look, Toby, you're a married man, and Alice lives alone.'

'She does not. There's Beth, large as life, doing crochet.'

'It's no good talking about Beth. She's a servant, and no protection against gossip.'

I finished my whisky rather fast. 'Phil, I don't concern myself with gossip. If Eve doesn't worry about my calls at Greyling, then why the hell should anyone else?'

'Does Eve know how often you go there?'

I was silent, thinking of my painting. 'I don't go to Greyling for sex, Phil. It's for art's

247

sake. I've been showing Alice my oils.'

'It's all very well to joke . . .'

'No. Gospel. I'm a secret painter. I keep my tack at Greyling to avoid rows.'

'People can't be expected to guess that.'

I was about to tell him that people could get stuffed, when the warning bell rang in the foyer.

What I did do was tell Eve about my painting. I said I was working to sell, a profit-motive any Frobisher could grasp perfectly. She accepted my relapse, and even came to Greyling once or twice, to inspect my efforts.

The second time, we found Frank Reppley there, talking to Alice about the Mission. Molly was planning a fête to raise funds for the Hospital, and Frank wanted Alice to write to firms in England for details of some special equipment.

Later, Frank offered to drop Eve off at a church meeting, and I stayed chatting to Alice. On impulse, I asked her what she thought of Frank.

She gave me a rather enigmatic look. 'He's all right, as long as he sticks to medicine.'

'Trouble is, he never does.'

'I can handle Frank.'

I never told her what Phil had said. I suppose I was scared she'd tell me not to come so often, and I didn't want that. I needed her too much.

A few months ago, I'd laughed up my sleeve at those people who danced round Alice's flame. Now I was no better than the rest of them, and the laugh was on me.

*　　*　　*

Looking back now, I can see I was to blame for what happened at Yellow-wood. I was the one who should have seen the forces building up, and how dangerous they were. I can only plead that no man anticipates a murder in his own circle.

I don't believe there are many people who make logical decisions and carry them through. So, I was unhappy at the Cottage, I was attracted to Alice, I imagined what it would be like to sleep with her. I knew I was heading for trouble; but I didn't think about a divorce from Eve, or change the surface pattern of my life with her. As I've said, we live one life in fact and the other in imagination, and both of them are real.

A crisis came on the last Friday in September.

The spring wind was blowing, gusting from the east, a dry and carping wind that churned up the red dust of the suburbs and deposited it in a film across town. Phil Rennie, Walter and I were having lunch at the office so that we could talk about a new line of machinery we were importing. At about a quarter to two, the telephone rang. It was Aunt Delia, and she sounded desperately worried.

'Toby? Darling, do you know where Frank Reppley is?'

'No.'

'There's a polo practice, isn't there?'

'Not until four.'

'Faith's been taken terribly ill. They can't find Frank. He's not at any of the hospitals, and most of the people on his afternoon round have no telephone. I've sent Mlaas out to look for him.'

'Are you at Reppleys' now?'

'Yes. Dr Moberley is here with Faith. It's her heart. She had an asthma attack, all this dreadful dust in the air, and her heart's collapsed. I tried to get hold of the girls, but Eve and Alice are both out, and Molly went to the Mission before lunch. We just have to find Frank. Dr Moberley says Faith may not . . . oh, Toby!'

'All right, Aunt Dee, don't worry. We'll come up and see what's to be done.'

The three of us drove to the Reppley house. It was a poky, ugly place, and the smell of drugs seemed to permeate it. Aunt Dee took us through to Frank's consulting room at the back. Open on his desk was his diary of appointments. The space from two to four p.m. had a line drawn through it, with 'rounds' written along the line. At the side of this was a scrawled list of some fifteen names, in many cases just the surname being given.

Aunt Delia said distressfully, 'You see, Faith is the only person besides Frank who knows what these names mean. His secretary's away.'

Walter was looking about him. 'What about files, there must be a record of all his patients. We might be able to work out who he's seeing this afternoon.'

We found a tray full of index cards and Walter started to go through them. Phil said, 'Won't the servants know where he's gone?'

Phil and I went through to the kitchen yard. The Zulu cook was sitting on the step eating a hasty meal of beans and bread. When I asked where the doctor was, he gave a wide shrug. The baas, he said, had left the house at one o'clock, on foot.

That seemed odd. We checked the shed at the back. Frank's pony-trap was there, and the automobile he disliked so much. The stables next door were empty. I asked the cook where the three polo-ponies were.

'Oh,' he swept an arm around, 'down there,

251

at the polo-ground. The umfaan took them, a long time ago.'

So Frank had intended to be at polo practice. But not this early. There were enough patients on his afternoon list to fill at least two hours, and he certainly wouldn't—couldn't—get to fifteen homes afoot.

Clearly he'd decided to spare his own ponies for polo. Then why hadn't he taken the car? The answer seemed to be that he'd calls to make at the homesteads scattered at the back of the Ridge, where the steep and sandy roads made a car virtually useless.

Phil said suddenly, 'What about the horses at Greyling? Frank might have borrowed one of them. The groom may know something. Why don't we go up there?'

'You go. I'll start visiting the houses on his list.'

The next couple of hours seemed endless. Walter and I called at place after place, found no sign of Frank, left messages in case he called. Back at the house, Dr Moberley and a trained nurse battled to save Faith. She was too ill to be moved to hospital. At four, Dr Leiper arrived with oxygen equipment. All the while, the hot and dusty wind keened and threshed in the tree-tops, like a Greek chorus.

It was close to sunset when we heard a rider

coming headlong up the drive. I reached the front door in time to see Frank tumble from Rollo's back. He thrust past me without a word and ran up the stairs.

*　　*　　*

Just before seven o'clock I left the Reppleys'. Walter and Aunt Delia stayed, and Molly had joined them. Dr Moberley suggested I go home and come back later, to relieve them.

'Frank must have friends with him,' he said. 'He's taking it very badly. He's even accusing himself of killing Faith, simply because he wasn't here when she started the attack. Rubbish, of course. As a medical man, he knows she could go at any time.'

'It's one thing to expect death, and another to accept it.'

'Aye, that's true.'

I walked home. At the gate I met Phil Rennie. He followed me inside.

'How is she?'

'Alive, but in a coma.' I felt tired and sad, the Cottage lights seemed dimmer than usual. I called, 'Eve,' and she appeared in the kitchen doorway, an apron over her afternoon dress. She came and kissed me.

'How is Faith?'

'Dying.'

She looked at me and her lips moved wordlessly. I said, 'Phil, you'll stay to supper with us?'

'No. I must get home.' But he didn't move. Instead, he said, 'What about Frank? Did you speak to him?'

'No. He's too upset.'

'So he bloody well should be.'

'You can't blame Frank.'

'I can and do. He's a swine.' Phil stopped and then blurted out, 'This afternoon, when I found him, he was with a woman.'

'What?'

Phil was shaking. I told him to sit down and tell us what had happened. It seemed that after he left the Reppleys' he'd gone up to Greyling and found it deserted. Beth Pottergill was nowhere to be seen. The doors and windows were locked. Phil ran to the stables, calling for Sipho, who tumbled sleepily down from the loft. Phil questioned him:

'"Has Dr Reppley been here?"'

'"Yes, 'nkosi. He came and went away again."'

'"With the horse?"'

'"Yes."'

'"Did he say where he was going?"'

'"No, 'nkosi."'

'"Sipho, this is very important. Mrs Reppley is very ill. Can you think where the
254

doctor can be?"

'The boy shook his head. Some flicker in his eyes made me glance into the harness-room behind me. I saw that two of the saddle-bars were empty. I asked Sipho:

'"Did the baas take two horses?"

'"Yes. Two."

'"With saddles and bridles?"

'"We saddled the horses here in the yard."

'I could see he wasn't telling me the whole truth. I said, "Listen, Sipho. The doctor's wife is going to die. You must tell me where to find him."

'Sipho didn't answer directly. He looked away from me and made a half-gesture towards the bush at the top of the Ridge.

'"Did he take the old road?"

'The boy nodded. I thanked him and went back home. I saddled a horse and took the back lanes to the top of the hill. No-one saw me go. By about four, I was on the old road, heading down into the Umgeni valley.

'It was out of the wind there, and utterly quiet. The sand was still damp from last night's rain. I picked up the tracks of two horses easily enough. I soon realised they were headed for the sawmill. I followed them there.

'I wasn't thinking coherently, I suppose. I didn't suspect anything. When I found Rollo and Slyboots tethered by the stream, I

255

dismounted and looped my reins over the same branch. I walked down towards the mill.

'I was at the back of the building. The window there is black with dirt. I couldn't see anything, but I felt someone was in there, watching me. You know how you can sense that?

'I stood still and shouted "Frank."

'There wasn't a sound. I went on round the building. On the north side there's a door. It was sagging open. I started towards it.

'Then he appeared. He was half-naked, he'd just snatched up his trousers to hold in front of him. He said, "Don't come in here."

'I said, "Get dressed and come out. I have to talk to you." I went back to the horse. I mounted my own and untethered Rollo. In a few minutes, Frank joined me. The sweat was running down the side of his cheekbones. He caught hold of my arm and said, "Phil, don't tell anyone. That woman is nothing, she doesn't mean anything to me. I've been mad but for God's sake don't let it ruin me." He was almost crying.

'I told him to shut up, that I hadn't come to spy on him. He stopped jabbering, and I said, "Faith is very ill. Moberley says it's her heart. You must hurry."

'His mouth kind of jerked. He snatched up Rollo's reins and swung up into the saddle.

' "Is she alive?" '

' "She was, when I left." '

'He didn't say anything more, just lashed Rollo and shot away towards town. I didn't try to keep up with him. I went home. I needed to think.'

I nodded. I'd been doing some thinking of my own. The urgent thing was to keep the story secret, or there was going to be one hell of a scandal.

'Phil,' I said, 'what about the second horse, what about Slyboots. Did you leave him at the mill?'

Phil's mouth twisted. 'Had to, didn't I? For the use of the lady?'

'Then where the hell has she taken it?'

'Home to its stable, no doubt.'

'To Greyling?' As his meaning came home to me, I understood why he was looking so sick. 'Don't be foolish, man.'

'I tell you I know what I saw. I saw the saddle on Slyboot's back. It was her own, the Mexican one. I couldn't mistake it. You know damn well she never lends it to anyone. The woman with Frank was Alice.'

I started to argue with him, but at that moment we heard footsteps on the front stoep, and a knock on the door. Eve went to open it. Walter stood on the threshold.

'Faith's gone,' he said. 'Toby, will you

come back there with me? Frank's broken down completely, and there's a lot to be done.'

'Of course.'

I followed him out of the house. Eve was still leaning in the doorway. As I passed her, she said gently,

'So now we know the truth about Alice.'

*   *   *

I spent the best part of the night at the Reppleys', and returned the next day . . . Saturday . . . to help make arrangements for the funeral. Molly arrived at about nine o'clock. She looked more strained than I had ever seen her. I knew how fond she was of Frank. She asked how he was, and I told her that last night he'd been in a bad way, but that Leiper had given him an injection, and he was still asleep.

She said, 'Faith and he were very close, in spite of the silly way he behaved.'

Her remark made me wonder if she'd guessed something of what had happened the day before. Molly had a sort of naive shrewdness about what went on under the surface of our lives.

I left her talking to the vicar of Faith's church, and went in search of Phil. He was at home. I came straight to the point.

'You're wrong about Alice, you know.'

He looked up with a quick hope. 'Why do you say that?'

'You're doing her an injustice. You wouldn't leap to conclusions if your emotions weren't involved.'

He shook his head.

'After all, Phil, you've nothing to go on but that Mexican saddle. One glimpse of it and you imagine that Alice was in the mill, hard at it with Frank on a pile of old sacks. It's too bloody unlikely for speech.'

'Is it?'

'Of course it is. You know Alice. Do you think that sort of escapade is in character?'

'Yesterday I wouldn't have thought it was in Reppley's character, and I'd have been wrong, wouldn't I?'

'Frank is a healthy male with an invalid wife who takes what he can where he can.'

'In that filthy place?'

'Rutters can't be choosers, old boy. But Alice has a perfectly good house of her own. If she wanted to have an affair, there'd be no need for her to buzz off to a sawmill. What's more, I don't believe she cares a rap for Frank.'

'There you're wrong. I've seen them together.'

'So have I and she treats him as no more than a friend.'

'Well, she would, in your presence.' Phil gave me a childish, half-sullen, half-pleading look. 'Frank's been after her for weeks. He's always up at Greyling.'

'So are you. So am I. Phil, you're talking like a damned schoolboy. You claim you love Alice. Can't you show a little trust in her?'

He rubbed a hand across his eyes. I looked at him, thinking there was a bitter irony in the situation. He thought I was arguing to comfort him, and I knew I was arguing to comfort myself. I said, 'Know what we'll do? We'll go up to see Alice, and set our minds at rest.'

'Good God, you can't just accuse her to her face!'

'I don't intend to. Come on.'

We found Alice working in her garden, setting bulbs in pots. When she saw us she stuck her trowel in the soil and hurried towards us.

'Hello. I didn't expect to see any of you this morning. Poor Faith, she was so kind to me. How is Frank?'

I told her. She listened with an expression of concern. She looked very pretty, her pale skin flushed from the sun, and the curls moist on her forehead. She turned and smiled at Phil.

'Thank you for bringing Slyboots back.'

Phil was stiff as a poker. 'I did not do so.'

'Then whoever did?' She seemed completely taken aback.

'I've no idea.'

'How extraordinary! Someone put him into the paddock late yesterday afternoon. I thought it was you.'

'Didn't Sipho see who it was?'

'No.'

'Did you ask him?'

'Of course. I wanted to know whom to thank. Sipho said he went down to the paddock and found Slyboots standing inside the gate.'

'Is he telling the truth?'

'I'm sure he is. I was angry with him for lending my saddle. He knows I don't like that. I ticked him off about that, so I'm sure he wouldn't have lied about Slyboots.'

I said, 'Perhaps he came home by himself.'

'But that doesn't make sense, Toby. Frank borrowed him, he wouldn't just turn him loose. And how did Slyboots open the paddock gate, may I ask?' She seemed to become aware of the tension in the air, and turned to frown at Phil. 'Did Frank have both horses with him when you found him?'

So we were trapped. Phil couldn't tell the truth. If he admitted that Frank had both horses, then Alice would want to know where

261

and how it happened that one had been abandoned. The safer course was to lie, and Phil took it.

'He only had Rollo.'

Alice smiled. 'Then that explains it. I suppose he left Slyboots with someone while he did his afternoon round. And when whoever it was heard that Faith was so ill, they just returned Slyboots to my paddock.'

'How would they know where to bring him?'

'Perhaps Frank left directions. Or perhaps they recognised my saddle. I haven't seen another like it in Durban, have you?'

She was looking directly at me as she spoke. Her face was calm and innocent, and yet there was something in her expression that warned me she was lying; lying, and urging me with the full force of her will to accept the lie.

I paused. Her mouth curved in the ghost of a smile. It was the smile of friend and conspirator rolled into one.

Now, her look said; now or never for us.

I nodded. 'I expect that was the way of it.'

We stayed talking a while, and then left. Phil walked with a jubilant swing. 'Thank God we went, eh? Rotten of me to suspect her. And I'm not Frank's keeper, after all. I intend to forget the whole thing.'

I kept silent. It was a silence that played

straight into the hands of a killer.

★   ★   ★

Faith was buried on Tuesday morning. Walter and I were among the pall-bearers. The service was held in our own church of St Thomas, but the burial was at the Central Cemetery in town. The long cortège, led by a hearse laden with flowers and wreaths, moved down Berea Road through the same hot and dusty wind that had helped to kill Faith. The weather expressed my mood; sadness, discontent, mistrust.

I'm not a religious man. I've never been able to take comfort in mysteries like resurrection. So a graveside is to me a place of finality, where illusion ends. I'd been fond of Faith, I envied those who believed they would see her again in some other life. I watched them, Aunt Delia and Molly and Beryl, weeping behind their black veils; Eve and Alice more composed. I watched Frank Reppley.

He stood a little apart from us. His eyes wandered. He seemed hardly to hear the words of the ceremony, and when it was time for him to scatter his handful of earth on the coffin Walter had to touch his arm to remind him. His face had the dull, dazed look of someone struggling against unbearable pain.

263

The burial over, the crowd of mourners moved to the cemetery gate. Eve and I stood with Beryl and Aunt Delia. Frank began to move along the line, shaking hands and accepting condolences; but when he was close to us he suddenly turned aside, as if he couldn't face us, and walked to the edge of the pavement. His face was streaming with tears.

Before any of us could move, Alice pushed her way through to him; took him by the arm and led him along the street to where her hired carriage was waiting; thrust him into it and climbed up after him. We saw her lean forward and speak to the coachman. The carriage started forward, swung in a wide arc, and headed back up Berea Road.

Back at the gates, the funeral party was left irresolute. I heard Walter speaking to the padre '. . . best thing to do . . . quite broken up . . . poor fellow . . .'

From beside me came a fierce whisper. 'Hypocrite! Hypocrite!'

I turned round, startled. Eve was staring after the carriage with an expression of fury. 'How dared he leave with her . . . after all that's happened . . .'

I caught hold of her arm. 'Eve. Be quiet!'

She dragged away from me. 'He didn't love Faith! He's a hypocrite!' In another moment she would have been screaming. I put both arms round her and pulled her against me, literally holding her silent. She began to sob. Molly came up to us and Eve turned and threw herself into Molly's arms. The two of them moved away and stood together by the cemetery rails, some yards away.

I waited alone, aware that more than one person had noticed Eve's outburst. I realised that she'd been far more disturbed than I thought by Phil's account of what happened at the sawmill. She couldn't reconcile it with Frank's grief today, she couldn't understand that he'd genuinely loved Faith. But somehow Eve must be warned to keep her mouth shut, or the whole scandal was going to break like a tidal wave.

The crowd thinned. Molly came over to me.

'She's all right. Take her home, Toby.'

'Did she say anything. . .?'

'Nothing. It's been too much for her, she shouldn't have come. Take her home.'

*   *   *

Eve swore she'd told no-one about Frank's escapade, and I was damn sure Phil wouldn't have spoken, and yet from that first week, the rumours started to spread.

They weren't specific. They weren't even hostile to Frank. Their tone was more pity for the sinner brought to repentance. Frank had played the fool but there was no real harm in him. Losing his wife had made him see the folly of his ways. Sad that his last memories of Faith must be tarnished by remorse. That sort of thing.

The gossips were busy with Alice, too. The poor doctor, they said, couldn't stand the loneliness, and was in need of company. Alice Frobisher had seen sorrow herself, she knew what it was to suffer a sudden loss, she could be comforter and friend in Frank's time of need. A bit soon, perhaps, but then who could judge how a man will behave in his grief?

So the talk ran, a little sharp, a little sly, but not yet dangerous. There was enough genuine sympathy for Frank to take the edge off the popular tongue.

Then I learned something that made me afraid.

It was about two weeks after the funeral. I hadn't been up to Greyling since then. I'd made a deliberate decision to keep away. I knew too much about Alice now, or too little. I felt she'd lied to me but I didn't know why. I couldn't believe she was Frank's mistress, yet I was tortured by doubts. I couldn't get her out of my mind and I knew I had to, so I stayed away from her.

But this night I couldn't go on with it. I was

alone at the Cottage, and I got to thinking about Alice, and the way people were talking, and I thought the least I could do was to warn her.

I went up to Greyling and the first thing that happened was that I saw a strange black groom in the stable-yard. I asked where Sipho was, and was told he'd gone, two weeks ago, no-one knew where. That frightened me. When black people disappear without a word, then you know they're running from trouble.

I headed for the house. Alice was sitting on the front porch, in darkness. To her right was a big sash window, with a lamp burning in it. There was a string of insects battering themselves against its glass mantle. I sat down on the top step.

'Alice, where's Sipho?'

'I don't know, Toby. He left, the day of the funeral.'

'Doesn't Mlaas know where he is?'

'Apparently not.'

'Did you sack him?'

'No. He just vanished.'

'Did he take anything of yours?'

'No. Just his own things.' She paused. 'Is that why you came? To ask about Sipho?'

'I came to tell you you're exciting talk.'

'People talk. It will pass.'

'Wouldn't it be wise to tell Frank not to call

so often?'

'He's so unhappy.'

'He'll be more unhappy if he begins to lose his patients. A doctor can't behave like this.'

'Like what?'

'Like a fool.'

She put out a hand to touch my wrist. 'You'll have to trust me.'

'Why should I? You don't trust me.'

'I do.'

'Not enough to tell me the truth.'

She was silent for a moment. Then she said, 'There are some things I don't discuss with anyone. I don't mean to hurt you, Toby.'

'Or Frank?' I knew I sounded bitter.

'Or Frank,' she said. She sat up straighter in her chair, and the shaft of light from the window fell across her face. I could see the long lashes veiling her eyes, the pale line of her cheek, and the faint, tender curve of her mouth. She had made up her mind. She had no more to say.

I got to my feet. I was angry with her, and with myself for my weakness. I said, 'You're headed for trouble. If that's what you want, then I can't stop you.'

And why should I try, I thought, as I made my way home? If she wanted to break Frank Reppley and herself, the silly bitch, then let her.

In this mood of hurt and anger, I kept away from Greyling. It was Phil Rennie who took decisive, and fatal, action.

★   ★   ★

It was a Sunday evening and, as usual, we'd gone up to Yellow-wood for supper, after which Aunt Delia and Molly went off to Evensong, leaving the rest of us to drink coffee and talk.

The wind had dropped, and we could look through the long funnel of motionless trees and shrubs to the orchard and the view beyond, where the sea was the colour of inkberries under febrile stars.

From this dark silence came Phil, pounding across the lawns with the force of a madman. He stopped outside the window of the drawing-room where we were sitting and glared in at us. It was obvious he'd been in a brawl. His left cheek was swollen, his nose bleeding, and his eyes shrunken and glittering. Walter hurried out to the verandah and drew him into the house. We saw them go through to the kitchen at the back.

Beryl, who was now eight months pregnant, got to her feet. 'Should I go and help?'

'Better not,' I said. It was only too easy to guess how Phil had collected that shiner, and I didn't want the girls onto it. Of course, I was wasting my time.

'He's been fighting,' said Eve, and Beryl nodded.

'I'll bet it was because of that woman.'

'Nonsense,' I said, and Beryl looked at me with bright hatred.

'It's not nonsense. You're as stupid as the rest of them about her. She's wicked.'

I tried to turn the question. 'Phil probably tangled with a pickpocket.'

Eve laughed. 'Oh, Toby, for heaven's sake! It's quite obvious Phil's quarrelled with Frank. They're both after her.' She came over and picked up my cup. 'More coffee?'

'Listen, Eve . . .'

'Yes, darling?' Her eyes mocked me gently as she bent over the tray to refill my cup; fair head shining, neck meekly bent; letting me know she would have her say when we were alone.

I shut up.

It was twenty minutes before Walter came back. He stood in the window bay, pulled off his spectacles and massaged the bridge of his nose with finger and thumb. 'Well,' he said, 'I never thought to see old Phil half seas over.'

Beryl squeaked, 'Phil drunk? I don't believe it.'

'Drunk,' said Walter, 'and apparently

disorderly. He went round to poor old Frank's place, and picked a quarrel.'

'About Alice,' said Beryl.

'Yes, and without the smallest justification. Phil's behaving like a jealous schoolboy. Alice has no intention of marrying him, that's quite clear. She's a perfect right to see whomever she wants. She's been helping Frank through a bad time, and Phil's taken it the wrong way. Believe it or not, he marched up to Reppley's place tonight and ordered him to leave Alice alone. Naturally Frank told him to go to blazes, and Phil apparently lost his rag and said he wasn't going to allow a man "of Frank's sort" to hang around her. He admits he started the trouble. The pair of 'em slanged each other up hill and down dale, and Frank lashed out and knocked Phil down. Phil climbed back and they indulged in a punching bout that was only stopped when Frank's servants heard the row, and rushed round the back. Which means that by tomorrow every servant on the Berea will have the whole story.'

Eve said loudly, 'Not the whole!' She walked towards the centre of the room. 'Phil knows the truth about Frank Reppley. Did he tell you tonight? Did he?'

Walter raised his hand. 'Eve, I don't want to discuss Frank, or anyone else. It's better for

271

people to think Phil was drunk, than that he was brawling over Alice.'

'Alice, Alice, Alice! That's all you're worried about. You're as besotted as the rest of them.'

'Alice is a member of my family.'

'She is not. She is an outsider. And you've no right to squander money on her.'

'What the devil are you talking about, Eve?'

'I'm talking about money, our money, Frobisher money, that you're getting ready to hand over to that...'

'You're crazy.'

'I am not crazy. I know what you've done. You've changed your will, haven't you, so that she'll get the same as Molly and me. Don't try and lie about it.'

Walter was now as furious as she. 'I've no intention of lying. But I'd like to know how you came by your knowledge? Have you been going through my papers?'

'Beryl told me. Beryl thought I had a right to know. And Molly. You won't hand over a penny to us when we need it, and all the time you're planning to give it to her...'

'Shut up!' Walter shouted at her so furiously that she backed away from him. He swung round to face Beryl.

'Well?'

Beryl stammered, 'I ... I ... may

have . . .'

'You went to my desk and read my will?'

'It wasn't locked . . .'

'. . . and having read my private directions to my solicitors, you then divulged them to all and sundry?'

Beryl burst into tears. She ran to Walter and clutched him. 'Walter, I'm so frightened. Send her away, please, Walter. If she finds out about the money, she'll harm you, she'll poison you, like she did Hugh.'

'For God's sake, Beryl, don't be such a nitwit.' He put an arm round her. His gaze came back to Eve. 'As for you, my girl, get it through your head that your inheritance is not altered in any way. Before Hugh died he was named in my will to inherit what I considered to be his share of my father's estate. When Hugh died, I decided to amend things so that she will receive what was due to him.'

'She doesn't need money. She's enough of her own.'

'And so have you, Eve, if you'll only learn to count your blessings. It's damn well time you grew up and appreciated your good luck. Settle down, have a couple of kids, and don't worry about the future. You'll do.'

Beryl was now sobbing helplessly. Walter said, 'Go upstairs and rest, love. Eve will take you.'

When they'd gone, Walter shook his head.

'God, what a mess. I'm going to have a whisky. Join me?'

Over the drink, Walter said to me, 'I've tried to talk sense into Phil. He told me what happened up at the mill. He's a bit of a prude, and seeing Frank spending so much time at Greyling ... really, he's just suffering from old-fashioned jealousy. He was lucky Frank didn't really hurt him. Anyway, he'll stick to the line that he had too much to drink, and lost his temper during an argument. I'll have to brief Frank, too.'

'Shouldn't you let sleeping dogs lie?'

'No. There's been rather too much of that. It's time to speak plainly. Frank must learn sense, Toby. He's our family doctor as well as an old friend, and we've a right to expect certain standards in his behaviour. I won't have him upsetting my family ... and that includes Alice.'

We heard Eve coming back downstairs. I said, 'I'm sorry she said what she did.'

'Forget it. I know Eve. We'll see you on Wednesday.'

'Wednesday?' My mind had gone blank.

'Molly's birthday. And now I come to think of it, we'd invited both Phil and Frank. One of 'em will have to withdraw. I'll sort it out, don't worry.'

274

Easy to say. Hard to explain to kind old Walter that I was now in a blue funk over what was happening to all of us. In six months we'd moved from unspoken love and trust to open quarrelling.

As Eve and I walked through the steamy spring night, I tried to talk to her. I met a stare of pre-occupation, as if she wondered what I was doing at her side.

And Alice? Alice was at the heart of our problems.

I remembered what Mrs Cunningham had said to me. 'Alice is a storm-point. Some people are like that, they attract trouble without meaning to.'

I had the feeling that we were being sucked into the vortex, and nothing we said or did could prevent our destruction.

*   *   *

The news of the fight leaked out.

The servants talked across hedges, and faster than summer lightning, their employers had the story.

On Monday afternoon Mrs Cunningham stopped me in the street. 'Toby, I'm very distressed. All sorts of rumours are flying about. I need a straight answer. Is there anything between Alice and Frank Reppley?'

'No.'

'Are you sure of that?'

'I am.' I was coldly certain that I had to make her believe me. She eyed me sternly and at last nodded. 'I spoke to Phil this morning. He's quite rabid, you know. I told him that he should apologise to Frank. He says he won't even meet the man, not under any circumstances. He can't see this attitude is doing Alice more harm than good.' She paused. 'I think Alice should leave Durban for a few weeks. Bart and I have invited her to go up to the farm with us. She's agreed to come. We'll be leaving on Thursday morning.'

'It's very kind of you.'

'No. I like Alice.' She smiled, patted my arm and went on her way.

That night Eve and I dined with the Rennies. Because the distance was short, and the night languorously warm, we walked there and back. It was after eleven when we entered the Yellow-wood property from the stable gates, and the lower windows of the big house were in darkness. However, as we turned the corner of the building we could see there was light flooding through the lattice-work of the side porch, and that two people stood there; Walter on the porch step and, facing him on the pathway, Beth Pottergill.

They were engaged in close conversation,

276

but at the sound of our approach, they both swung round. Mrs Pottergill stared at us for a moment, then with a smooth movement gathered up her skirts and hurried away down the front drive. Walter, without a word of greeting, turned and went into the house. It would have been a trivial enough encounter had I not seen their faces.

Walter looked ill, stricken. And Beth, as she looked at us, wore an expression of virulent hatred.

*   *   *

Eve had seen that look, and been frightened by it. As we made our way through the orchard she clung to my arm, as if she expected Beth Pottergill to spring out at us.

'That woman. Did you see? She hates us. We've got to get rid of her.'

'Don't be silly, you're imagining things.'

'I'm not, I'm not! What was she saying to Walter? I don't trust her. I shall speak to Mother tomorrow.'

She was shivering. All that night she was restless. At dawn she fell into a heavier sleep. I looked at her face on the pillow, the feverish colour and damp forehead, and knew that if I didn't watch out she would be ill again.

I spoke to Walter next day, and asked him

what Beth Pottergill had been doing at Yellow-wood. He answered brusquely. Beth had been there on private business. He couldn't discuss it. When I tried to press him, he said,

'I'm sorry, Toby. I can't talk to you about it.'

His voice was as gentle as ever, but his eyes evaded mine. I had a sick feeling he knew how I felt about Alice. Then, as if to reassure me, he dropped an arm round my shoulders. 'Frank has landed us in a crisis,' he said, 'but we'll weather it if we keep our heads. You must trust me.'

That was all I could get from him. He went into his own office and shut the door, telling the staff he was not to be disturbed. I put my head round the door at lunch-time, and saw him sitting by the window, his hands to his temples. He was a thousand miles away. I withdrew without speaking to him.

At about three o'clock he went out, and returned at four with a number of parcels and four bottles of champagne. He asked me to come through to his office, set down his purchases, and said abruptly:

'I've decided I must look for a new doctor to attend the family. I shall tell Frank he's no longer welcome at Yellow-wood and I'd like to know I can rely on your support.'

'You've changed your mind rather suddenly, haven't you? A couple of days ago . . .'

'I've had time to reconsider, since. We can't hope to remain friendly with both Philip and Frank. I believe Phil has a far greater claim to our loyalty.'

'Surely if you allow things to settle down . . .'

'No Toby, I'm afraid that won't do. I shall break with Frank. Of course, you will do as you think fit, but I do urge you to weigh Phil's claims against the other.'

Of course it was clear which I would choose. Phil was a lifelong friend, worth a hundred Frank Reppleys. I said:

'Molly will be upset, she thinks a lot of Frank.'

'Molly is my main reason for giving Reppley the boot. He's not a fit companion for a young and impressionable woman.'

'Have you told her that he won't be at the party tomorrow?'

'I'll give some excuse. I don't want to spoil her birthday. I'll explain in due course.' He rubbed a hand wearily across his eyes. 'Blast, I forgot to call at the chemist.'

'Feeling mouldy?'

'It's not that. I forgot to pick up the packet of antimony. We've run out. No matter, I'll

279

collect it on the way home.'

*   *   *

Eve and I reached Yellow-wood at six-thirty on Wednesday evening. Walter, Beryl and Aunt Delia were sitting out on the terrace.

'It's so hot,' said Beryl. 'I'm sure it's going to storm.'

Part of my memory of that night is the feeling of heat and tension in the air.

I asked where the birthday girl was. 'Upstairs, dressing,' said Aunt Delia. 'Molly would be late for her own funeral.'

We sat drinking sherry. Phil Rennie arrived at seven, driving a trap with Alice and Beth Pottergill as passengers. I went to the horse's head while the women alighted.

'Very grand,' I said to Alice, 'to employ a white coachman.'

'At twelve midnight,' said Phil, 'I change back into a white mouse.'

Alice looked charming in a dark green dress. She carried a packet wrapped in silver tissue, and a velvet cloak. She called Beth to her side.

'Beth's made some petit fours for Molly. She asked for them specially, and this is the last chance. You know we're going to the Cunninghams' farm tomorrow?'

Mrs Pottergill showed us a little woven punnet packed with the sweetmeats; coloured squares and diamonds, miniature fruits with sugary leaves, pigmy pastries oozing cream. Aunt Dee exclaimed over them.

'I'll take them to the kitchen, ma'am. Rufina will mebbe be glad of a hand with the serving tonight.'

'Bless you, Beth, I'm sure she will.'

Mrs Pottergill went into the house. Alice linked an arm through Aunt Dee's, and we walked back to the ring of chairs. Eve was sitting there, glass in hand. When Alice greeted her, she did not answer.

'Eve!' I leaned over her chair. 'Behave yourself!'

'To her? Why should I?'

She spoke in a vehement whisper. I said, 'It's Molly's birthday, for God's sake!'

'Send Alice away.'

'What?'

'Send her away.'

'How can I?'

'You'll risk us all, for her!'

'You're being an idiot.'

'Am I?' Eve stared up at me. Our faces were close. 'Am I, Toby?' She pushed me aside and got to her feet. 'I'm going to talk to Molly.'

'I'll come with you.' Smiling serenely, Alice gathered up cloak, gift and purse. She set off

281

after Eve, who didn't trouble to wait for her.

'Oh dear,' said Aunt Delia, who had not noticed our exchange, 'I think it's starting to rain. Walter, dear, we'll have to move indoors.'

★   ★   ★

It was almost half an hour before the girls rejoined us. Molly was rigged up in a new blue dress and smiling like ten to two, but she looked unhappy. I guessed she was thinking of Frank.

Neither the champagne, nor our best efforts, could make the party go with a swing. There were so many conversational pitfalls that by the end of dinner everyone was thoroughly nervy. I saw Walter bend forward once or twice, as if his stomach was troubling him.

We went into the drawing-room for coffee. Beth Pottergill's petit fours were on the tray, and each of us took one. Most of the women and all the men drank peach brandy.

It was just before nine-thirty when Walter got to his feet and went out of the room. I was talking to Alice and Phil about the new house. The others had moved to sit in the bay window.

Less than five minutes later we heard an

upstairs door flung back with a crash. There was the sound of plunging uneven footsteps. Then Walter's voice, raised in a scream.

'Toby! Toby! Hurry!'

★   ★   ★

I ran out into the hallway. Walter was at the top of the stairs, clutching the rail. As I watched, he collapsed sideways across the upper landing, his knees pulled up to his chest. I went up the stairs three at a time and knelt beside him.

He was gasping raucously, the pupils of his eyes dilated. I raised his head on my arm and he clawed feebly at my coat.

'Doctor. Poison. Packet.'

Phil, who had been close on my heels, turned and plunged back to the telephone in the lower hall. Beryl passed him on the stairs, calling over the banisters for the servants to come. She flung herself down beside Walter, snatched at his hands and began to chafe them.

'My darling, what is it? What have you taken?'

He drew in a long retching breath, lurched sideways and vomited violently. I said to Beryl, 'Hold him a minute.'

She took my place supporting Walter. I

went into the main bathroom, the door of which stood open. The light was off, and I snapped it on, looking about me.

It was a large room, converted from the dressing-room next to the master-bedroom. The bath was on the right, and directly opposite me on the inner wall, was a cupboard, now hanging ajar. I looked inside it. On the lowest shelf was a wide-necked glass bottle, open to show the white crystals within it. The screw-cap was missing and I found it on the bathroom floor. Picking it up, I saw that a blue and white jam-label had been glued across it, bearing the printed words, BROMILON SALTS FOR INDIGESTION.

There was a glass on the bathroom table with some dregs of liquid in it, and beside that a small teaspoon to which some white crystals clung. I touched a fragment to my tongue, and at once spat it out, my mouth burning.

I went back to the landing and said to Beryl, 'I think he's taken antimony. The stuff he gives the horses.'

She began to whimper. Molly, who was now beside her, got to her feet and drew her away, and Phil and I and Mlaas picked up Walter and carried him into the guest chamber at the head of the stairs. As we lowered him onto the bed, he spoke my name. I bent close to him and caught the thread of his voice.

'Tell them accident. Take care of Alice.'

Then he was seized by a violent spasm and seemed to lose consciousness.

By this time the whole house was in uproar, voices calling, people running about. Aunt Delia came in with some milk and we tried to get Walter to swallow it, but it kept dribbling back, soaking the sheets under him. Every now and again a spasm shook him, and he would scream and vomit. The vomit was streaked with blood. There was nothing to do but support him and try to ease him. I was aware of Aunt Delia and Molly, at the bedside, and of Eve standing like a wraith in the doorway, her eyes on Walter. I asked her if the doctor was coming and she nodded. 'Phil called Frank. He's on his way.'

I turned to Molly. 'Go downstairs and call Dr Leiper as well. I want two opinions.'

She went without argument, though she gave me a scared look.

Walter lapsed once more into unconsciousness, and I went out onto the landing. Beth Pottergill and a black housemaid were there, cleaning up the mess where Walter had been sick. I said sharply, 'You should have let the doctor see that. They may have to take tests.'

Beth sat back on her heels and looked at me. 'When I got here, they'd already put everything down the lavatory. I'm just washing the carpet.' There was a deadly coldness in her voice, as if I were a mortal enemy.

At this point, Phil Rennie came and joined me. I took him through into the bathroom and showed him the Bromilon bottle, with its content of antimony crystals.

'The light was off when I came upstairs,' I said. 'I don't think Walter switched it on.'

'You mean he took the stuff without looking properly?'

'You can see fairly well by the light from the landing. I think he must have come up, poured himself a measure of what he thought was Bromilon, knocked it back. Then when it burned he rushed out and shouted for help . . .'

It was possible. Walter often took medicines. He knew where they were kept. The Bromilon crystals and antimony were very similar in appearance.

Phil said, 'You mean, an accident?'

I shrugged. 'I'm going to lock this place.'

The bathroom had two doors. The one to the landing I now locked. Phil and I went through the other, into the master-bedroom shared by Walter and Beryl.

The bedroom was tidy. Two cloaks were laid across the bed. One of dark blue satin, I knew was Eve's. The other, green velvet, belonged to Alice.

Phil said, 'Is that what you're going to say? That it was an accident?'

'That's what Walter wants us to say. He told me it was an accident. He also said, "Take care of Alice".'

'"Take care?" In the sense of "watch out"?'

'No. I think Walter means we must look after her. See she isn't accused of murder.'

'Oh my God.' Phil sat down on the edge of the bed and stared at the two cloaks. 'If Wally dies . . .'

'Pray he doesn't.'

He nodded. 'But how could it have happened?'

'That jar in the bathroom is labelled "Bromilon". That means one of two things. Either Walter, when he brought the fresh supply of antimony home this evening, put it into the wrong bottle. Or else someone switched the caps on the bottles.'

'If that's the case, then there should be a bottle full of Bromilon, but with a cap marked "Antimony".'

'Yes. It would be in that cupboard over there.' I pointed to a serpentine chest of drawers by the window. 'That's where Walter keeps anything dangerous. Rifle-bullets, revolver, and the antimony.'

Phil went over to look. 'It's locked. No key.'

'It will be on his key-ring. Come with me, we'll get it.'

We went to the guest-room. The women had covered Walter with blankets. Above them, his face shone waxen, the lips livid. Aunt Delia hurried up to me.

'Where's Frank? Walter's dying.'

'Coming, as fast as he can.' I took her hands. 'Aunt Dee we need Walter's keys.'

She was too distraught to argue. She fetched the keys from Walter's coat that now lay on a chair. Phil and I took them back to the other bedroom and unlocked the serpentine cupboard.

The jar was there all right, the cap labelled 'Antimony', but the contents Bromilon.

We left it where it was, relocked the cupboard, went out and locked the bedroom itself. I gave the key-ring to Phil. He put them into his pocket with an almost shamefaced expression.

'Toby . . . if it comes to the police . . .'

'We needn't discuss that.' For I knew that if it came to an interview with the police, I would lie to them. Phil, being Phil, would not.

We went downstairs together. Alice was standing in the front hall. Phil mumbled something to her, then hurried on to the front

288

verandah, where Molly and Eve were waiting for the doctors. I stopped beside Alice.

Her lips moved stiffly. 'How is he?'

'He's been poisoned by salts of antimony.' I watched her face and saw a stillness there, the look of someone awaiting a death-sentence.

'They'll say I did it.'

I made no reply. She seemed about to speak again, then drew back.

'I'd better leave. I'll be at home if I'm wanted.'

She started to move off. I caught her arm.

'I must tell you. Walter spoke to me. He said it was an accident and that I must take care of you.'

Her eyes filled with tears. She shook her head dumbly.

'You mustn't crack up now,' I said.

Before she could reply, we heard the sound of wheels on the gravel, and Frank Reppley's pony trap came dashing up to the front door.

★   ★   ★

Frank Reppley strode into the hall with the others trailing him like Gulliver's fleet.

'Where's Walter?'

'Upstairs. The front guest-room.'

He turned his head. 'Phil, there's a box of equipment in the trap, will you bring it,

289

please?'

He started up the stairs, saying over his shoulder, 'Did Walter speak?'

'Yes. He told me it was an accident.'

'I'd like you to call a second opinion, Toby.'

'I've done so.'

His dark eyes met mine. 'Who?'

'Leiper.'

'Good. Do you know what the poison was?'

'Antimony, I think.'

'Did he vomit?'

'Yes. Unfortunately it was cleared away.'

'Who did that?'

'Beth Pottergill. I've locked the bathroom, with the antimony bottle and the glass he used inside.'

'That's wise.'

We reached the landing. Beryl came hurrying forward and threw herself at Frank, weeping.

'Help us.'

'We're going to, Beryl.' Frank was the good physician now, calm and soothing. But could he be trusted? Could anyone be trusted?

He went into the sick-room. I waited at the door. I watched Frank push up Walter's shirt-sleeve, administer an injection. His eyes were bright and absorbed, his hands deft. Phil and Molly came upstairs with a box containing rubber tubing. Frank began to set up the stomach-pump.

Leiper arrived, and with him a uniformed nurse. The sick-room was cleared of everyone but Walter and the professionals. The house grew quiet, waiting.

Most of them went into Aunt Delia's bedroom. I didn't join them. Instead, I walked to the back of the house, where there was a servants' staircase. I stood on the landing, at the window overlooking the stables, and thought.

*   *   *

Fear is a strange thing. It both deadens and stimulates. So that night, while my body felt the curious inertia of shock, my mind was turbulent with all-too-vivid imaginings.

A few yards from where I stood the doctors were deciding our future. That I knew. If they saved Walter we were all saved, if they lost him we were lost. Death by antimony poisoning meant another inquest. It meant the revival of Hugh's tragedy, and of all the old scandal. It might mean . . . I realised with a strange feeling of detachment . . . a trial for murder.

I leaned my forearm against the glass of the window and saw, not the darkened stable-yard, but a scene in full sunlight; Walter measuring out the antimony for the horses, while Alice watched him.

Her voice came back to me: 'I've seen enough of poisons to last me a lifetime...' and again, tonight, 'They'll say I did it...'

As they would, of course. If Walter died, who would believe his gallant attempt to say it was an accident? 'Hugh first,' they'd say, 'and now Walter. Too much of a coincidence.'

They would cry vengeance; as I should, Walter being my friend.

I could feel the sweat breaking out over my body. I wiped my face, trying to set my thoughts in order.

Walter must have collected the new supply of antimony from the chemist yesterday afternoon; taken it up to his room, decanted it into the bottle, locked the bottle in the cupboard.

Between, say, five-thirty yesterday, and dinner tonight, someone had switched the Bromilon and antimony bottlecaps. That person would have to have access to Yellow-wood, and the keys on Walter's key-ring, which he would relinquish only to someone he trusted. One of us, in fact.

That person might have been Alice. She had entered the master-bedroom, to lay her cloak on the bed. She knew Walter possessed antimony, probably knew where he kept it.

Walter had named her to inherit under his will.

But why should she, a rich woman . . .

Yet, they'd say, if she could kill Hugh for no reason, might she not kill again? What had Beth Pottergill told Walter, two nights ago? Something that made him look ill with worry. Something about Alice, perhaps.

I couldn't think straight.

I needed a drink.

I slipped down the servants' stairway, and made my way to the dining-room. It was dimly lit by the lamps on the sideboard. I went over to this. In its central mirror, whose frame was carved with serpents and flowers, I caught sight of myself and of someone else; a woman standing near the door. I spun round.

It was Beryl. She came slowly into the room, her hands pressed into her armpits, as if she were cold.

'He's going to die, isn't he, Toby?'

I drew her to a chair. 'Sit down. You mustn't talk like that, Beryl.'

'He'll die. I didn't mean to harm him. I did everything for the best.'

'What did you do?'

She raised blank eyes. 'I should have gone to the Police. I see that now. He wouldn't listen. I told him she was wicked. He wouldn't listen, and now he's going to die.'

Suddenly I understood. 'You sent those letters to Phil Rennie, didn't you?'

She nodded. Grief and fright had washed away all her prettiness. She said simply, 'I thought they'd send her away ... if they understood how wicked she is. Now she's killed Walter.'

Crossing to the sideboard, I unlocked the liquor cabinet, and lifted out the brandy bottle. I splashed a generous amount into two glasses, and carried one to Beryl. 'Drink up.'

She did as she was bid. The stuff made her gag, but she stopped crying.

I leaned over her. 'Listen, Beryl. Walter's alive. You've done enough damage, sending the letters, now pull yourself together. Go upstairs and pray for him. Do anything you like, but keep your mouth shut. Understand?'

The rough words seemed to get through to her. She nodded and stumbled to her feet. I saw her cross the hall and move heavily up the stairs.

I went back and took a long pull at my own brandy. I was thinking about the letters. Beryl had been crazy enough to send those. Might she have been crazy enough to plant the antimony, in an attempt to incriminate Alice?

No. Nobody could be that imbecile.

And yet, there was a germ of truth in it. What if the attack on Walter had been made

294

with the specific intention of throwing suspicion on Alice? Here she was, a ready-made suspect. If Walter died, then by noon tomorrow the whole town would be talking. Before such a jury Alice had no chance of being found innocent. She would be destroyed almost as effectively as she would be by a hangman's rope. No decent house would be open to her. She might leave Africa, but the story would follow her. This woman, they'd say, was twice mixed up in a poison case.

I thought about it. If this was the motive, then it cast new light on the possible criminal.

It might be any member of the Frobisher family anxious to protect his or her inheritance against Alice's claim.

It might be Beth Pottergill, believing that by such action, she could cut Alice off from the Frobishers, and have her to herself for the rest of her life.

Beth might be jealous enough to attempt murder. I didn't doubt that. But there were two factors which seemed to rule her out.

One: I did not believe that Walter would have lent her the key to his cupboard.

Two: If by some strange chance he had lent it to Mrs Pottergill, he would have tried to tell me so, in those moments before he lost consciousness. There was no reason for him to protect Beth Pottergill.

The guilty person might be Frank Reppley. Walter had learned something about Frank in the past two days, something of a serious enough nature to make him bar Frank from Yellow-wood.

And, my God, in the confusion of the moment, we'd called Frank in tonight.

I ran up the stairs, and knocked on the sickroom door. Frank answered, in his shirtsleeves.

'I want to speak to you,' I said.

He followed me out onto the landing.

'What is it?'

'How is Walter?'

'Very ill. Alive.'

'Make sure he stays alive, Frank.'

His face went scarlet, then pale. 'What d'you mean?'

I lied then. 'Walter told me who was with you at the sawmill. If you don't want to face a murder charge, save Wally.'

He said nothing. His eyes swivelled past me, to the doorway of Aunt Delia's room. Molly was standing there in her blue party dress. She came forward and put a hand on Frank's arm.

'Frank? What's wrong? Is Walter. . . ?'

'No.' He put an arm quickly round her shoulders. 'It's all right. Go back, Moll.'

She gave me one scared look, then

296

retreated. I left Reppley standing there, and went back downstairs. It was as I reached the lower hallway that I realised I had something in my hand.

The key to the sideboard.

The key, I realised, that might unlock every door.

★   ★   ★

I left Yellow-wood by the back gate and headed for Greyling. I can't describe how I felt, my thoughts were in a jumble that night. I acted by compulsion.

The lights were on in the little house, and the door stood open, as if I were expected. I went straight into the livingroom. Alice was sitting in a straight-backed chair, with some mending piled on the table beside her. Beth Pottergill was on the sofa, poring over a book, a Bible I thought. They both rose as I entered, but neither of them spoke.

I went over to Alice. 'Sit down.'

'Walter's dead?'

'Sit down!'

Beth Pottergill said furiously. 'Don't you talk to her like that!'

'Shut up,' I said. 'There's no time for jabbering. Alice, I want you to listen carefully

297

and tell me the entire truth. Understand?'

'Yes.'

'This key.' I held it out on my palm. 'Have you one like it?'

She studied its curly design. 'Yes. In the tall-boy.'

I went over to the piece of furniture. It was carved with the same flowers and snakes as the rest of the serpentine suite. Its key was in place in the lock. I removed it, replaced it with the one I held, turned it. The lock clicked back. The keys were identical.

Both women were watching me intently. I said, 'Either of you could have unlocked the cupboard where Walter kept the antimony.'

Alice shook her head. I said, 'Think now. Did you go into Wally's bedroom tonight?'

'Yes. Yes I did. Beryl told me to. She told me to put my cloak on her bed, and I did. Next to Eve's.'

'Were you in the bedroom with anyone else?'

'No. Beryl was busy downstairs. Beth was in the kitchen. Eve and I went up to see Molly, and I took my cloak and Eve's to Beryl's room. We stayed in Molly's room, after that, and went down to the drawing-room together.'

She was looking very white. Mrs Pottergill hurried over and stood beside her.

'Don't be afeared, my dear. They're only

trying to put upon you. And this one,' she stabbed a finger at me, 'he should be ashamed, accusin' you . . .'

I ignored Beth. 'Alice, it looks very bad for you. I believe that Walter was poisoned tonight because of something he knew.'

'What?'

'The identity of the woman who was with Frank Reppley at the mill, last Friday.'

'And?'

'The woman in question rode your horse, with your saddle on it. A saddle you don't lend. And Sipho, who might have been able to tell us who was with Frank, has disappeared.'

'I told you, Toby. I don't know who took Slyboots out.'

'You're lying!'

'No.'

'You're lying, Alice, and it's too late for that. And if you won't admit the truth, perhaps Mrs Pottergill will. Perhaps that's what she told Walter, at Yellow-wood, on Monday night.'

Alice swung round. 'Beth? Is that true?'

'I went there.' The woman was whey-faced but truculent still. 'It was for your good, I went.'

I said, 'The woman at the mill could have been you, Alice. Or Beth.' I spoke as insultingly as I could, meaning them to be

299

angry, but Beth reacted.

'Are you calling me a whore?'

'There was certainly a whore at the mill with Frank. Because of her, Walter Frobisher may die. I'm going to find out who she was, I don't care how.'

'You bloody toad!' Mrs Pottergill ran at me like a fury. 'Trying to blame us, you dirty filth. You and your snot-nosed Frobishers, murdering swine, the lot of you, and trying to put it on my poor lady.' She was weeping, she struck at me again and again with her clenched fists, so that I had to grab hold of her to fend her off. Alice shouted above the uproar:

'Toby, you've no right to threaten Beth. She's my friend, my dear friend.'

'And Walter is my dear friend, and tonight somebody poisoned him with corrosive. I think it was one of you who did that. I think that last night Walter warned off your friend Mrs Pottergill, and that tonight, while we were at dinner, she slipped up the back stairs, and went to Walter's cupboard, and switched the bottles.'

'No. No, I never!'

The woman was hysterical, throwing herself back and forth in my grip. I shook her.

'Tell me the truth, you bitch.'

'I am telling you. I'm telling you. I never . . .'

300

She went limp, sagged backwards into a chair. Alice bent over her, smoothed the damp hair back from her forehead, soothed her like a child. The hysterical sobbing ceased. She raised her face.

'I never told him who, Miss Alice. I never . . .'

'It's all right, Beth. Listen to me. I want you to tell Mr Rourke exactly what you said to Mr Frobisher.'

I waited. Beth slowly turned to me. 'I told him . . . "they want to hurt Miss Alice," I told him that.'

'How can they hurt me?' asked Alice.

'Say you're . . . a murderess. Say you're wicked . . .'

As Alice began to shake her head I interrupted. 'That may be true. Someone may be trying to harm you.' I looked at Beth, draggled and pathetic now. 'What did Walter say?'

'He said . . .' she fixed her wide grey eyes on me '. . . said nobody should be allowed to hurt us. He asked me if I knew who had brought the horse . . . Slyboots . . . back to Greyling . . . that day. I told him I never knew who. But I said that perhaps Sipho knew.'

'I see.'

Rage quickened in her again. 'Sipho knows and so do you know, Mr Rourke. You don't fool me.'

She leaned back on the sofa and closed her eyes. Alice got up.

'You'd better go.'

I went out onto the verandah, and she followed me. I was aware of her as one is aware of fire too close to the skin. She stood in the half light, frowning up at me, frightened, but not defeated. I had not broken her formidable will.

'What will you do?' she said.

'I'm going back to Yellow-wood.'

She hesitated, then said quietly, 'Do one thing for me, Toby. If Walter lives, come and tell me yourself? You won't let . . . anyone else do it? I couldn't bear that.'

I nodded. 'I'll come myself.'

*   *   *

I went back to Yellow-wood, but not to the house. Instead, I walked past the stables to the servants' quarters. All the doors were shut. A trail of creeper swung a little at some faint stirring of the air. The crickets had fallen into their hour of silence.

I tapped lightly on the door belonging to Mlaas. There was no answer. I had the feeling that all along the building the black people lay awake, listening but making no sound.

Something made me turn back towards the stables, and there, a shadow against darkness, was Mlaas himself. His knob-kerrie was in his right hand. He beckoned to me to come away from the quarters, along the path that led through the orchard. I followed him to the patch between two silvery plantain trees. He raised a hand in salute.

'Nkosi.'

'I see you, Mlaas.'

'The master is very sick.'

'Yes.'

'He may die.' It was not a question. I was a young man, about to be given the advice of an older and wiser. I listened in silence.

'I've waited,' said Mlaas after a pause, 'too long, it may be. Someone tried to kill the master. A very wicked act. But it doesn't surprise me. There has been a wickedness in the house for a long time.' (He used the word 'tagati', which is a spell, but a spell implying human malice. The Zulus understand that malice is of itself the most virulent poison in the world.)

'There has been tagati,' I agreed.

'I thought it might go away. I've watched it. It is because of the woman from the far place, but it is not her doing. You thought it was her doing?'

303

'For a little while.'

'Yes. I too. Not any more.' He sighed, seeming to search his mind. When he spoke again, it was on a different tack.

'You want to know about Sipho.'

'Yes.'

'He came to me. He was afraid. He had seen something at Greyling that frightened him. He wouldn't tell me about it. But I've heard a lot of talk, about the doctor and a woman. I think Sipho saw that woman.'

'What did you do?'

'I sent him away, to my brother's house. It's not far. Tonight, when the master was taken ill, I called him back. And I made him tell me the name.'

Old Mlaas lifted his head. In the darkness I couldn't see his eyes, but I could hear the sadness in his voice. 'It's a hard name to speak, 'nkosi.'

And so, to spare him, I said the name myself.

★   ★   ★

It was past three o'clock.

I circled the house, making for the front verandah. Frank Reppley's trap was still drawn up to the rail, the pony drowsing between the shafts. As I approached, Frank

304

himself came out of the main door, walking wearily. He had reached the top step when a woman came running after him.

'Frank! Wait! I have to speak to you.'

He faced her. 'I never want to see or hear of you again.'

'Frank ... my darling ... please.' She fumbled at his hand and he jerked away with such a wrench that she toppled sideways and had to grab at the verandah post to save herself.

'Do you think I'll countenance murder?'

'I did it for you.' She followed him down the steps. 'I'd have money, Frank, more than she has. We were happy once, weren't we?'

He shook his head vehemently. He was unloosing the reins, backing the horse, climbing up into the trap. 'Mind away!'

'I didn't kill him.'

'You can thank God for that, not yourself.'

'It's quite safe. I'd never tell about us. No-one else knows.'

He had turned the trap and was already heading it down the driveway. She began to stumble after it. I caught hold of her.

'Eve,' I said. 'You must come home now.'

★   ★   ★

Back at the Cottage, I tried to talk to her.

She showed no remorse for what she'd done. I don't think she looked on it as attempted murder. At first she tried to deny her affair with Frank, but after a while admitted that it had been going on for months, and added, smiling, 'You won't be able to prove anything, Toby.'

'I will. I will be able to prove that Sipho saw you bring Slyboots back to the paddock, that Friday.'

'Who'd take the word of a black stable-hand, against mine!'

'Eve, don't you understand that because of what you've done, Walter may be dead at this moment?'

Suddenly she was furious. 'He deserved it. He was horrible to me. He never gave me anything I wanted, although it was our money. Yet he'd have given it to Alice.'

'Hugh's share only.'

'Hugh's dead and I'm alive. It's my money, not hers. I told you to send her away. You couldn't see that she was taking what belonged to me. My money!'

'And Frank? You were afraid of her getting Frank, wasn't that it?'

'Frank cares nothing for her. He loves me.'

It was a child's reasoning, of course to imagine that if she removed Alice, all would come right. I think the attack on Walter was made more on a childish impulse than by careful plan. She told me that she'd done it because she was 'fed up'.

'Walter sent Frank away. I could see he'd found out about us, and meant to interfere. I decided to teach him a lesson.'

'How did you switch the bottles?'

'Oh, that was easy. On Tuesday evening I just went to Yellow-wood and switched them. I used the back stairs. No-one saw me.'

'Which key did you use?'

'The one from our desk.' She pulled it from her pocket. 'I always carry it with me. I don't like people prying among my possessions.'

*   *   *

The dawn came. Eve went to bed, and slept. I walked up to the big house and spoke to Leiper. He told me Walter was probably going to be all right, but he was still very ill.

From there I walked to Frank Reppley's house. He was up, sitting on the front porch. He seemed to be expecting me.

I said, 'I've spoken to Eve.'

He looked at me warily. He was scared, but still ready to try and out-smart me. 'Eve is mentally unbalanced. You should know by now not to believe all she tells you.'

'Listen, Frank. I haven't come here to

argue. You slept with my wife, you got tired of her, and you left her. Now you'd like her to take the blame for what's happened. So I'm telling you, you won't get off that lightly. What Eve did was done because of you. You share the guilt with her. From now on, you're going to take orders, not give them. And the first order is that you will keep your mouth shut about what's happened, for the rest of your life. Understood?'

'What if there's a police case?'

'We'll worry about that if it happens. If we keep our heads, it won't. Walter is alive, and Leiper thinks he'll pull through. Leiper's already guessed some of the truth, and I intend to tell him the rest. We'll need his advice, and because he's ten times the man you are he'll think of his patients before himself. I don't need to remind you that Walter and Eve are both his patients.'

'What will Walter say?'

'Walter has already made it clear he wants people to think it was an accident. You are going to support that theory in full. Then, in a few months' time, when things have settled down, you are going to leave Durban.'

He started to protest, but changed his mind. 'Very well, I agree.'

'To everything I have said?'

'You have my word.'

'You break it, and I'll break you.' As I turned to go, he got up quickly.

'And Eve? What will you do about her?'

'That doesn't concern you.'

As I went back to the Cottage, the light was soaring over the eastern sea. At the gate of the orchard, I found Alice. She looked fresh, tidy, and calm, and nothing to do with my world. I stopped in front of her, and she said, 'They tell me he's going to live.'

'Yes.'

She glanced at the Cottage. 'Toby, I tried to warn you last night, but I couldn't speak openly in front of Beth. Leave things alone, Toby, don't ask questions. It will be better that way.'

'That's no use now. I know about Eve.'

'I see. I'm sorry.'

I understood that she had known for some time, perhaps even before the mill incident. She could have cleared herself if she'd wanted, but had kept silent to spare me. She'd done me a great kindness and I couldn't even thank her. I felt leaden all through.

'We'll talk another time,' she said, and I nodded and went through the gate to Eve.

* * *

It was several days before Walter was well

enough to see me alone. I sat beside his bed and we talked. He told me he'd guessed Eve had switched the bottles. He knew her better than I.

'She's always been . . . irresponsible. She and Hugh. And lately, I've felt she was ill. In her mind, I mean. I guessed it might be something to do with Reppley. Then Beth Pottergill came round, on Monday, and told me Sipho had seen the woman with Frank, and it obviously wasn't Alice. I put two and two together. I told Frank to clear out.

'Then, on Wednesday, when I swallowed that stuff, I realised it must be Eve who'd done it. You and she were the only two people who knew Beth had spoken to me.'

'You'll have to do something about her, Toby. She can't be allowed to do . . . any more damage, you know.'

'I know. I've spoken to Dr Leiper. He says she'll have to have treatment, by specialists. He says that, as a doctor, he can't keep silent unless she's under restraint. He told me about a place in Switzerland.'

'An asylum?'

'A hospital. They've had some cures. And it's better than any other solution, for her.'

Leiper helped us to make the arrangements. At the end of November I took Eve to Switzerland. Aunt Delia and the others knew where we were taking her. Perhaps they guessed why, but they never spoke of it. In those days, people would do anything to avoid a public scandal, and they didn't discuss relations who had to be certified.

The book of Eve was closed, and put away on the shelf and, in time, forgotten.

*   *   *

At this point, Toby Rourke's manuscript ended.

Philip Rennie lifted his head and gazed about him with an almost bewildered air.

Someone had drawn the curtains and lit the fire. Mrs Riggs must have come and gone without his noticing. His hands felt cold. It was past midnight. He got up and moved closer to the hearth, warming himself.

Such a long time ago.

Did it matter what he did?

Toby had left the story for him to finish. And yet, what was there left to write?

Those people from a long-dead world, the world of two wars ago . . . many of them were dead now. Aunt Delia, of old age; Molly, of enteric fever, at the age of thirty-one; Frank Reppley at Vimy Ridge; Eve in Switzerland; and now Toby himself.

The living, Walter and Beryl, were grandparents, pillars of society. They certainly wouldn't want to resurrect the past.

The only people to consider now were Alice and her sons.

Philip lifted his head to consider a framed photograph on the mantel. There she was, a picture taken many years since. Smiling beside Toby in a Swiss garden. She'd lived with him for several years before they could marry—Toby would never divorce Eve and Alice understood that he felt responsible for her. Alice had two children born out of wedlock.

I couldn't have lived on those terms, thought Rennie. I was never the man for her, and thank God she knew it, if I didn't.

He remembered the last time he'd seen her, it had been on the shores of Lake Geneva in ... what was it ... 1920? She told him that Eve was dying.

'We go to the hospital every day. Toby is the only person allowed to see her, now. She doesn't recognise him. She has no contact with anyone. And she won't eat. She believes, poor thing, that someone is trying to poison her.'

★　　★　　★

Rennie went back to the desk and re-read

Toby Rourke's last letter to him. 'I've been arrogant enough to think I could look after myself and those I love, and leave retribution to other men . . . thank you for this last office . . . and for the many good years we shared.'

Rennie glanced again at the photo on the mantel. Alice stared back at him with that look of amused challenge so typical of her.

He picked up the manuscript, carried it to the fireplace, and fed the pages, one by one, into the flames.